“I admit I
for wantin
Devlin said. r
marry; I should like to know why.”

“I am quite content to live out my days surrounded by family and friends. It provides me independence, as well,” Nicole answered.

It seemed a well-rehearsed answer. Perhaps, like him, she had deeper reasons that she did not wish to share. “But suppose you fell in love with a man who would allow you the freedom you desire?”

“I can just as easily turn the question back on you. Would finding a woman who would not curb your independence change *your* mind?”

“I have assumed that meeting such a woman is unlikely. However, I cannot say with certainty what would transpire should such a woman exist and should we care for each other.”

“That is where we differ, Devlin.” The sadness in her voice was audible; she seemed tired and quite unguarded with him. “I believe I would remain adamant.”

Instinctively he knew the conversation was closed.

MARY MOORE

has been an avid student of the Regency era since the 1970s and is a member of the American Christian Fiction Writers' historic fiction community as well as a member of the Faith, Hope and Love and Beau Monde chapters of the RWA. She has been writing historical fiction for over fifteen years. Mary had to put her writing on hold due to some health issues, including a bout with breast cancer. She is now even more excited about her writing as she incorporates her struggles throughout her books, dedicated to encouraging others in the Lord and using her talent to His glory. A native of the Washington, D.C., area, Mary and her husband now live in the beautiful Blue Ridge Mountains of southwest Virginia, with their black Lab, Darcy. When not writing, Mary enjoys time with her husband, watching romantic movies, reading and weekend getaways. Mary would love to hear from you. You can reach her by visiting her website, http://marymooreauthor.vpweb.com.

The Aristocrat's Lady

MARY MOORE

Love Inspired

Recycling programs
for this product may
not exist in your area.

™ LOVE INSPIRED BOOKS

ISBN-13: 978-0-373-82886-9

THE ARISTOCRAT'S LADY

www.LoveInspiredBooks.com

Printed in U.S.A.

"For I know the plans that I have for you,"
declares the Lord, "plans for welfare and
not for calamity to give you a future and a hope."
—*Jeremiah* 29:11 (NAS)

To:
Jesus Christ,
May God Get The Glory

and

To Craig
My husband and my best friend

"…Love is not love which alters when it alternation finds,…No!
It is an ever-fixed mark that looks on tempests and is never shaken…"

William Shakespeare

Chapter One

Lady Nicole Beaumont sighed as she walked along the terrace of the Elizabethan mansion. The air was surprisingly cool and lightly blowing over the palatial gardens behind the house. It was an immediate remedy to the stifling heat of the ballroom behind her. Tracing her hand along the marble railing, she reached the landing that led down into the meticulously patterned walkways. However, Nicole did not descend. She only listened to the sounds coming from the lake, the focal point of the famed park. She could hear the soft gliding of ducks as they floated across the smooth water. She smiled when she perceived one quacking truant dip its head into the cool pool only to bring it up again in a flurry of feathers.

The smell of roses was strong where she stood, and it took Nicole's thoughts back to her own home in Gloucester. Roses had always been her favorite—she grew the most beautiful and unusual varieties.

She sighed again as she stood against the sculpted balustrade. London had been so much worse than she had imagined. Why had she allowed her mother to convince her it would be good for her to visit Town during the Season? Everything was at a faster pace, and her problems seemed magnified in the unending bustle of the city. Her incapacities only reminded her of her endless limitations.

This night she was attending a ball at the home of Lord and Lady Swathmore. It was their "country" home, though less than five miles outside of London. Nicole's mother had been overjoyed at the invitation. Nicole had come to hate such fetes, but at least at Swathmore Hall there was an escape to fresh air. The past week had been spent in an endless round of soirees and balls in the sweltering heat of London, where the grand houses were bunched against each other like fancy flint boxes stacked in a row.

On this terrace Nicole could imagine she was back at home, and thought of the peace God had finally given her. She could, for a few moments, pretend the accident had never happened. The night air made her think of evening rides on Solomon. She could not ride very often, and never without her faithful servant, Toby, alongside. But she had to consider the good: now that the rides were more sedate, she could spend her time in prayer and contemplation. It had taken too long to be thankful for that, but she looked for those boons from life now.

Town had not brought Nicole the pleasure her mother had hoped for. Her disability overrode any enjoyment anticipated.

She castigated herself at the thought. Nicole had

never truly imagined the trip would provide her much pleasure. Even her dismay at facing the height of the Season had been easy to set aside when she thought of the time she might devote to charitable endeavors that must abound. What she found had shaken her faith in her fellow man. The richest and most lavish city in Europe cared nothing for the poor among them. She had met people who did not give as much as a farthing to help others, while spending hundreds of pounds on a coat cut from the cloth of the famous Weston. Her altruistic intentions met with nothing but disdain. She sent up a silent prayer asking God for the direction He now so often showed her.

Suddenly, Nicole became aware that she was not alone. It came as quite a shock to realize she was so consumed by her own thoughts that she had no notion of the additional presence. She always tried to be very sensitive to her surroundings. Concentrating in earnest, she determined that her silent companion was a man. She could smell the pungent aroma of his cigar mixed with a cologne unfamiliar to her. The fragrance of roses in the air must have overpowered the scents he exuded. Or perhaps her slow pace had only now brought her near enough to notice it.

Unfortunately, the new smells only added to her nostalgic homesickness. Her father's one vice had been his delight in "blowing a cloud," and the memories associated with that pungent pastime were both happy and sad. When she was near him, the smell of horses and books often wafted over her, leaving a sense of security and stability. These were etched in her memory as clearly as every physical trait he possessed.

The cologne worn by Nicole's unknown companion on the terrace was subtle and she liked it. She hated the practice of some of those who avoided bathing. Instead they dowsed themselves in scent, as if *that* made it better!

Focusing again on the present, Nicole sensed the man was behind her, probably up against the house in the shadows. She remained at the terrace railing and heard the ducks quacking at some disturbance in the distance. Her disquiet fled as she realized her servant, Toby, was close by.

She considered her actions carefully before deciding her best exit. She could easily turn and saunter back the way she had come, returning to the ballroom. But she was ever so reluctant to give up the quiet, cool atmosphere of the terrace for the sweltering heat in the crowded room. Her innate sense of justice also required that she beg forgiveness for interrupting someone else's solitude.

Therefore, Nicole turned slightly and said in a low and clear voice, "I am terribly afraid I must beg your pardon for intruding upon you. I was so enjoying the peace and quiet that I did not realize until just this moment that anyone else was present. Please forgive the interruption. I will allow you to finish 'blowing your cloud' in peace." She made a slight curtsey and turned, her hand retracing the smooth surface of the banister to the double doors she had earlier exited.

The man's low chuckle stopped her.

His voice was deep, and at the moment, dripping with sarcasm. "Let a vision of beauty that is also well versed in such slang get away? Absolutely not! I am charmed and incredibly curious as to how your knowledge was acquired."

Sarcastic or not, she knew a desire to stay and hear more of it. His voice was vibrant, Nicole thought decidedly, and certainly that of a gentleman. His words and manners were quite different from those of the simpering dandies she had met inside. However, she did not know how to respond to his jousting so was momentarily undecided as to her next move.

His lazy drawl interrupted her thoughts. "You have no need to apologize for interrupting my solitude. Studying the profile of a beautiful woman against the backdrop of a full moon is much more a pleasure than an intrusion."

Nicole could feel herself color at his words. And she knew that in the semidarkness of the moonlit terrace, he could have little knowledge of her facial features. She had not heard such compliments in a long time and thought he must be very adept in the art of flirtation. She was glad for the darkness that covered her confusion. She had not responded to either of his statements and she felt awkward and tongue-tied.

The gentleman exhaled the smoke of his cigar then continued his preposterous flirting. "I realized quite soon that you were not aware of my existence, a severe blow to my ego by the by, so I determined to enjoy the view."

Nicole spoke with wonder in her voice. "Why then

did you not make your presence known? I should have left you to your thoughts *and* your cigar that much sooner."

"At the risk of knowing your first opinion of me will be that I am an arrogant lout," he answered, "I thought you had perhaps followed me here. I kept silent, hoping you would tire of your search and return to the dancing."

She frowned at his logic. "Had I come in search of you, I should have called out to you in the hope of gaining your attention. I would not have stood by silently." Her mind was so far from her calculating counterparts in London, his reasoning made no sense to her. She continued in naive explanation. "In any event, I would not have followed you at all, knowing I could speak to you when you returned to the ballroom. It would be quite obvious that you wished a moment alone when you left it, would it not?"

Lord Devlin sounded almost bitter in his reply. "I have very often found that the women who seek me out are not the least interested in conversation."

She wondered at his comment.

"That is," he drawled, "until her father, or a conveniently placed brother, is within hearing. They then become quite interested in talking, in loud voices and with crocodile tears."

He explained further and with no little sarcasm. "My dear, their desire for 'solitude' is quite insincere. And their 'conversation' consists of one word…compromise. You see, I am up to every rig."

In a flash she turned toward him, her clenched

knuckles on the balustrade the only indication of concealed fury.

Nicole gasped at the realization that this man had the audacity to assume her on the catch for a husband! Her temper flared, and her mother's reminder that her tongue would one day get her into trouble went unheeded. Nicole ground out in a low and dangerous voice, "Have no fear, sir, I have no brothers, no father, no uncles, not even a distant cousin of the male persuasion waiting to cause you such distress. As I have no idea who you are *and* no interest in marriage, forced or not, you are completely safe from me."

She never raised her voice during her biting speech. "Furthermore," she continued acidly, "as you have clearly pointed out your arrogant tendencies, I am surprised *any* female would willingly sacrifice herself on the altar of marriage to you."

She turned to go, but was sorry for losing her temper with a total stranger. Her nature demanded she make an apology, though her heart balked at the idea. She said a quick prayer, asking God to help her convey her sincerity. "I am sorry I intruded. I will leave you to the solitude of the terrace," and in her pique she added, "without feeling trapped and without childish temper tantrums." She did not bother with the required curtsey, but slowly walked away.

In an instant shock replaced her anger…he was laughing at her! It brought her up short, and she turned back toward him to find out what had amused him so.

"If you do not be quiet," she shushed him, "you will bring a crowd from the ballroom and cause just the sort of scene you have been trying to avoid." She heard him push away from the wall of the house, and it took only one long stride to reach her side.

Nicole turned back toward the gardens behind the house, still blushing at her outburst. She felt his hands lightly on her shoulders turning her to face him; she would not, however, raise her eyes to his face.

He tweaked her chin with his thumb and forefinger saying, "Put your claws away and cry peace with me. I deserved every bit of that masterful set-down. Indeed, several of my acquaintances would have paid a king's ransom to hear it! I sincerely beg your pardon."

In an apologetic voice he continued, "I realized you were not one of the many 'title hunters' in attendance tonight. Even as I intended to introduce myself to you, you became aware of my presence and we came to blows. Can you pardon me?"

Nicole heard the sincerity in his voice and, not knowing why, believed it. She gently responded, "It seems that we have stepped upon each other's toes in our efforts for a moment alone. I do accept your apology and would ask in return that you forgive my wretched tongue and temper, both of which flare up far too often for my mother's peace of mind."

She discovered that close proximity to this man made her heart do strange things, made her wish for other than what God intended for her. She determined to leave his presence as quickly as possible. "I really must get back inside. My mother will undoubtedly be looking for me. It was a pleasure to make your acquaintance." Nicole turned to go, but once again his voice stopped her.

"I beg to differ, ma'am," he said close to her ear. "I have not yet *made* your acquaintance, and contrary to your need of fresh air, I had the distinct impression you were hiding from something. If not hiding, you would have remained had I not been here."

Nicole did not respond, but let her thoughts run rampant. She could almost feel him studying her profile so she turned away. With the intuition she had developed, she knew he was not a man in the first blush of youth. Now that her initial anger had subsided, she began to see the humor in the situation and felt an intense wish to stay and converse with this man. She knew it would be quite improper, but the inane pleasantries she had been forced to endure at recent soirees made her long for a normal and intelligent conversation with someone who had no preconceived notions of her. Truth to tell, she asked herself if a moonlight discourse with someone she did not know *could* be considered a normal conversation.

However, it was too late, and she was beyond rational thinking. She wanted to pretend she was whole and that an interesting man found her company enjoyable. She raised her head at the sound of the agitated ducks.

The gentleman broke into her thoughts. "You will think me mad, indeed I am beginning to agree with you, but since you lost your temper with me, you have... I cannot explain it, you have withdrawn. Despite what they say killed that woebegone cat, I find myself curious. Indeed, I have wanted to ask you why such a beautiful woman attending the most exclusive house party in London would be here on the terrace instead of wrapping every man in the room around her little finger." He continued, sounding puzzled. "In fact, while you did not know I was here I even heard a sigh or two."

It was now Nicole's turn to chuckle as she turned back toward the house, leaning her back against the railing. Suddenly Nicole felt she could be herself. "It appears you consider yourself quite perceptive, sir. I admit I *may* have sighed at the pure joy of the fresh air, however, that is where I draw the line. That borders on a fit of the vapors, and I assure you I have never resorted to those." She raised her nose just slightly in the air, appearing to snub him. His surprised bark of laughter confirmed to her she had met a kindred spirit amidst all the trappings of London.

"I am Nicole Beaumont, and I admit to a small amount of despondency because I miss home. The breeze on my face was a feeling I had almost forgotten since arriving in London."

She felt him beside her now, leaning his back against the railing. "Where is your home, if I may be so bold, and what makes you miss it so?" She knew the need to return to her mother, but did not yet wish to go.

For just an instant, Nicole wondered if she could be completely honest with this man. Finding herself shocked at the thought of telling the gentleman all about herself on less than half an hour's acquaintance, she simply answered, "The quiet here reminds me a little of home, a chance to put London's glitter into perspective."

"Those seem very serious thoughts for a beautiful young woman at an exclusive ball. Are you one of those Methodists who eschews the upper classes?"

She was pensive for a moment. "No, I am not. I cannot despise Society when God has placed me here. But I feel…sorrow that what is important in Society is what is transpiring in the ballroom. I see little evidence that much else matters except to see and be seen."

"I *see* that getting to know you could take a bit more time than the space of a ball."

Nicole smiled at his restraint. She knew he would have little patience for such words had he not been intent upon flirting with her. Would she be missing the one chance she had to tell him about her beliefs? It was clear the conversation would never fit into the short space of time on a moonlit terrace, so she answered his question. "My home is in Cheltenham in Gloucester. My father's estate is there, and I am securely attached to it and its inhabitants." She had almost forgotten he was present. "The scents of the garden were making me nostalgic as well. I am afraid I am quite the enthusiast when it comes to roses and I had a decided curiosity toward Mr. Repton and his work here."

She had to rein her thoughts in once again. "Unfortunately, I could not leave the ballroom earlier when I could have strolled through the famed atrium he created for Lady Swathmore. I understand his acclaimed work with fountains is represented here as well." She smiled unevenly as she said, "What a pity it is a sight that only the rich and prestigious may see."

She shook off her melancholy. "However, the smell of the roses was enough to carry me back to the country. Believe it or not, I even miss my chores!" She chuckled at the last. "Since my father died I have been helping to run our estate. The new earl has not yet... taken an interest in his new home." She shook off that thought. "I am even more amazed at how much time is taken up in London with nothing getting accomplished!" She stopped on this comment, embarrassed again for going on about a subject of absolutely no interest to anyone but herself.

"*I* am amazed that I have only now had the pleasure of meeting you!"

Nicole was not in the least surprised. "We have just spent the past five hours in the same house and we have not met." She left unsaid her purpose to avoid as much of the company as possible. "Unlike you, I am surprised that even though the same people attend the same affairs night after night no one gets better acquainted. I have come to the conclusion that the hosts of such events only count them a success should their drawing rooms be so overcrowded that guests need only spend a few moments in each other's company!"

"I can see," he said, very seriously, "each time we begin a conversation you will twist it so that I get no answer at all." His stature changed and he became less flirtatious. "I apologize in advance for once again sounding arrogant, but whether I wish it or not, I usually come into contact with the new crop of belles each

Season. Had I met you sooner, I would know more about you now than that you are attached to your home and that you are a follower of Mr. Repton. I, too, have a particular interest in his work, although I find some of his designs too intricate and symmetrical for my taste. Much more to my liking are some of Sir William Townsend Aiton's ideas in the royal gardens."

She let out a little gasp of surprise.

"You see, even on so short acquaintance we have much in common, and I am not the conceited simpleton you think me!"

He left the topic, however. "Do not imagine I have forgotten the provocative comment you made about having no desire to marry. That in itself makes you different from every other woman here."

The gentleman placed his finger under her chin and gently turned her head toward him. It was too intimate a gesture for a first meeting and it embarrassed her. "Your attention seems bent solely upon this stone terrace. Oddly enough I would prefer it to be on me, despite my earlier attempts to send you off posthaste."

Nicole could not raise her eyes to his. She was afraid her confused emotions might show. Why would this man, who by his own admission was much sought after, show interest in her? Did he intend to add her name to a list of conquests? She had foolishly admitted she had no males to protect her, though she knew Toby would not stand idly by and see her hurt.

His hand still cupped her chin, and it made Nicole feel decidedly strange. She had never felt such an immediate connection with a man and she could not explain it. *Lord, protect me from this gentleman and from myself,* she prayed quickly. This is what it could be like, if her malady did not exist.

She turned her face back toward the candlelit ballroom. She knew God's plan for her did not include marriage, but in her daydreams, she still saw it all. She would meet a man she could love who would share her humor and appreciation for the country. She dared to conjure up someone who would appreciate her family ties, but especially her love of God. He would accept her, defects and all.

Dream though she might, she was much too practical to dwell on what could not be. She must rely on the verses in Jeremiah that now gave her confidence. *For I know the thoughts that I think toward you, saith the Lord, thoughts of peace, and not of evil, to give you an expected end.* Her expected end did not include marriage, but God promised His peace would accompany it.

"You must forgive me. I meant no insult." He resorted to humor again. "I do believe you and the moonlight have conspired to bewitch me!" Flirting followed close on its heels. "I do not believe that I have ever spent half an hour with a woman without once hearing the latest gossip or being asked to give my opinion on a new bonnet. Your conversation pleases me. I believe I have determined Society to be a dead bore."

Nicole could almost hear his mind working, and somehow she knew he would continue with a preposterous statement.

"Let me assure you, however, if you should wish to discuss bonnets, I trust I could hold my own."

She tried to hold back her laughter, but said in a choked voice, "I have no doubt about it, sir." Nicole was confused, to say the least. First he made her laugh, then angry, then laugh again! She made an instant decision that there was a great deal too much disparity in their lives for such a friendship to prosper. Her heart fought her stubborn head, but she could not afford to let go of the plans she believed God intended for her life. "I accept your apology then, but I really must go now. Do forgive me."

Suddenly Nicole heard her mother's voice as she came out into the darkness from the sparkling ballroom. "Nicky, dear, are you out here? There you are! I have been looking everywhere for you and was starting to worry. I knew you wanted to sneak out to the gardens and was afraid you might have gotten… Oh dear, who are you?" Her mother was indignant. "Nicky, what can you mean standing alone in the dark with a man?"

"Mama, nothing untoward happened. I came out for a breath of fresh air. You know how easily the stifling heat drives me out of doors. Unfortunately, I interrupted this poor…um, gentleman…seeking the same."

Nicole heard his muted chuckle at her obvious hesitation before using the word "gentleman" and rushed on. "I was just excusing myself to return to you."

The "gentleman" was back on familiar ground, however, and began a charming assault on Nicole's mother. "Please, ma'am, let me introduce myself to you. I am Jared DeVale, Lord Devlin, at your service. Your daughter and I were just discussing bonnets when you came out. I was hoping she might help me decide on something perfect for my grandmother."

Nicole commented under her breath that she did not believe for one instant he *had* a grandmother. It reached his ears and caused a delighted gleam to enter his eyes. How wonderful it was to have someone understand *and* appreciate one's sense of humor.

Nicole knew that once her mother learned he was a London lord, she would change from indignant to indulgent on the instant. The time had come to end this meeting and put the whole episode behind her. "Lord Devlin, I am afraid that my mother, Lady Beaumont, has probably called for our carriage by now. She knows how these late evenings tire me."

Lady Beaumont's surprise at a statement made by her daughter, who had more stamina than a regiment of soldiers, made her uneasy.

"It has been a pleasure discussing…ah…bonnets with you, my lord, and I pray you will give your dear grandmother our regards."

"I certainly shall, my lady," he said, chuckling out loud. He then added, "Lady Beaumont, I hope that you will allow me to call on you in London next week. Ladies, you have my compliments." With that, he bowed and passed them into the house.

As Nicole and her mother linked arms and walked back toward the ballroom, Nicole vowed she would forget this night had ever happened, and she would certainly never think again for one moment about Jared DeVale, Lord Devlin!

Chapter Two

"Lord Devlin! Dear Nicky, he is only the most sought-after man in all of London. And an earl! Of course he may call on us if he wishes. I only pray that you do not get your hopes up *too* high. No doubt he offers such compliments as a general rule and cannot remember even half the people he meets." Nicole and her mother were in the carriage on the way home after bidding farewell to Lady Swathmore.

"Nicky, you must at least have *heard* about him. I vow I hear something new of him wherever we go." Her mother's voice changed to a discreet whisper. "I declare he is even more handsome than rumor has it. His raven-black hair makes him most dashing. He is reputed to have the bluest eyes in all of London. Such a pity I could not make them out in the dark. I recall someone telling me that he once caused a young lady to faint with his intense gaze. I suppose she must have been quite a goose to have been so overset." Nicole could only smile at her mother's words. "I thought his hair a trifle too long to be quite fashionable," her mother continued, "but young men are of a different stamp than in my day. However, most of the ladies seem to like it very much. Tell me, Nicky, what did you think of him?"

Fortunately, her mother did not require an actual response.

"Apparently he is still quite popular, though he is considered somewhat haughty and standoffish." Lady Beaumont finished her descriptions of the gentleman with a sigh. "Nicky, were I twenty years younger I should be vying for his attentions myself!"

Nicole could hold her laughter no longer and leaned over to hug her mother. "I believe you would win his heart immediately, did he know it," Nicole bubbled.

She had known from the timbre of Lord Devlin's voice and his natural arrogance that he must be much sought after. But now that her mother had expounded on his reputation, Nicole could be sure it had just been a moonlight flirtation and she could forget it ever happened. In any event, she supposed she could try.

"Mama, this whole evening was a disappointment to both of us. Sitting out all of the dances is becoming excruciating, especially when I am stuck in conversation with the likes of Lord Stokes. I do not make friends of my own when I sit with the dowagers all evening. My only pleasure was to be the cool breeze on the terrace, yet what was the outcome? I am accused of trying to compromise some haughty lord into marriage! I am weary of this and wish to go home."

"What in heaven's name are you talking of?" Her mother stared in question but continued in complaint. "Really, Nicky, you will say anything to shorten our stay, and you promised you would try to enjoy it. *You* are the one who set the conditions during this trip. *You* vowed no one must know of your condition and now *you* are complaining because it hinders you from enjoying any of the events. Why can we not admit your situation and get on with it?"

Nicky reached over to her mother and hugged her again. "Mama, I am sorry to be such a disappointment to you. I know you think if I told everyone about the accident things would be better. But do *you* not see that they would be so much worse? Now I am only relegated to the dowager section and can still sit out dances with some conversation. If Society knew about me, no one would know how to treat me. People would ignore me because they would not know what to say to me."

Nicole continued in a tired voice, "Mama, anyone here who would accept my inabilities would be friendly enough, but then I would be cosseted to death. You know that is worse than anything for me. You promised if I agreed to come to London we could keep it a secret as long as possible. That gives me the illusion of having a normal Season."

Lady Beaumont sighed and took Nicole's hand. "My dear, I only want to give you the chance to meet someone you could love and trust, as I did your dear father. People are not intentionally mean or cruel, just ignorant of differences they do not understand." She gripped Nicole's hand tightly. "Every man you meet will not be like Michael. What he did was abominable. When you meet the man God intended for you, he will appreciate the strength and courage you have shown and will love you as much as we do."

She hurried on. "We must also have faith that Dr. Morrison will give you a brighter prognosis for the future." She patted her daughter's hand in sympathy. "Now no more talk of going home. We will be back at Beaufort Hall soon enough."

"Very well, Mama. Why do you not rest until we get home. You know Chelsea may have fallen asleep in one of our beds and will want a full account of the ball when we get there." Nicole had yearned for solitude on the drive home, but her mind betrayed her by reliving the wonderful time spent on the Swathmores' terrace. Since the drastic change in her life, Nicole had come to the conclusion that she must remain unwed and was unwavering in her decision. Her mother's mention of Michael only confirmed it.

Michael had been the first man she had really loved. He was a doctor and she had thought so highly of him. She had looked forward to sharing a life helping others and raising children among the families and friends in Cheltenham. She had thought she had found that with Michael. But when she had had her accident, he had become more and more distant until he had finally asked her to release him from his promise. He needed a helpmeet, he had said. She could no longer be that. With a heart that only she'd known was broken, she had released him. That's when she had learned that the disability that had so affected her life, making each day harder to cope with, also made her a burden. She had determined she would not be a burden to her family, and she had become resolved never to be a burden to a husband.

Tonight, however, had reminded her of what her life could have been, and she realized that her conviction might cause her as much pain as the daily reminder she had to contend with.

She did everything in her power to turn her mother's mind from the meeting with Lord Devlin, yet now she herself could think of nothing but the enigmatic man bent on furthering an acquaintance with her. While such reflections made her seriously regret a solitary future, she determined that God would help her effectively convince others that she was content in His plan for her, and she was striving for that contentment daily.

Despite her protests to the contrary, Nicole *had* heard of the renowned Lord Devlin. Since she spent much of her time with the dowagers, what she had heard had not been favorable. A major complaint was that he took an active interest in his estates rather than giving them into the hands of bailiffs. And the soldiers! Well, they could not even speak of his association with those of such low descent.

These were comments Nicole had overheard, but none were characteristics that made her think less of him. Indeed, she had secretly desired to know more of the man who flouted the conventions of Society and followed his convictions.

She had long ago built a wall around her own heart. It was not enough to stop her innermost attachments, but for protection from just such a hurt as she had set herself up for tonight. She thought once again of the pleasure she'd had being treated as a desirable woman. It proved that her self-constructed armor was still impervious to an irresistible gentleman on a moonlit terrace!

She allowed him that small entrance into her inner sanctum and knew he might be the man with the power to penetrate it completely. Her only other option was to create a more indomitable edifice around her heart that would affect *all* who would seek to gain her love, not just prospective suitors. Her nature balked at that thought. She had been given a heart for God, and she intended to follow the dictates of that heart.

Upon arrival at the townhouse, Nicole bid the servants good-night and climbed the stairs. Toby, her personal servant, accompanied Nicole to her bedchamber. He never retired until he was assured of her safety. "Thank you, Toby." He was a gentle giant and she loved him dearly. She put her hand on his arm to stay him a moment, but embarrassment made her keep her face averted.

"Toby, I want to thank you for the time alone on the terrace this evening. I know you were close by. Maybe close enough to hear parts of my conversation with Lord Devlin?" She did not wait for his answer. "I know it was you disturbing the ducks!" She had startled him, but she only laughed. "Do not worry. I truly appreciate your restraint when I am sure you felt the need to interrupt. It was quite pleasant having a normal, relaxed conversation for a change. I believe the gentleman even flirted a little, do you not think so?"

Toby's brow furrowed as he said, "I couldn't 'ear

most of what you said, Lady Nick, and you know I don't go in for no eavesdropping. I know you can take care of yourself most of the time." They reached her door, and he waited to be sure she was safely inside before he left her. She could hear Chelsea's even breathing; the girl was asleep on the divan.

At a touch Chelsea came awake with a start. She rubbed her eyes and stifled a yawn. "Oh, Nicky, what time is it? I vowed I would be quite grown up tonight and not fall asleep. Confound it! Here I have done that very thing."

Nicole hugged her, laughing. "There were several ladies snoring softly at the ball. You were not alone, pet!"

"Nicky, never say you sat with the dowagers again all evening," cried her sister. "I prayed and prayed God would give you a good time for a change. Papa always told me if it was for the good of someone other than me, my prayers would always be specially answered."

Nicole put on her most impish smile and chuckled at her sister. "You are a little minx! Your prayers were not only answered, they must have given even the angels enjoyment! Where should I begin? Lady Swathmore's turban kept tilting side to side until footmen were following behind her at each step to make sure she did not topple over.

"Old General Thomas, God bless him, was seated next to Mrs. Ballingham-Smythe at dinner. He is as old as the hills and deaf to boot. Every attempt on her part to talk to him only brought the reply telling her to speak up. After several go-rounds she finally threw up her hands in despair and knocked a platter of turbot right out of the footman's hand."

"I do not believe one word, Nicky. You are making the whole thing up to please me."

"Upon my honor, sweetheart, it all happened as I said. Why, even the haughty Miss Letitia Preston was upset because she had to open the ball with the young Duke of Crawford. He was the highest ranking title there, you see, and she complained that her pink dress and his red hair would clash!"

"Nick, you know that was not truly the enjoyment I prayed for. I prayed for you to enjoy yourself with a special companion or a new friend."

"Very well, minx—if you must know, I did meet a nice gentleman tonight. I enjoyed the evening much more than usual. Now do not go into whoops, I am only telling you this to show you that Papa was right and God does listen to your concern for others."

"Oh, Nicky, tell me all about it!"

"He was a mere mortal and I met him when I went out on the terrace to get a breath of fresh air. We had a very nice conversation, and since Toby was not with me, Lord Devlin was not aware of my accident. We had a nice pleasant conversation about the Swathmores' gardens."

"You call *that* the answer to my prayers?" Chelsea groaned in exasperation.

Nicole sat up straight and knew she had to be honest with her worrisome sister. "Darling, when all you desire is a little normalcy and it comes along in such a nice and unexpected fashion, believe me, it is a very special answer."

She could not help thinking back on the evening as she continued. "Lord Devlin was exceptionally kind and made me laugh. You know, more often than not I find myself laughing *at* London gentlemen, not *with* them."

Nicole came out of her reverie and smiled dearly at Chelsea. "That is all there was to it, minx. Now since I told Stella not to wait up for me, would you like to help me change for bed?"

Nicole discovered she was glad to have the company. She suddenly feared the quiet of the night and the subject her thoughts might continue to dwell upon. She could only pray silently for God's strength.

While Nicole was regretting her decision to have Chelsea as her abigail, Lord Devlin was sitting alone in his coach, his own thoughts far from restive. He was going to his grandmother's house only two miles beyond Swathmore Hall.

His grandmother was the only relative he felt any fondness for. Indeed, she was the only person he truly loved, as much as he could understand love. Knowing he would be so near tonight, he had informed her through the post that he wished to stay the night with her after the Swathmore fete.

She would want to discuss the ball, but he was not sure he was prepared to talk to anyone about the sudden departure of his usual boredom after meeting Lady

Nicole Beaumont. She was a very special woman, of that he was certain.

Discounting his impressions of her physical charms, it was her wit and intelligence, along with her innocence and experience, that made him think of her as more than a beauty. His own mind told him repeatedly that innocence and experience in one package seemed a conundrum, but he felt it nonetheless. Could he believe that such a desirable woman was truly disinterested in marriage or the social whirl?

But as his coach pulled up to the dower's house, his thoughts changed direction and settled on the woman who had been mother and father to him for most of his life. His grandmother seemed to get a little frailer each time he saw her now, and he knew she could no longer get out of the Bath chair she had once used only as a convenience. She was more special to him than she would ever know.

Lady Augusta, the dowager countess, was his fraternal grandmother and had always tried her best to shield him from his father's harshness. Devlin's mother had been too weak to stand up to the fifth Earl of DeVale. Even Devlin's marriage had been loveless. But his grandmother was strong and her protection had often spared him unjust punishment. They soon came to share a love built on respect and caring that he had never felt before or since.

Indeed, he always looked forward to time with his grandmother. Thinking about it now, he realized he had grown up hearing of his grandmother's great dependence on God. Lady Nicole also broached that subject.

But as Devlin grew and became more and more embittered with his father and society in general, his grandmother's beliefs seemed incongruous in the world he lived in.

He supposed his grandmother's faith in a supreme being had kept him from overt surprise when Lady Nicole had indicated the same. But he believed as a young, beautiful woman in the midst of a London Season, it would be a simple matter to trust in an all-loving God. She had not seen enough of the world to be jaded as he had.

His grandmother was convinced there was still a woman for him who would unlock his heart, and she often castigated Jared's father for the tangle he had made of her grandson's life.

Devlin looked forward to recounting to Lady Augusta the details of the Swathmore ball, especially an incident with a platter of turbot, but he did not think he would yet mention the mysterious episode on the terrace. He had not convinced himself that it was not all a trick of the moonlight!

He entered his grandmother's drawing room and found her comfortably ensconced in her Bath chair near the fire.

"Jared," she said with a loving smile. "I am so glad you have come."

Devlin leaned down to kiss the weathered cheek then brought both of her fragile hands up to his lips.

"My lady," he reproved her, "what are you about, to give up your rest to wait upon me? I should never have asked to come had I suspected you would jeopardize your health over it!" Pulling a covered footstool closer to her chair, he sat before her.

"Goodness, Jared." It was the lady's turn to scowl. "What an abominable greeting." She had feigned anger, but she soon looked at him with her dazzling smile as she squeezed his hand. "My dear, you must not scold me. Tell me all about the ball. Indeed, I shall surprise my neighbors by knowing all the gossip before they do!"

An image of a dark-haired beauty on a moonlit terrace flashed through Devlin's mind. He decided that despite what he had just told himself, sharing that unexpected encounter would not only please his grandmother, but would possibly help him dispel the air of mystery he had put upon it.

"It was no different from any other of the balls I have attended over the past ten years. I did meet an unusual woman. She left, however, before she could become a dead bore."

She casually asked him while taking a sip of her tea, "Did you set up a new flirt, dear?"

Devlin laughed out loud. "Grandmother, you are a complete hand!"

"You avoid my question, Jared."

Devlin laughed again and held up both hands as if to ward off a blow.

"Then tell me, dear, who is it that piqued your interest tonight?" Lady Augusta watched a faraway look come into her grandson's eyes. She was now certainly intrigued.

"Your description is quite apt, Grandmother. Lady

Nicole definitely 'piqued my interest.' The sameness of such events is becoming tedious. Dare I admit I was in a dark corner hoping to avoid notice?"

"If what I hear is correct, you very seldom avoid notice."

"When I was young I found all of the attention quite diverting. I enjoyed the antics some women went to just to get my attention. Fainting spells and sprained ankles were a common occurrence when I was by." He looked at the older woman with a mischievous glint in his eyes. "I would know, do they teach women those maneuvers from a young age, or must you invent such ploys as you go along?"

"Do not be impertinent, Jared. You know very well I despise such artifice."

He was obediently contrite. "I apologize, ma'am." He continued with his train of thought. "But after Vivian, I no longer saw such machinations as humorous, and I can no longer even pretend to be flattered by them. These women have no knowledge of me beside what they have heard through the gossipmongers. Yet it seems not to matter as long as I am a wealthy earl." He stopped, downing the rest of his brandy all at once.

Lady Augusta patted his hand. "I gather the someone you met tonight was quite different?"

"To own the truth, Grandmother, I do not know. I know that while we conversed she had no idea who I was. However, I do believe that had she known, she would not have behaved any differently. I suppose the fact that she did *not* fawn over me explains my notice of her." He hoped he sounded nonchalant to his grandmother.

"You begin to interest me greatly, Jared. Why would she have acted differently had she known who you were?"

"I am afraid I was a bit…ah…starched up, and she gave me quite a set-down. I believe you would have liked her immensely!"

"Jared, what in the world…?"

"Do not be alarmed, I did nothing too outlandish!" He winked to reassure his grandmother. "I am only aware that had I behaved so to someone knowing my identity, I cannot help but believe they would have playfully rapped me with their fan and called me a shocking tease. It was quite diverting to be put in my place for a change.

"It made me wish to further the acquaintance. However, soon after she left the ball with her mother, and I had no opportunity to determine whether her indifference was only another creative attempt at catching a husband or a shocking decline in my wit and charm." He doubted he would ever know the answer and was a little surprised that he wished it otherwise.

"Do not worry, I have not lost my wits," he continued, striving to stay away from deeper ruminations. "Having an interesting, intelligent conversation with a female not intent on fawning on me was quite pleasant."

"She sounds quite spirited," his grandmother remarked cautiously.

"Yes, I believe she must be, but I own she was quite

composed after our initial encounter. I am inclined to believe the set-down was a little out of character for her. She was quite reticent thereafter and never looked me in the eye. It was fleeting, but I thought you would enjoy knowing my evening had not been quite as boring as most."

He would have been quite surprised to hear Lady Nicole making the same explanation to her little sister back in London!

Chapter Three

"Lady Nick?"

"Yes, Toby?"

"There's a caller waiting for you in the blue drawing room. Lady B sent me 'ere to fetch you."

Botheration! In the early mornings Nicole was free to do as she wished. That wish entailed spending time in the small garden she had lovingly tended since their arrival in Town. Many mornings she would just sit and appreciate working with the flowers and herbs, especially their fragrances. She was now able to separate each smell. She delighted in the sweet perfume of the roses as well as the pungent, tangy scent of the thyme.

Now her only solitude was to be interrupted.

"Toby, Mama would have a fit of the vapors if I greeted anyone dressed like this. Could you please let her know I have gone to change?"

Stella helped Nicole change into a dark blue morning gown with an Empire waist and a high white ruffled collar. There was a white ribbon tied around the empire waist, which hung to the floor and accentuated the collar. The sleeves were short blue puffs with the same white ruffle at the hem. Stella did not have time to curl her hair, so she just brushed it until it shone, then pulled it up in a blue-and-white ribbon.

Toby took her arm at the bottom of the stairs, taking her to the morning room. "Do you know who the caller is?"

"Nope, can't say that I do. Didn't feel it was my place to ask. Your mother sent me for you before she went into the drawing room."

"I suppose it makes little difference. Thank you for your help."

Nicole knocked on the drawing room door, then opened it and entered, saying, "I am sorry for the delay, Mother. As you know I was working in the garden and had to change my…"

"Darling," Lady Beaumont said, interrupting her daughter in an obvious state of agitation, "only see who has called on us this morning." Her voice sounded distraught as she added, "You remember Lord Devlin?"

The look on Nicole's face must have been identical to the one her mother had presented, for Lord Devlin laughed and said, "I see I have caught both of you ladies quite by surprise this morning." Since Nicole did not move in his direction, he walked to her and raised her hand to his lips in a light salute.

Nicole was nervous, and her thoughts were running rampant. What was he doing here? It had been over two weeks since they had met! In those first few days she had lived in dread *and* in hope of having him call. She'd spent days after the ball trying to remember what had been said in the shadows of a moonlit balcony.

She finally decided that she did not give a hang *what* he was like, as it appeared he would not further the acquaintance. As the days passed into weeks, she accepted his defection. Her mother told her not to compare the men she would meet to Michael. Yet the only other man she had been attracted to since Michael had reacted the same. So she had convinced herself to keep him as a special memory and nothing more. Now he was here, and she was not prepared.

"Mama, I am sure you have ordered some refreshment for his lordship. Shall I check on what is keeping it?"

"Darling, I did offer, but Lord Devlin said he could not stay but a moment." Indecision was evident in her voice.

Lord Devlin was enjoying himself immensely. During Nicole's deafening silence, he had ample time to reassure himself that he had not imagined her beauty. She was not in the first blush of youth, but she looked in daylight as she had in the shadows! The Empire design kept him in the dark as to her figure, but her hair was long and chestnut with a few tendrils escaping the ribbon in back. Her eyes were large, thick-lashed and *very* brown.

He wished he could just sit and study all the nuances Lady Nicole presented. He watched her as she wrung her hands in her lap. He watched her foot tap under her skirt, and imagined that sitting still in her chair was driving her to distraction. Yes, he was enjoying himself to the hilt!

"I did mention to your mother that I cannot stay. I wished, however, to call upon you and ask if you would do me the honor of driving with me this afternoon. I want to apologize for not calling on you sooner. I went to visit my grandmother in Beckenham after the ball that night. Unfortunately she was not feeling as well as I had hoped, so I remained with her an extra week."

The flash of outrage on Nicole's face vanished quickly, but his intense study of her did not allow it to pass unnoticed. She still doubted that he had a grandmother at all!

"My lord, I would be honored to drive out with you today. However, I find the crush of carriages during the five o'clock hour puts quite a damper on the excursion." She seemed to be bored. "I have come to wonder why anyone actually calls it a drive?"

The chit was being impertinent, and he could not wait to see where it led!

"Perhaps if we go a little earlier, we might truly enjoy it. Oh dear, I should not be putting you out so," she said, though he did not think her sorry in the least. "I am imposing—please forgive me. Perhaps we may go another time."

The impudent minx was actually giving him another set-down! She acted as though she did not care a jot whether she was seen driving in his curricle at the fashionable hour! Now he knew why he could not forget her. She was original and quite able to handle herself...and him!

Two could play at such a game, he thought. "Six

o'clock would be better for me, my lady. It will be a little cooler then as well." At her barely perceptible acquiescence, he rose. "Thank you for your time this morning, I look forward to this afternoon." He bowed, and turned toward the door.

Nicole's mother stopped him in the doorway. "Perhaps, my lord, since you will be driving with Nicky so late, you would care to stay and have supper with us afterward? I know it would be unusual," she said in a small stammer, "however, it is our 'at home' night, and you would be very welcome. We are quite informal on such evenings. We would not expect you to change from your driving clothes."

Devlin's instinct was to give a cool denial and stop any pretensions early. But he was intrigued by the beautiful Nicole and decided to withhold presupposition at least until after the drive. He could always "remember" a prior engagement if it became necessary.

Lord Devlin shocked Nicole by saying, "I would be charmed, Lady Beaumont." As he walked out the door he said, "Lady Nicole, my carriage will call for you at six."

Several hours later, the usually composed Nicole was in a state of high fidgets. *Drat the man!* she thought. She stamped her foot in vexation. Why could he not have taken the hint to go away? His appearance had upset her entire notion of priority!

And what was her mother about, inviting him to dinner? He was a famous Corinthian! He did not do "at homes" with a countrified family he had seen only twice. It must be so unusual that it amused him to accept. He was likely ruing the day he had ever expressed an interest in calling on them.

It was too late now, however. She only hoped it would not prove too embarrassing and that he would allow them to get through the last few weeks of the Season in relative obscurity. With his standing in Society, he had the power to make them the laughingstock of London. Home looked even more tempting!

Nicole finally settled on a russet driving gown and Stella chose a matching spencer and hat. Her dress was very simple, and she tied her hair in a loose chignon at her nape to keep it from blowing during the drive. She was in the foyer pulling on her gloves when a knock sounded at the front door. Geeves bowed gracefully. "Your lordship."

Devlin came to Nicole immediately and raised her gloved hand to his lips in a swift kiss. He did not hold it overlong and she complimented him on his promptness.

"On the contrary," he said in a teasing tone, "I believe my groom will like you immensely. He will be amazed that he will not have to keep the horses standing. I have sometimes driven ladies who are *not* known for being ready beforehand."

"My lord, do not be absurd. I do understand the importance of a late entrance at a ball when just the right dramatic flair must be achieved," she said, raising her nose to highlight her words. "But even *I* know better than to make a famous Corinthian keep his horses waiting!" She smiled, hoping he found her diverting in return. "You will note my astute awareness that you *are* a famous Corinthian. It is new knowledge, I will admit. I was not previously aware there was a specific title for such a sportsman before I came to London, but I am now cognizant of how important your horses must be to you." Nicole finished her absurd greeting by taking his arm and asking, "Do you not then normally drive out with intelligent women, my lord?"

Devlin laughed aloud at Lady Nicole's teasing while trying to reconcile it with her attitude of cool pride earlier in the morning. He must remember to expect the unexpected from this fascinating woman. But all he said was, "You would be surprised, my dear, very surprised."

As they took the first step out of doors, Nicole begged his patience for one moment. "My lord, may I let my mother know what time you envision returning for supper?"

"If you are up to it, my lady, I propose that instead of going to the park where we might still run the risk of congested pathways, we take a leisurely drive through London. I daresay we should not be much more than an hour or so. I brought my curricle rather than my phaeton so we could converse easily. In my curricle, I may pay more attention to my companion than to my driving."

"I would enjoy a drive through Town very much," she said. Nicole then turned to the butler and said, "Geeves, would you let my mother know an hour or so for dinner, and would you please let Toby know we are ready to leave."

Lord Devlin was confused. "Toby?" he asked. "Is there someone else joining us? It may cause us to be overcrowded."

Who the deuce was Toby? he asked himself. He was trying hard not to show his vexation. He had truly been looking forward to this time alone with her, and now it was being ruined by someone he had never heard of.

"Oh dear, I am so sorry, my lord! Toby is my servant. Actually, more than a servant to me—he goes with me whenever I leave the house. He will ride in the back with your groom if that is acceptable, and I assure you he will not crowd us or inconvenience us in any way."

He was not pleased. "I have apparently given you some cause for concern if you feel the need to provide your own chaperon," Lord Devlin said coolly. "Let me put you at ease, my lady. I am not in the habit of seducing young ladies of Quality in broad daylight."

She put her hand on his arm and said softly, "Forgive me, my lord, I had no intention of making you angry. Toby is not for propriety, and I am sorry if I gave you that impression. You see, I was in an…accident two years ago and Toby serves as my personal servant whenever I am out, in the event any special need should arise." She took her hand off his arm and turned away, red and flushed. "I have come to take Toby so much for granted that I sometimes forget to inform others when making plans. I will certainly understand if you wish to cry off from the drive."

Suddenly, Devlin felt like the worst cad. Why had he jumped to such conclusions without any basis? Why had it made him so angry that she might be bringing someone else? And why, after she explained about the accident, did he still resent the servant? *He* wanted to meet any special needs that might arise, though he had no idea what those might be.

These were new emotions for him, and it piqued his curiosity even more. He had been intrigued at the outset, anxious to know her better, and this was his opportunity.

"Lady Nicole, if we are to be friends as I hope, you may as well know now that I have a terror of a temper and it does not require much provocation. It is I who owe you an apology for jumping to conclusions, and I beg your forgiveness. Your servant is welcome to come along and I certainly have no plans to cancel our engagement, unless you are wishing me at Jericho."

Nicole turned back to him with a dazzling smile that made him quite happy she had not changed their plans. "Now that your groom really will be angry to have his horses kept standing, you will surely lose his approval on your taste in driving companions!" Then in a more serious vein she added, "You have certainly seen *my* temper flare and forgiven my outbursts. I can do no less for you."

Toby, the manservant who was six feet four if he was an inch, was up with his groom and offered with a grunt, "A great pair of grays, Guv'nor. Ain't never seen a better-matched pair."

Lord Devlin humbly thanked the servant, who was, by the by, the first to take the liberty of commenting upon his cattle. He noticed a small, almost thankful smile appear on the face of Lady Nicole. Was there no end to the mysteries surrounding this woman?

Devlin handed her into his equipage and walked around to climb in the other side. He began to steer clear of the busy Berkeley Square traffic and to move toward the outskirts of London.

Nicole purposely complimented him on his grays *and* his driving skill. She had secretly been concerned he might be a bit too sporting for her capabilities, but he made her feel very safe. She hoped the compliment would do much to appease their earlier contretemps.

He seemed to be concentrating minimally on the task of driving, but had not yet opened the conversation. She, therefore, resorted to humor and questioned him in a whisper, "May I ask you about something you said earlier, my lord?"

"You certainly may, my lady."

"I would be interested to know when it *is* your habit to seduce innocent females, since it is not during daylight and not before dinner."

His loud crack of laughter booming from the curricle drew the stares of several pedestrians on Berkeley Square, and not a few comments on the lack of gentility in young people today!

Lord Devlin was an excellent tour guide. He spoke freely of London's more interesting sights, and she appeared to listen closely to his words without the silly interruptions usually accompanying such an outing with other females. When he pointed out the famed Drury Lane Theatre, he felt her excitement increase though she did not speak. He thought he could not be mistaken in her reaction. "Have you had an opportunity to visit the theater since being in Town?" Devlin inquired.

"No," Nicole replied, softly. "I have often dreamed of attending Drury Lane, but Mama has not allowed us the time on this trip." She laughed and shook her head. "I shall put myself beyond the pale by telling you that as a child I wished to be an actress. I was quite downcast for several weeks and took my parents seriously to task for being wellborn!"

"I have a new respect and compassion for your mother and father, my dear. Had I been your sire, I may have resorted to locking you in your room until you reached your majority."

Devlin had a difficult time keeping his eyes off her face. She made no reply, but her smile seemed to shine directly from her heart. What an unusual woman! She truly enjoyed his light banter, unlike the females who tittered and slapped his arm while declaring him a horrible tease.

Conversation ceased for several moments as Lord Devlin maneuvered his team through the busy city streets. Very soon they were past the outskirts of London, and Devlin chose a path along the Thames which he knew was less traveled.

"The roses and honeysuckle smell simply wonderful," Lady Nicole said. Her eyes closed in the enjoyment of it. "I do not believe I have been to this part of the city before."

The voice of her manservant sounded from behind them. It momentarily diverted Lord Devlin's attention.

"There's them yellow roses you love so much over to the right, my lady."

"Ah, Toby, thank you," she said as she turned her head in that direction.

Perhaps, thought Devlin, she was one of the very progressive elite who allowed their servants much freedom. He knew his grandmother gave her servants much license; she believed them to be her equals in God's eyes. More likely, Lady Nicole's accident had given him more prominence than was usual. Devlin was certainly puzzled by the enigma.

He slowed his horses to a sedate trot. The almost deserted lane allowed him to turn his full attention to the lovely woman beside him.

"The time has come, my lady," Devlin began. "I have waited patiently during the past two weeks to hear all about you. I would like a history of Lady Nicole Beaumont, and I shall not hesitate to quiz your charming mother should you try to dissemble."

Nicole seemed easier in his company today, but still showed signs of reticence. She would make a teasing comment with a sparkle in her eye, then her countenance would change and he sensed an inner turmoil in her. He would take an oath she had been happy just seconds before, then as quickly, her thoughts seemed to take her deep inside herself.

He had been intrigued since meeting her, yet he admitted that her many facets might require more attention than he had ever invested in a woman. He had promised himself that after his marriage to Vivian, he would only enter into a relationship with all the cards on the table. He knew he must marry again eventually; as head of the family he must produce an heir. But he justified that at the age of one and thirty he had plenty of time.

He decided he was on the verge of a relationship with this woman, he just did not know yet of what nature. Confound it! This was the third time they had met, but he felt so drawn to her that he was sure he had to know her better.

Devlin had told her he wished them to be friends. But he had never been simply friends with a female. Truth to tell, he would not have believed such a relationship possible had not his own best friend, Lord Hampton, had such a friendship with the woman he had eventually married. There had been the rub! Peter had been adamant that they were just friends for years. The problem was, it had ended in their marriage. Beth was a wonderful woman, but Devlin found it hard to believe that their relationship as friends had only been the natural incline of deeper feelings. Peter even went so far as to say that having been friends first only increased the satisfaction in their marriage. Devlin felt only doubt.

But it was no use. He had allowed his curiosity to override his judgment, and he knew he would be unable to dismiss the intriguing Lady Nicole. He told himself he only wished to enjoy the remainder of the Season with a light flirtation. He would feel no remorse, as both of them had clearly dismissed marriage the night they met.

He felt her forcibly lighten her mood next to him. She apologized and drew his attention back to his earlier request. "My lord, there is no mystery *or* excitement to my life. I am afraid you shall be terribly disappointed if you have truly been waiting weeks to hear of it!" Her laughter delighted him. He found he enjoyed making her laugh and that, too, was a new feeling to him.

"I have no reluctance to tell you, my lord, I only fear boring you to tears. I would not be able to face my family should you send me home alone in your curricle."

"You are trying to throw me off the scent, my dear, but to no avail. I am inclined to be gregarious this afternoon. Tell me about your home. Or you may talk of your parents, how well you watercolor—whatever interests you." He paused for a moment. "And as we have agreed that we shall become fast friends, I would be honored if you would call me Jared."

"My lord, you cannot be serious?" she asked incredulously. "You know how very improper that would be. Why, the first time anyone heard me call you such, I would be labeled forward and be ostracized from the little of the *ton* that accepts me now." She thought he must be teasing her again, so she smiled as she said, "Or is that your diabolical plan?"

He was perfectly serious in reply, however. "Perhaps you could use my name when we are alone, as now, and my title when others are present?"

"I am afraid you give me far too much credit! I should not be able to carry it off, *my lord*," she said. "I would be standing next to one of the patronesses of the hallowed halls of Almack's and say, quite without thinking, 'Jared, pray tell me how your dear grandmother is.'" She smiled wickedly as he burst out laughing. "There would not be enough smelling salts in all of England to revive the matrons!"

"Minx," he said, in a mischievous tone. "Very well, I shall forgo your downfall in Society, *for now.* But I beg a compromise. May we not agree on Devlin? Your address of me in public, as in private, will prevent the censure of the great ladies of Almack's."

"That seems fair, my lord…um, Devlin. In return, you must know that the ones closest to me do not call me Nicole. My friends call me Nick or Nicky. Should it please *you,* feel free to address me as such." She laughed a bit as she continued, "Indeed, you quite remind me of my father when you refer to me as Nicole. He is the only one who ever did so."

"Do not fly up into the boughs with me. Despite your strict sense of propriety, you will not deter me from calling you Nicole. You see, I believe I can safely use your Christian name in private yet appear quite formal in public. And I defy anyone to call such a beautiful woman Nick!"

He lowered his voice to a thoughtful timbre. "If it would not offend the memory you have of your father, I would greatly cherish the honor of calling you Nicole."

She underwent another mood change, but it did not appear to be a dark one as before. He leaned closer to hear her softly spoken words and quickly had the thought that he liked the physical closeness communicating with her required.

"My lord…I mean Devlin, if you are sincere in your wish, you may certainly call me Nicole." With downcast eyes she continued, "Indeed, I think my father would have liked you very much, and would be glad to know that someone carries on the tradition. And thank you for the wonderful compliment."

He thought she was trying to cover embarrassment by teasing him. "Had you ever seen me at home riding astride Solomon, you would have no trouble addressing me as Nick!"

He determined to keep her thoughts buoyed. "If *that* was a wonderful compliment, I believe you have been hanging around some very dull dogs. It appears I will not have to pull out all of the stops to impress you. And I think I should give a king's ransom to see you riding astride!" Her smile satisfied him.

He teased as well, but he was acutely aware of times she faced an inner struggle and would gently nudge her back to the present with a common question or remark.

"Very well," she laughed. "You must forgive my wandering mind. There is so much to enjoy that I hate to spoil it. I would much prefer to hear about the places you have traveled or people you have met." Nicole paused, chewing on her lower lip. "To own the truth, I should even like to know about your clubs and…Tattersalls! Why do they think a woman should not purchase her own horses?" She seemed to shake herself mentally. "In any event, as those places are closed to women, I have no way to picture them."

Devlin laughed wholeheartedly. He thought she

might be expecting a set-down and was pleased to see the smile on her face.

"I hope, Nicole, we shall have many more such outings and I promise to tell you all of the secrets of a man's world in London. Today, however, we are talking of you."

She was embarrassed at first, but she did as he asked. "I am three and twenty years old, so you can see that I am quite on the shelf! I grew up on our estate in Cheltenham. Beaufort Hall is such a beautiful place, and my father was only really happy when he was there. The only time he went to Town was to do his duty as a Member of Parliament."

Nicole averted her eyes, a habit he noticed she frequently employed. "He believed the love of God, sincerity and loyalty, friendship, caring for others, and honesty to be the Golden Rule of one's life and not the exception." She stopped for a moment, and then added, "I only wish it were possible for us to live up to those standards." She reddened and finished, "I am afraid I often fall short."

Devlin felt the need to reassure her. "I know some of the world do not concern themselves overmuch with honesty and loyalty. However, we cannot assume the guilt of others. You and I have already decided upon candidness, have we not?"

Nicole's brows furrowed for an instant, but it was gone so quickly he was not entirely sure it was ever there.

"If only we *could* live with complete honesty, what a better world it would be." She gave a pregnant pause, and then continued, he thought, in a sardonic way. "We would have to tell poor Lady Swathmore her turbans were monstrous and Sir Richard that his famous waistcoats were abominable."

He chuckled at the picture she presented, though her words did not convey what she had actually been thinking. He wondered at the kind of problems this lovely woman faced that sometimes seemed to take her somewhere else, while all the time remaining in his presence.

"What else would you like to know, my lord?"

"When you spoke of your father, a distant memory came to me about your parents. I believe your mother is the daughter of a viscount, is she not? And she was his only child, I think?"

"Yes, she was. Her father had been somewhat displeased not to have a male heir, but he did not disdain the distant cousin who would inherit the title. As several of my grandfather's estates were not entailed, he specifically willed property and a generous dowry to Mama. But when she married Papa, she gave up the glitter of Town life to live with him at Beaufort Hall."

"But your father, he was one of…seven, if I remember correctly."

"You *are* correct. Father knew he would inherit the title, but he often lamented being the oldest. Had he not been, I believe he would have been a member of the clergy. He was interested in education and spiritual matters from an early age."

Nicole sighed in frustration. "Are you *sure* you wish me to go on with this?" she queried.

"By all means, I assure you I am riveted."

"My mother's parents were not happy with the match. They did not like that she was 'buried' in the country away from all her friends *and* the diversity of Society. But Mama had been spoiled from birth, so she could not be gainsaid. She immersed herself with father's people and, for the most part, has always been quite content there."

She let out a breath, happy that he had his information. However, he was not quite finished.

"I assume their happiness increased tenfold with the birth of their baby daughter?"

"Your sarcasm leaves little to be desired, my lord." She pretended hurt feelings, but he saw the amusement in the appearance of one lone dimple.

"I was not being sarcastic, and I thought we agreed on Devlin."

She hurried on before he could speak again. "My parents had a heart for children." They had already planned a school for the little ones of the local gentry and the tenants who could spare them.

"My father was the most giving of men—of his time, his money, even just his ear—and I loved helping him tend the estate. It was a wonderful childhood. Unfortunately my mother's parents were killed in a carriage accident soon after I was born." She did not go to her dark place at these words. He wondered at it. But her eyes crinkled with her smile and she said, "Ten years later we were surprised by the birth of Chelsea."

Devlin felt the old questions coming to the surface as they sometimes did when he was with his grandmother.

How could she believe a loving God would take her grandparents in a carriage accident so suddenly when they had only just begun to enjoy being a family? He wanted to ask her because somehow he thought she could explain it to him in a way his own grandmother could not. They were almost back in Berkeley Square, and somehow he knew it would be an intense conversation; perhaps it would be better saved for a later date.

She had already been speaking again during his thoughts. "…yes, you may groan at the word. I am quite the bluestocking!"

How very different she was from anyone he had ever met! All the more because she had no way of knowing that being well-read was not disparaging in his eyes. And despite her horrified whisper, he knew she really did not care whether she had horrified him or not. He could not come up with the proper rejoinder before she started again.

"But the Bible has always been my favorite book. I love the idea that man could, with God's help, achieve the wisdom of Solomon. Indeed, that is how my horse got his name!"

He somehow felt her every nuance, that she felt pleased when he understood when she was serious and when she was teasing.

"There is not much more to tell, to be honest. The rest is a little hard for me to talk about. My father got sick when I was seventeen, and he never recovered. I treasure the last few weeks I had with him." She kept talking, but he noticed the lone tear that ran down her cheek. "Of course Mama was devastated, and though

Chelsea could not quite grasp what was happening, she knew her world was changing. It was one of the darkest periods of my life."

Devlin was completely silent, allowing her time to get her composure. He also dimly locked away in the back of his mind her statement that it had been *one* of the worst events of her life. Confound it! Were there more? Had this "accident" been even harder for her? He suddenly thought he might never get to know the lovely young woman buried under the protective layers she had constructed. And it disturbed his peace of mind. He wanted to know it.

"We had to move to the dowager house, of course. It was not an easy time, but it has become the norm for us now. The new earl is not married, and enjoys Town life, so he is not much at home. He is happy to allow me and Mama to continue our attention to the estate and its tenants." She gave a relieved smile. "May we now end this retrospective of my life once and for all?"

He laughed and hinted that, on the contrary, he had only just begun.

They had arrived back at the house, and he took her hand to help her down. They stepped into the foyer and divested their coats and hats to Geeves. "Stop, stop, I vow you are as tenacious as a hound during the hunt. I refuse to waste one more minute discussing such things." Why did he feel there was so much she was *not* telling him?

"At dinner, sir, turnabout will be fair play. You shall have to tell me all about *your* life! My mundane existence can be of no possible further interest to you."

But mundane would never be a word used to describe her life if he was any judge. He sensed a reserve in her; she skirted around areas he would have delved further into. He did not know *why* he was genuinely interested in knowing more, he only knew that he *was*!

Chapter Four

She was true to her word during dinner, and most of the conversation had centered on his life. He believed he had handled it adeptly. His conscience nudged him, reminding him of things he had purposely omitted, that he had not shown the integrity they had agreed upon. He tried to determine if omission equaled lying and he decidedly convinced himself it did not.

Lady Beaumont hurried them both upstairs to freshen up before dinner, and as he came back down, he paused, not knowing precisely the direction he should go. He heard a haunting melody coming from a room to his right and he took the liberty of going in. Lady Beaumont stood in front of the fire, warming her hands while Lady Nicole sat behind the pianoforte, her eyes closed, playing a piece he had never heard before. He watched her play with so much feeling. He was mesmerized!

"I hope I have not kept you waiting long." He watched as Nicole rose from the piano bench, quite flushed, then he addressed her mother. "I have been listening to your daughter's playing with much pleasure. She is quite accomplished."

Lady Beaumont thanked him prettily and herded them to the informal dining room like a mother hen.

The "informal" dining room was charming, and Devlin knew without a doubt this must be Nicole's favorite room. It was at the back of the house and the outside wall was constructed completely of French doors. He could see that lights had been set up along the veranda that glistened, as well, in the garden beyond the balcony. He deduced that the sun must flood this room with light and warmth in the mornings, and he thought his grandmother, too, would love it.

Nicole began to tease him almost immediately about his childhood and he believed the conversation went well, that he made his life sound perfectly normal. He told her about growing up at DeVale Priory, "a cavernous pile of bricks that my parents enjoyed boasting of." He admitted to a sort of loneliness in being an only child, but he flattered himself that he made it sound quite mundane. He finished his story with the simple fact that his childhood had centered on riding lessons and tutors.

When Nicole asked about his parents, he related facts, though admittedly not in the greatest of detail. He candidly told her he had seen little of his parents when he was young. They were very powerful in London's social throng, so they lived there much of the year.

He so much wanted to tell her more, and tried to determine if he would have, were they alone. He found himself feeling uncommonly comfortable with her, and he felt strange tendencies to talk about things he had never shared with anyone else. Truth to tell, knowing her gift for listening intently, he deduced that she was able to fill in many of the gaps on her own but she did not gush with sympathy. There was no doubt she felt it; she just knew how to contain it.

He smiled to himself as she said, "My lord, I should like to hear more about your grandmother. I do so hope she is feeling...better."

The little minx! She still did not believe he possessed a grandmother, and she thought she was trapping him in front of her mother!

"Mama, may we remain a little longer? When we get to the drawing room, Chelsea will be there and all co-herent conversation will certainly be impossible!" She said this with a smile to show there was no malice in the words. "I am eager to hear all about Lord Devlin's grandmother. She sounds like such a dear."

"I should not mind, Lady Beaumont, if you do not." He barely stifled a laugh at her startled reaction. If he was willing to talk about her, Nicole must now know there *was* a grandmother! Still looking at her plate, she smiled and nodded, acknowledging defeat.

"A mind reader," he said, clapping his hands slowly. "You have hit the nail on the head, my lady. She was always caring of me, and I got to spend much time with her when my parents were in Town. I will own she often tried to protect me from my parents and tutors when I...ahem, used bad judgment in my behavior."

Her laughter conveyed her thoughts.

"You may tease all you like, my lady, but if you think that she always gives in to me, and does not give me a piece of her mind more often than not, no doubt you would be pleasantly surprised."

Nicole laughed out loud at his absurdity.

"May I suggest, Lady Beaumont," he said, "that we now go to the drawing room where I may meet your other, possibly more charming, daughter?"

Lady Beaumont became flustered with his teasing and could not tell whether to take him seriously or not. Devlin was almost overset when she gave a great sigh as she mumbled, "I am afraid, Lord Devlin, if you are truly hoping that Chelsea takes away any bad impression of the family, this evening is truly doomed."

But despite Lady Beaumont's predictions, the rest of the evening passed very pleasantly. Truth be told, more than pleasantly.

Nicole's sister delighted him from the moment she was introduced to him. He thought how odd it was, considering he had little experience with thirteen-year-old girls. They enjoyed tea and dessert, and Nicole's sister even convinced him to play a game of spillikins, which he had not played since he was a boy, *and* which he conveniently lost to her.

When Lady Beaumont had finally chided Chelsea that it was past her bedtime, Devlin decided to take his leave soon upon her heels. However, when he looked at Nicole, she was staring serenely into the fire. Her laughter and swift rejoinders convinced him she was aware of all that went on during the game, but he noticed that much of the time she was quiet and thoughtful. Instead of following his instincts, he acted upon a heretofore unknown desire to extend the evening.

Devlin addressed Lady Beaumont with a pleading air. "My dear ma'am, I know I should depart and allow you to seek your beds, but I wonder if I might ask your indulgence awhile longer. I could not help but notice your beautifully lit garden, and I hoped Lady Nicole would honor me with a brief view of it from your portico. We discovered the night we met on the Swathmore terrace that we shared an interest in things horticultural. I promise we will not actually venture onto the grounds. However, I should appreciate the opportunity to get a closer look than I had from the dining room."

He knew his request was odd, and should Nicole's mother be of a matchmaking bent, he *could* be jumping into the proverbial frying pan. But he believed Nicole's intent never to marry, and he had actually invited her mother to join them to dash any hopes he might have raised.

"I am sure you do not need me along for a few moments of fresh air," her mother had kindly answered. "Indeed, I should only be in your way." He was caught unawares as she then finished, "Toby will be chaperon enough, to be sure."

He had hoped his astonishment had not shown as she bid them both good-night and cautioned her daughter not to stay outside long enough to catch a chill.

He had learned from the afternoon not to let his confusion over the servant cause an outburst of anger, but he felt the need to defend himself anyway. In a polite but serious tone he stated, "I promise I do not intend to compromise you by my request, Nicole." He had risen and gone to her chair to take her hand and place it upon his arm.

She shook her head and laughed as they wandered onto the terrace. "My lord, you must stop seeing Toby as a threat. I've tried to explain that Toby is a fixture in our lives and we often take his presence for granted. In fact, you have made me quite conscious of the fact that we do not appreciate him as we should." Before he could respond, she laughed again. "Be assured my mother would never have allowed this *without* Toby's presence."

Devlin had to lean closer to hear her words, a habit he had come to enjoy in earnest. She led him to a bench at the end of the terrace. "Would you like to sit a moment?"

Devlin could not see the large servant, but he assumed her lowered voice meant that he was near and that she did not wish him to hear their conversation.

Nicole instantly began to talk of the garden now twinkling in front of them. Her love of it was very obvious to him, and his own interest was piqued by their mutual pursuit.

"It was Mr. Benson, our gardener, who thought of interspersing the plants with covered lanterns so it could be savored by day or night. He allows me the honor of the plants on the veranda, but the garden is his domain." She sat quietly a moment. "I feel so close to God when I am out of doors. I am amazed that His creation is available to us just by sitting amidst a small garden."

He had waited for such an opening, when alone, to

discuss this God she and his grandmother allowed to pervade their lives. Would now be the time?

Quite unexpectedly she said, "Devlin, close your eyes." She leaned her head back against the rough brick while closing hers. He was so surprised he had not even time to enjoy her use of his name.

"I beg your pardon?"

"Oh, for heaven's sake, I am not a lunatic! Close your eyes and tell me what you smell."

He felt a little foolish, but did as he was bid. "I suppose flowers would be too obvious?"

She giggled, then shushed him. "God has given us five wonderful senses. What a waste not to use them all. Try again."

He sat with his eyes closed and wondered if she was a little more than he bargained for, when suddenly a specific scent overcame him. "I believe I smell roses. Are we near roses?"

"Yes, yes!" she exclaimed as if she were a teacher happy with her student's progress. "The trellis next to us has climbing roses. They are my favorite."

He felt exuberant, just because he had pleased her! He suddenly anticipated a continuation of this exercise.

"But they are the flowers that are closest to you," she said. "You must try again, but now you must get past the roses. Try to determine some others."

His pleasure quickly dissipated. It had proven harder than it seemed, and he had worried about disappointing her. His only hope was to turn the tables.

"What do *you* smell, Nicole?"

She took a long time to speak and he wondered if she

had heard him. He opened his eyes to await her reply and decided he was content to simply watch her.

"I, too, smell the roses. But when I get past the roses I can smell grass, freshly scythed. And, of course, I smell the fishpond. When the passion flowers fall into the water, it changes their scent. It goes from a cloying sweet one to an amazingly pungent one. But flowers are only a part of it. I can smell the smoke from the chimney and the new hay from Mr. Loft's stable. It makes me think of the country and wagon rides."

She had grown quiet again, but seemed perfectly relaxed.

And he had been surprised. He had been able to smell those things, too, when she had pointed them out. He was sure he would never view his horticultural interest in the same way!

But Nicole began to speak again. "I can picture Mr. Keats in such a setting as this when he wrote,

'And in the midst of this wide quietness/A rosy sanctuary will I dress/with the wreath'd trellis of a working brain/with buds, and bell, and stars without name...'"

Then she had told him, a little shyly, "I also smell you. I mean, your cologne. I am not familiar with it but I remember it from the night we met on the terrace. So it evokes memories of a lit cigar and the faint aroma of leather and horses." She suddenly sat up straight but did not look at him.

"What are you about letting me...ramble on like

this?" Her cheeks flamed and she knew he could see it in the well-lit garden. "I believe I may have to stay off moonlit terraces with you, my lord. I promise I am usually much *more* proper and much *less* fanciful."

"You were not rambling, my dear, and I thought we agreed on Devlin. I do believe I shall never take a simple garden lightly again." He paused a moment, then went on, "I admit I had an ulterior motive for wanting to share your terrace."

This had lifted her face, and he noticed questioning apprehension in her posture. "It is nothing untoward or nefarious, Nicole." He did take a more serious turn, however. "I know it is not my business, but you say you will never marry. I should like to know why." He went on hurriedly, thinking that even as he asked it, he felt a niggling desire that it were not so. "I find it surprising that such a delightful, intelligent woman should disdain that illustrious institution."

He sensed another of her inner battles raging and felt a little remorse that he had broken the pleasant mood. Once again, she surprised him.

"I do not suppose my reasons much different from your own. I am aware that is a great presumption on my part, as we have not yet discussed your reasons for avoiding it, but I suspect that both are based on the general premise that we should be better off unmarried."

"That is very vague, Nicole. If you would rather not confide in me, you may certainly tell me to mind my own affairs."

"I have no reluctance to discuss it. It is more that while you may understand my overall desire to escape the institution…as a man you may *not* comprehend additional personal reasons."

"As a man I may not. As a friend I would certainly try."

"That was very prettily said, sir." She sighed and gave a resigned shrug to her shoulders. "I suppose I should most object to relinquishing my freedom. I believe one reason is a result of my upbringing. My father allowed me such free rein, and you already know how much I enjoy sharing the daily management of Beaufort Hall with Ben, our bailiff. I have yet to meet a man who would allow me that partnership."

She was relaxed again, but her thoughts had turned inward. He did not wish to interrupt her contemplation. She finally said, "I thought once that I had, but it came to nothing."

He was surprised that jealousy had been his first response; he knew instantly he had no right to be so. "You have had your heart broken and fear it happening again?"

She laughed softly. "Michael has no bearing on my decision. We were engaged for a brief time, but he found… *We* found we did not suit." She took a short pause. "No, it is a matter of freedom, as I have said. I should be quite content, I think, to live out my days surrounded by family and friends. But it provides me independence as well." She forthrightly asked him, "Does that shock you, my lord?"

It seemed a well-rehearsed answer to him. Perhaps, like him, she had deeper reasons that she did not wish to share. He wanted to ask more about her broken engagement, but she seemed reticent. Instead, he simply replied, "No, Nicole, that does not shock me. You are an intelligent woman and there is no reason you should have to hide it. However, I would assume that as a female you might regret the loss of having children. In fact, as a male I sometimes feel the loss. Of course I must provide an heir at some point, but I flatter myself that children would be a joy to me, even now."

"It has been a very serious consideration, Devlin. To own the truth, it is the only cause of melancholy whenever I reflect on it. You understand what is due to your name, and you meet every eligible woman in Society. Eventually, it will happen for you and you will have that happiness."

He was frustrated that the newness of their acquaintance denied him the liberty to investigate further, while actually feeling as if he had known her for years. He decided to try a different tack. "Suppose you fell in love with a man who would allow you the freedom you desire?"

"I can only say that the freedom you understand differs extremely from mine. But I can just as easily turn the question back on you. Would finding a woman who would not curb your independence change *your* mind? Would the hope of children to carry on your name override your aversion to marriage?"

"I honestly do not know. I have assumed after reaching the ripe old age of one and thirty that meeting such a woman is unlikely. However, I cannot say with certainty what would transpire should such a woman exist and should we care for each other."

"That is where we differ, Devlin." The sadness in her voice was audible; she seemed tired and quite unguarded with him. "I believe I would remain adamant," she said.

Instinctively he knew the conversation was closed.

"I believe I am beginning to feel a little cold, my lord. I think it time we returned to the house."

She had risen as she spoke, so he had no choice but to take her arm and escort her back inside. He did not wish to leave on what seemed a disturbing note, so he stopped their progress on reaching the terrace doors.

"I would like you to know," he said, "I have spent a most pleasant day in your company. I should very much like to further explore our friendship. May I importune on our short acquaintance and ask if that is your desire as well? And, yes, I readily admit that a friendship between the genders is *not* an everyday occurrence."

"I should like that, too, Devlin. However, I believe only time will tell whether we are destined to be such friends."

She had summarily dismissed him as she called to the butler for his hat and cane!

Chapter Five

As they waited for the butler in her foyer, Devlin thought that as recently as a fortnight ago he would have found an evening spent in such a way a sad trial. Could what Peter had told him be true? Could a woman be as close a friend as any man? He was bemused. Though he had so much pleasure in the evening, he was afraid he might need to completely avoid her if this obsession did not soon leave him.

As he donned his greatcoat, he lamented the fact that he would not be able to see her for the next two days. He needed to finalize his speech for Wednesday, and when he told her as much, his reason caused a stir he was not expecting. Her introspective attitude completely disappeared, and she became as excited as a child in a candy shop.

"You are addressing Parliament? On what topic will you speak? Can anyone come to hear it? Oh, why did you not tell me earlier? I should have loved to have heard more about it."

He was bowled over to find her so interested. If he

did not know her better, he would have taken it as a ruse to get his attention. She seemed so genuinely impressed that he was sorry to disappoint her. "I am afraid that the subject would not be of much interest to you. More importantly, they do not allow women on the floor. There is, of course, an upper gallery, but it is usually filled with local merchants trying to discover anything the government is proposing that might hamper their business."

He had seen her frown of disappointment and offered, "I would be happy to take you there on a day when we are not in session so you could get a glimpse before the end of the Season."

"Thank you, my lord," she said, trying to sound excited. "That would be delightful."

Her agitation was obvious. She could not possibly be interested in the actual workings of the government, could she? He had been oddly proud when she had reacted so favorably to his speech, but he could not understand how he had dampened her excitement with his last words. It was almost as if she were angry at him. He had never met a woman who was interested in his political activities. Perhaps he was making too much of it, and she was only disappointed that he would not be able to meet her on the morrow.

Before taking his leave, he gave his thanks for a lovely evening and, hoping to bring the smile back to her face, asked if she and her mother would be interested in attending the opera with his party three nights hence. He was not sorry he asked once he noticed the sparkle return to her eyes. He remembered her uncommon interest in Drury Lane and felt guilty at how little it put him out.

He had already begun to look forward to seeing her again and sharing her first theater experience. She had mentioned on their drive that when her mother had been adamant about the trip to London, it was the one thing she had promised herself she would do. She had emphasized the statement with a wistful "somehow." He felt an intense feeling of joy that it was he who would make it happen for her.

Now, sitting in his library, he gave his thoughts free rein and began to think about the way she had looked tonight. She had been wearing the same russet day gown she had worn for their drive, however, she had dined without the spencer. The top of the dress was overlaid in a golden lace which, with the russet outlining, set her hair color off to perfection. Even in a simple knot at the nape of her neck, her hair seemed to highlight the lovely creaminess of her skin.

But he could not put his finger on the elusiveness she exuded. It was in evidence so often, he thought he should be able to understand it. Then she would revert to a teasing manner and completely divert him.

His tumultuous thoughts were interrupted by a knock on his front door. Devlin's butler entered the library and announced that Lord Hampton was in the foyer and wished to see him.

"Peter here at this hour?" he questioned. "Of course, show him in."

Devlin immediately rose and went to his friend. He

greeted him with a hearty hug, showing the closeness between them. "What in the world brings you knocking at my door at this hour, old man?" he exclaimed. He handed his friend a brandy and steered him toward a chair by the fire. "Is everything well with you?"

Peter's outburst of laughter surprised Lord Devlin. "Drat, Dev, I have been waiting for *you* all evening at White's, where we were supposed to meet for dinner three hours ago! You will forgive me, I am sure, for having started without you."

Devlin ran his hands through his hair and closed his eyes. "Great guns, Peter, was that *this* evening? I sincerely apologize, old man, it completely slipped my mind." He refilled his glass from a decanter. "Truth to tell, Peter, I do not know which end is up at the moment. Looking back now, I certainly should have spent the evening with you, then I would not be in such a quandary. Will Beth comb my hair with a footstool if I keep you here a little longer?"

Devlin proceeded to tell his friend about meeting Nicole and of their subsequent time together. He admitted that he had been sitting for over an hour reliving the recent evening and had come to no conclusions.

Before Peter had come, Devlin had been ruminating on the marriage of his friends Hampton and Elizabeth. They had begun their relationship as friends. Had they remained the best of friends, he would not be so confused. The friendship had ended in marriage, however, and Devlin had no plans for marrying any time in the near future. When he thought about cutting Nicole before it went any further, he knew how much he would miss her wit and intelligence.

As he ran his hands through his hair for the third time, Peter asked him, "Does *she* believe you are friends, or that you are courting her?"

"No, on the contrary, she has made it plain that she does not intend to marry."

"I do not see the problem, Dev." Peter chuckled. "It seems you have stumbled upon a pot of gold! You have found a woman who accepts you for what you are, warts and all, and is not seeking a leg shackle." More seriously he added, "I can remember telling you that a woman friend is sometimes more interesting to be with than a male chum because of the extra insight she brings to every occasion."

"You do not have to sing Beth's praises to me, Peter. I have always declared you a lucky fellow in your mate."

Peter rose and walked to the fireplace to warm his hands. "I tell you true, Dev, I see things through a second set of eyes—eyes of an exceptionally intelligent, witty woman, even if I do say so myself, but my point remains the same. If neither of you is counting how many times you have walked out together or danced together, it can be a rewarding, and, more importantly, an honest relationship.

"Stop worrying, old man. The Season is over in a few weeks, and I assume you will be heading back to the priory for estate matters. She will no doubt return to her home in wherever-shire. Yes, yes, I know, you are afraid once this type of closeness develops will you be unable to give it up. Listen to me, you *will* know by then what you need out of the relationship. But I warn you, if being a friend remains as a strong desire, it will be more difficult the longer the distance and the more time between visits."

Peter then took on an injured pose and asked, "By the by, Lord Devlin, is this paragon the reason I was stood up this evening?"

Dev laughed as Lord Hampton had intended him to.

"You would not have believed it had you seen it with your own eyes. I spent half the evening playing spillikins with her little sister in the drawing room!"

Peter laughed, too. Devlin knew he was wondering about his friend whose heart had been encased in stone years ago after his disastrous marriage. Had Dev finally found the woman who could erase the pain of his past?

Lord Devlin felt he may as well empty his budget. "Peter, old boy, I have to admit that she is beautiful. At times I have wondered…if we can be friends when I sometimes feel so drawn to her self as well as her brain."

"Now that, old boy," Peter touted, "is the *only* problem with a female friend!"

Nicole lay contemplating her evening with Lord Devlin. She could not remember ever feeling so comfortable with a man, especially one who, if considered by actual number of meetings, was a virtual stranger to her. She appreciated the fact that he only wanted to be her friend. To be sure, he flattered her and flirted with her at times, but she knew he was not interested in marriage now. And that was definitely not God's plan for her. They could enjoy each other's company and their common interests without commitment.

When he had invited them to the opera, Nicole had been overjoyed. She so loved all types of music and had immediately offered a grateful prayer heavenward: *Thank You, Lord, for allowing me this diversion. It is an entirely selfish desire, but I know You are bringing these treasures to me to be savored over the years. I want Your plan for my life, Father, but I thank You for this special friend You have given me for now. I will endeavor to make whatever happens be to Your glory.*

Nicole did not shy away from the truth. She enjoyed his company. This day had proven that. But she knew little of his character. She noticed that he never mentioned God, another reason they could only be friends, but she felt she must know more of his makeup and his moral fiber. Perhaps God had given her the opportunity to learn more of him by attending his speech in Parliament. She might then get a feel for the best time to talk to him *about* God.

It was not an easy decision to make, and Nicole knew Toby would do all in his power to prevent her. To own the truth, the thought of going caused her no little trepidation. The crowds were a serious threat to her well-being, and she would need all her courage to go. She had accepted her infirmity, though she confessed to sadness over the decision she had to make for a solitary future.

No, Toby would not accept a trip to Parliament without a fight. And she knew she would have to face her own deeply buried fears if she truly wished to hear Devlin's speech. Yet she decided it was worth the risk. She would know if his speech were for some selfish topic only for the rich and spoiled, or whether he had more depth than he showed the world.

Nicole knew people rarely showed anything other than what they appeared to be in ballrooms. She herself was a prime example! But she could not help but notice that many were so selfish and greedy on the outside, so delving deeper did not seem necessary.

She was also more than a little put out. Devlin would not even bother to tell her the topic of his speech; he assumed she would not be interested. But Nicole knew that taking his seat in Parliament seriously, assuming it *was* seriously, already made him vastly different from most. This might be the only opportunity she had to really *know* him. Yes, it was a risk, but one she would take.

"Lady Nick, it would be too dangerous and you know it!" Toby was not in a good mood.

"Toby, I *do* know it but..." She hated the infirmity that had to be considered before *every* decision. "Yes, I know it, but this is important to me. Toby, I sometimes think you know me better than anyone else. Can you not understand why this is so important?"

She could feel Toby's frustration. It was stronger than she had realized.

"Sure I know why!" She heard the hardness in his voice and waited for...she knew not what. "It's for 'im. You're willing to risk everything for 'im!"

His forcefulness cowed her somewhat. "Toby, please do not be angry at me. You have heard enough between us to know I am happy in his company. But I must know his mettle. He only shows me what he wants me to see. This is my chance to see if he is…more."

Toby barked, "You can't *see* anything!" He paced back and forth.

She knew it would be a battle royal to convince him. "Toby, do not worry…"

"*You are blind!* Miss Nick. Tell me 'ow I can 'elp but worry?"

She was shocked at his outburst. Her eyes filled with tears. He'd finally said what they usually avoided saying.

He stopped, breathing heavily, and then he broke down. "I'm sorry, Lady Nick, truly I am. I never shoulda spoke to you like that. I jest get so scared." He dropped down on his knees before her and spoke in his usual gentle manner. "Why can't you jest tell the guv'nor the truth about your sight?" Nicole could hear him clear his throat to hide the tears gathering in his own eyes. "Missy, if you was ever to get 'urt on my watch, I…would die, I would jest die."

A tear trickled down Nicole's cheek. She wiped it away. "Toby," she said softly, "you must not apologize. You are my friend, my very dear friend. You may speak to me of anything on your heart. I am sorry I have been such a trial lately. I have been so selfish."

"Aw, Lady Nick, don't. You're not a trial. Say anything, rake me over the coals, but don't go all cold on me. I'll train somebody else to take care of you, I swear, but don't freeze me out. I'm begging, my lady."

Nicole's heart thawed at the words of her beloved friend. "Toby, I am the one who should be apologizing. I know you are only worried for my safety. You, more than anyone, know how much what I cannot see scares me to death. Other than the places I have memorized, I feel paralyzed for fear of falling or being caught up in a crowd without you. I have nightmares about it quite often." Her voice became very small. "I try to make things work, being...blind, but sometimes I wish I could just forget about it. I fear I still want to be normal, Toby."

"Lady Nick, it ain't fair and never 'as been. There's bad folks everywhere deserve this more'n you. Sometimes I can't understand 'ow you still trust in that God of yours. But I won't stop you...from feeling normal, that is. If'n you wanna go 'ear your gent give a speech, I'll take you. But you must promise me, Lady Nick, promise me you'll do everything I tell ya to when I tell ya to, else that nightmare of yours will come true."

Nicole smiled at him from the bottom of her heart. "Thank you, my friend," she whispered. Then a little wistfully she said, "Toby, he is not 'my' gent and please, never, ever think about leaving me again."

As their carriage arrived, she was still trying to calm Toby. Inwardly, she kept trying to calm herself.

"You will be at my side the entire time, and we can sit in the very back of the gallery. It cannot be so crowded there, and it will be easier to leave. I promise

I will listen to everything you tell me. There must be *some* women who come to support their men. We could sit where they sit. We would not be conspicuous there," Nicole pleaded with him.

Toby may have given in, but he was still deadly serious. "'ave I got your word the minute I say we need to be leaving, we go? You won't go a questioning my judgment?" His English became worse the angrier and more worried he got.

"I promise, Toby. Thank you so very much." *Thank you, Lord, for getting me over this first hurdle! Keep us safe, Father.* She wanted Toby to allow her to hear the speech, and she thought this might just be a step in overcoming her own cowardice.

When they stepped from the carriage, the Parliamentary guards were directing dignitaries and visitors to the correct entrances. Fortunately, Nicole was so engrossed in making this work that she did not care what others around her were doing. She heard the buzzing voices, but Toby noticed the surprised stares and began to rethink the outing. "Lady Nick…"

A guard stopped them, questioning their intentions.

"Sir, we are here to listen to Lord Devlin address the House," Nicole said in her haughtiest voice. She hoped it would intimidate the man.

It did not.

"Mum, you may enter to the left there. That door leads to the upper galleries. But if there is not enough room for all of the gentlemen who wish to attend, the women must make way." The guard was insolent, even adding under his breath, "Women in Parliament! Next they'll be asking to join the gentlemen at White's!"

"Toby, let us go. Be sure we are in very secluded seats, and we shall leave as soon as Lord Devlin speaks."

Her thoughts turned from leaving, however, as soon as they entered the indicated door. Nicole held on to Toby's arm tightly, but excitedly whispered, "Toby, do you not feel awed? Tremendous decisions are made here that affect all of England." Her tone was reverent and her senses heightened as she concentrated on the power that seemed to emanate from the room itself. Oh how she wished she could see it!

"I'm more concerned with getting you settled, my lady, so don't be distracting me with your talk of 'igh and mighty England." Toby mumbled that the "upper gallery" didn't seem that much safer than the crowd below. "I don't know, Lady Nick, you can still see right good from back 'ere. What if one of them gents from down there notices you?"

"Do not worry, Toby," she said again as they settled into the hardback chairs. Nicole could smell the wood-paneled, hallowed halls of the famous room. She imagined the great and heated debates that had gone on there. A sense of wonder overwhelmed her.

In the midst of her awe, she heard his voice from the floor below in a clear and powerful tone. She had not been listening to the much-regulated procedures of the institution so she missed his introduction. Unexpectedly, his voice made her tingle and the pride she felt in knowing him caused her heart to race.

"Gentlemen," Lord Devlin began in a deep baritone, "I am aware that the topic I am about to address is not important to most of you, so I will be as brief and concise as I am able. However, I shall do my utmost to make you understand my views. And I pray that after you have heard me, you will seriously consider voting for the veteran reform I propose for next month."

Devlin spoke in a voice she had never heard from him. He was obviously good at public speaking, and he sounded convincing and forceful. The resonance of his voice was masterful. She waited with bated breath for his expansion on the topic.

Suddenly his words stopped, but she could hear him moving about, directing quiet comments to specific individuals. When he spoke again, he did not sound the least bit nervous, but authoritative and deliberate.

"Many of you know my views on pension payments for the soldiers now returning home from the war in France." His voice reverberated around the quiet room. The silence was almost immediately broken by groans from spectators below and around her. Truth to tell, she had a difficult time keeping a groan from escaping her own lips. She sat stunned, hoping against hope that he was on the side of the poor soldiers. She prayed he did not align himself with the many who felt the returning soldiers should cope on their own. She quickly turned her attention back to his speech.

"All of us in this room owe our very freedom to the men who are returning now and who valiantly, and *voluntarily,* fought to keep that freedom. For too many years these brave men have been coming back to their homes and families who have tried to hold things to-gether without them. *I* believe they should begin re-ceiving a stipend from the government to help them get back on their feet."

Nicole's heart thundered an applause that would have drowned out any actual ovation!

But such an ovation did not occur.

A male voice from the floor below interrupted her thoughts with a loud bellow. "You will break us, man! We have not the funds to pay men for doing duty they have already done. They were paid while fighting!"

A gavel sounded while a stern voice reprimanded the gentleman who had interrupted. "Let me remind you, sirrah, that Lord Devlin has the floor."

Devlin patiently answered his detractor, "I am aware, my lord, that England's coffers could not stand up to full pensions for all of our fighting men. What reason would I have to bankrupt England's treasury? That is not my intention. Many who fought were your own younger sons and thereby had some wealth of their own to come home to. My bill is intended for those in need, and all I ask is that you read it and digest it before next month's vote."

It irritated Devlin that these rich and powerful men begrudged stipends to the war veterans. However, now was not the time to show his disdain. He continued in an authoritative tone, "My proposal is for three sepa-rate groups of returning soldiers. The first group is men without families who come back whole and perfectly capable of working. In those cases, I propose we would not have to pay any pension at all. We would set up a government bureau to specifically get these men settled into jobs as soon as possible. We have such agencies to find middle-class females employment, yet we have no such provision for our men."

Nicole could not have moved a muscle if she tried, so intent was she on hearing his next words.

"The second group will be those men who are whole and unhurt but have families who have been trying to keep their farms or businesses going while they were away. I propose in those cases, the families be paid a monthly stipend for six months to one year. It would be capital they could invest back into their living." The members started to rumble once again. "Consider, gentlemen," he had to speak louder over the din, "that many of these soldiers are tenants on our lands. That can only help *us* in the long run."

He must have felt the impatience of the crowd that even she could discern. He did not take a breath as he continued. "Gentlemen, you will need to read my proposal fully. When you read it, I believe you will conclude that my range of figures for the stipend amounts are well worth the effort these men gave us. All I ask is that we recognize that those men risked their lives for us all. Some of them have been gone for years at a time. I do not see that one year of monetary help from us would be too great a drain on our resources."

Nicole jumped as a voice very near to her in the upper gallery shouted down to Lord Devlin, "I can't wait to hear your third part, Guv'nor. Do we give them all silver plates to eat on, too?" A riotous guffaw started in the gallery as merchants and businessmen slapped each other on the back in agreement.

The gavel pounded several times along with a shout of the stentorian voice behind the bench: "Order, I want order, now!" As the crowd quieted, the voice continued, "We will have no more of these interruptions from the gallery, or it will be cleared immediately. Is that understood?"

Toby nudged Nicole. "It may be time to go, Lady Nick. I think 'is lordship 'as seen you and 'e looks worried."

"Toby, he is worried because he cannot make this roomful of selfish fops understand his plan." She didn't give Toby time to start in again as she listened to the raised voices below.

"Lord Devlin, are you going to continue?" the harsh speaker asked.

"Yes, your grace, I apologize. The third part of my plan *will* be the hardest and most costly for England, yet I believe the soldiers have paid no less a price." He paused for emphasis. "The third phase consists of two groups. First are men who will come home, but will not be whole in body. They will have lost limbs, or sight, or have been too seriously injured to work. The second are families of men who were lost in the war. Without the heads of their households, many have been thrown out into the streets, or worse, into debtor's prison. In my opinion, these groups deserve pensions for *life*."

The uproar was incredible. It reverberated off the oak walls and seemed to echo back upon him. "For life?" one voice called over the tremendous noise. "You are mad!" cried another. A third yelled, "How are we supposed to pay for the problems we have in America if we are funding soldiers who are no longer fighting?"

Suddenly one man stood up and the others quieted for him. "Lord Devlin, what you propose is outrageous. Why, on some of my estates, several poachers have already been caught because you give them the excuse of 'not being able to find work.'" The "hear, hears" chimed in around the room. "What have you to say to that?"

Nicole was so proud of him. He kept trying to convince a room full of opposition, while at the same time trying to still the crowd into reason. "I agree with Lord Faversham. Poaching *has* begun, and as far as I am concerned, a criminal is a criminal whether veteran or not. However, my hope is that this plan will keep the soldiers who cannot work from turning to a life of crime."

He seemed to recognize that they were losing their patience. He finished his speech very quietly. They *had* to lower their voices to hear him. "Gentlemen, I appreciate the time you have given me today and ask that you consider my words as you read my proposal. I spent some time with our soldiers on the continent and have personally seen the hardships they bear. I will not tax your patience with those details now, but I would ask that we not make them face conditions just as hard when they return to the home they fought for." He turned and faced the bench. "I thank you for your time, and I bow before your grace and this House."

Conversation broke out everywhere, and Toby demanded they leave. Nicole was compliant; she had heard enough. Lord Devlin was not like the other men she had met in London. He was an honorable and just man who would fight for a cause, whether popular or not. In her eyes, that was much more important than handsomeness or charm.

She kept hold of Toby's arm, occasionally brushing into others because of her thoughts on Devlin's speech. They finally entered the light of day, and Toby ordered their carriage before the bulk of the attendees had left the building.

Nicole suddenly heard her name called through the milling crowd and recognized Lord Devlin's voice as he neared them, almost out of breath.

In a dangerously low voice and with tightly clenched teeth, Lord Devlin spoke to the pair. "Lady Nicole, what do you think you are doing here? Confound it, woman, no one knows when a speech will incite a riot. You should never have come." He had her by the arm, and she could hear his anger very close to the surface along with what she thought was a tinge of concern in his voice. "Toby, why have you let her come here?"

"Didn't *let* 'er do anything, my lord. I told 'er myself she was asking for trouble. When Lady Nick gets an idea in 'er 'ead, it's more than me that can stop 'er. Think I ain't never tried?"

"*I* should have found a way of stopping her," Devlin muttered as he handed her into her waiting carriage and stepped in after her. "I will escort you home, ma'am. I still have a few choice words to say to you."

Toby chuckled as he climbed onto the top with John Coachman.

Inside, Nicole clapped her hands then rested them against her heart. "You can be as angry at me as you want. I do not care. I would not have missed that for anything in the world. You were magnificent, my lord, and I am so proud of you. You fought for justice for your fellow man, and I know how hard that is to do in the face of rejection and disapproval."

"Nicole…"

"No, listen," she interrupted before he could berate her. "I was amazed at your understanding of the soldier's plights. Will you tell me about your proposal in more detail? When did you visit France? I should like to hear about it. I always hear people glorifying war but I am aware it always seems to be done by men who have never actually experienced battle."

"I begin to understand Toby's frustration. I must remember to apologize to him." He ran his hand through his hair. "I am not going to get through to you how stupid it was to go there alone, am I?"

"I was not alone. I had Toby and the Lord," she said absently. She could not get her mind off his words, and she could only wonder at him for wanting to be *her* friend! Oh, how she wished she knew more of him so they could talk beyond the everyday platitudes. She felt they could be even better friends, eventually allowing her to reveal her own secrets to him.

He continued his tirade with much less air in his sails than before. "You had a servant? And it was a lone servant at that." Devlin ran his hands through his hair in frustration again. "Toby would not have been able to fight an angry mob and get you to safety at the same time, despite your hero-worship of him. And I have yet to see your God pop out of nowhere to stop an oncoming danger. Do you not understand how worried I was when I saw you in the gallery?"

"But Devlin, none of that happened. We are all fine. You worried over nothing." She clapped her hands again in delight. "You let me believe you were telling me all about yourself last night at dinner. I think it is I who should be angry at the moment!"

Then he laughed in total surprise. "I only know of one other woman who would have done anything as harebrained as you have done." His laughter ended, but his joy did not. "My grandmother is also the only other person who would have been proud of me for it."

"Devlin, those men must be convinced! They must believe the truth and necessity of your plan." She chewed on her lower lip as she contemplated her own role in that endeavor. "Do you think it would help if I set about entreating their wives? They could then influence their husbands. Women are much more sensible, you know. They would understand completely the need for such funding."

"Nicole, I beg you, slow down." She knew he was trying to curb her enthusiasm. "More likely, you would be given the cut direct for even discussing it. You have played least in sight this Season, so you do not know how few influential women are interested in politics. In all honesty, interference from the ladies might only put up their husbands' backs. You must not get your hopes up. You heard them, almost no one agrees with me on this."

Nicole smiled knowingly. "You take such a defeatist attitude, sir!" Then she, too, grew more serious. "God can do anything, my lord. He *can* convince those men to do the right thing. He *can* change their hearts."

He smiled at her unshakable faith, thinking his grandmother would also have said that. "I will happily leave it in God's hands, then, and no longer worry over the matter. But Nicole, *my* understanding of your God is that He also allows things that do not always coincide with our desires. If I must leave it in His hands, you must as well."

"It is as you say, my lord," Nicole said with quiet dignity. "I thank you for reminding me God has many ways to accomplish His purpose." She bit her lip and continued very seriously, considering her words carefully. "Devlin, may I ask… Do you think… Oh, botheration, the part about the criminals. The ones you mentioned that have been caught for poaching. It is usually their only means of food, you know. We cannot treat them the same as someone who steals as a trade." Nicole's voice was pleading at the end.

"Nicole, you are the only woman I know who would have come to hear me today. Even my grandmother may have found it too tiresome. You are the only woman I know who would sympathize with me without waiting to see how others reacted before taking my side. I am very glad we share a common bond. You, Lady Nicole, are an indomitable force to be reckoned with!"

She interrupted him. "Do you not see? Your solution would keep them from becoming criminals…it must pass."

"Nicole," he said sternly, "I do believe we need to keep crime under tight rein. Therefore, the laws must be the same for all. We cannot allow motivation as an excuse. We have no way to determine the truth of someone's state of mind. Therefore, we could not enforce laws if some were allowed to break them."

"Devlin, can we…I…pray about it now?" Nicole leaned forward and grasped his hands. "Do not worry, my lord, I will pray for both of us." She lowered her head and closed her eyes as he watched.

"Dear Father, Your sons are coming home from fighting a terrible war. We thank You for bringing them home, and we ask that You convince the hearts of these powerful men in Parliament as they decide the fates of many. We pray Your provision for them until this bill is passed so they will not need to resort to poaching to feed their families. Lord Devlin faces a foe in this battle no less fierce than Goliath, when David fought him. But David defeated Goliath to prove even the smallest of us has Your mighty power inside us."

Nicole talked to God as a friend.

"We know You purpose what is best for us and for Your plan in this world. We close now in thanksgiving and praise."

She opened her eyes and addressed Devlin. "Thank you, my lord. It always gives me peace if I can pray when it is fresh in my mind." She let go of his hands. "Now, where were we? Oh, yes, poaching! There is another thing that I have never understood. Why is poaching, a small crime, if a crime at all, punishable by death or deportation, when cheating a green youth out of all his money at the gaming tables is chalked up to teaching him a lesson for the future?"

Sitting opposite him as they debated, Nicole was very glad she had put her fear aside to hear his speech. As they took the long way home, she began to think she would risk much for the friendship of this particular gentleman!

The next day Nicole berated him. "Devlin, you purposely misunderstand me!" Nicole abruptly pushed back against the bench and crossed her arms in front of her in frustration. They were in Hyde Park discussing his speech of the day before.

That morning a large bouquet of the palest mauve roses was delivered to the townhouse. Chelsea crowed in delight, seeing that the card was addressed to Nicole. She ran up the stairs two at a time, lifting her skirts high as she raced to wake her slugabed sister. Chelsea could not hide her pleasure at the thought of Nicky with a beau *or* her curiosity as to his identity. She knew who she wanted it to be, and she could not stand the suspense.

She jumped on Nicole's bed, crying, "Wake up, Nicky! You have an admirer."

Nicole, still half-asleep, listened as Chelsea described the beautiful flowers, exclaiming at the unusual shade.

"Chelsea, do quit," Nicole mumbled. "Let me sleep a few moments more."

Nicole rarely stayed abed once awake, so Chelsea sensed the gift had no significance. She could not have known that her usually practical sister wished only to relive the previous day's adventure, pleasure and…uncertainty.

"But I have brought you the card, Nick. Perhaps it is a love letter," she said, making kissing noises with her mouth.

At Chelsea's continued prodding Nicole finally gave in, saying, "Very well, read it to me, imp."

Chelsea clapped in glee and hastily broke the wax seal in her eagerness to open the card. "'Dearest Lady Nicole,'" she began. "'I pray you will accept my meager thanks for a splendid evening with you and your family as well as your unexpected show of support yesterday…'"

Nicole interrupted her sister by abruptly sitting straight up in bed, saying, "What?" She could not explain the fluttering of her heart when she heard Chelsea read Lord Devlin's words. Oh, how she wished she could read the note herself, keep it a secret in her heart, to savor the words. She was afraid her impetuous prayer had given him a dislike of her. She slowly returned to Chelsea's words.

"'…I hope you will join me for a drive in the park this afternoon. I should like to pick you up at three o'clock as we are both wishful of missing the crush of the fashionable hour. My man will await an answer.'" Chelsea sighed in a lovelorn manner. "Oh, Nicky, he salutes you as 'Your Devoted Servant' and…wait…there is a postscript."

Nicole did **not** wish to feed Chelsea's imagination by asking her **not to** read the rest, so she silently prayed it said nothing outlandish. She had already been frightened that Chelsea would ask what yesterday was about, but it seemed she was too excited to notice.

"The postscript says," her dramatic sister continued, "'I hope you enjoy the roses. I went into the shop, closed my eyes and waited until the right fragrance struck me.'" Chelsea scrunched her nose in question. "What on earth can he mean by that?"

Nicole blushed at the remembrance of their evening on the terrace, but felt a great deal of satisfaction that he had not made fun of their exercise that night. "Chelsea, run down and tell Lord Devlin's servant I shall be ready at three o'clock."

"Nicole?" Chelsea's voice reached through her fog.

"Yes, sweetheart?"

"Why do you not tell Lord Devlin you cannot see? He seems awfully nice to me, and you wouldn't need Toby with you all the time."

Nicole took a moment to formulate her reply. How could she explain feelings she did not always understand herself? She did not wish Chelsea to fear rejection, yet she was setting the example for that exact thing. Chelsea could not seem to understand the concept of normalcy as yet.

"Darling, I do not like to put someone to so much trouble. Toby already knows how to help me." She felt God's quiet conviction, and for the first time in her life, she was afraid to listen to it. "It is as we talked about before we left home. I do not want to put people to extra trouble while I am here."

"But he already likes you, goose! He would not…"

"Chelsea, it is just better for now. Why don't you run down and tell Lord Devlin's man that I shall be ready."

Chelsea's exuberance could not long be subdued, so she kissed Nicole's cheek and ran from the room. Rising from bed, she knew she must remember to restrain her imaginative sister in her belief that a love was blooming between her and Devlin.

But in *her* heart, she could imagine.

Nicole was ready at the appointed time, despite frantic last-minute changes. She was happier than she wanted to admit when Devlin arrived to take her for the drive.

They proceeded to the almost empty park, and Lord Devlin suggested they walk for a while. Nicole hated that her lack of sight prohibited a long leisurely stroll. It could only happen if she were brazenly forward to Lord Devlin by leaning on his arm all afternoon. They were not at that level of friendship yet! Instead she asked if he could find somewhere for them to sit and talk. He led her to an isolated bench shaded by a large weeping cherry a fair distance from the path.

They immediately relaxed into an easy banter after Nicole thanked him profusely for the wonderful roses. It was not long before they returned to the topic of Lord Devlin's speech the day before, and it was that which led to her frustrated outburst.

"I believe you take delight in deliberately misunderstanding me!"

Her fury only made him laugh. "Nicole, there is no need to become so heated. It is not something you and

I may resolve. Therefore, it is not a matter of such importance as this."

"That is where you are wrong, my lord."

"We are back to 'my lord' again," he said, running his fingers through his hair.

Nicole continued as if she had not heard him. "It is an integral component of the plan you presented, and almost as important as the pension payments themselves. And I believe with God, all things are possible." Nicole was passionate to make him understand.

"But, my dear, we do not agree. I believe poaching to be a crime whether caused by need or by malice. I have no wish to include this debate in what is already an unpopular bill." He hesitated a moment and said, "And did we not put it into your God's hands only yesterday?"

She was so pleased he had not made fun of their prayer the day before, but her passion for the subject made her overly animated. "How can such an intelligent man be so bird-witted?" The minute the words came out of her mouth she realized her *faux pas* in addressing him so and apologized immediately. "I told you, did I not, that I am the despair of my mother!"

Once again he could only laugh and say, "You are quickly becoming the despair of me!"

She then became serious. "I wish to tell you a story, my lord." Her voice had calmed to a serene level, and he waited silently. She spoke again. "But I must beg your pardon. I have no desire to quarrel with you, I promise. Are we friends again?"

"Sweetheart, you are not likely to lose my friendship because you raise your voice *or* because you disagree with me. I hope I have more loyalty than that! Once again I question the bumpkins who surround you if they have given up after a single disagreement!"

"Very well," she said, a little relieved. "My father found an ex-soldier lying in the woods near Beaufort. He was injured and only barely alive. He brought the man to our home, and my mother and I took on the task of nursing him. His condition was grave. He had been shot, you see, in the chest." Her eyes were looking back in time, and she sounded as if it had only happened yesterday. "Michael...Dr. Perry removed the bullet, but the poor man had lost so much blood that he died only two days later."

Nicole had paused, but with an air of sadness went on with her story. "He had just returned from fighting a month before. He had gone to his home and learned that his wife had died and his two children were being passed from family to family in the neighborhood. Overwrought over the death of his wife, but needing to care for his children, he sought work. There is no need to tell *you* jobs are scarcer than ever."

Nicole waited for some response from Lord Devlin, but as none came, she continued, "He had performed odd jobs and had been able to keep his children fed for a short while, but his income and his hope dwindled when he and his little ones went two days without food. He crossed through the woods hoping to find work on a neighboring estate. When he was on his way home, he found a dead rabbit lying on the ground and he took it, thinking only of his family."

She closed her eyes a moment to fight back her emotions, but soon gained a semblance of control. "It seems the owner of the estate felt he was losing too much game to poachers, so had set the dead rabbit as a trap. Mr. Richards was unfortunate enough to be in the wrong place at the wrong time. He was shot by the gamekeeper and left to die—all perfectly legal because poaching is a capital offense." Nicole could only think that God's tears overflowed at man's cruelty to man.

Lord Devlin took her hands into his own and felt the icy coldness in them. "I am sorry, Nicole," he said. "I hope you know me well enough to know I believe no one should take the law into their own hands. Mr. Richards should have had a trial with the local magistrate and received whatever punishment was decided upon there."

"No!" Nicole burst out. "Please try to imagine watching your own children starve." She stopped and squeezed the hand still holding hers. "Can you not see a major difference in a man so desperate he takes an animal already dead than a man poaching to sell the skins for gain?"

"Of course I can, Nicole. However, I see a difference in motivation, not in crime. I am sorry, but I still believe criminal behavior should be categorically wrong. Who may prove a man's motivation? Who may determine a man's inner reasoning? I hate to even say this, my dear, but who is to say Mr. Richards told you the truth? No, do not attack me. I ask you to use the same reasoning ability you ask of me."

Nicole was struck by his words for a moment. How

could he be so very determined for justice at all costs, yet not know the loving God who teaches that kind of truth? He had been so condescending in the carriage ride home yesterday. She did not care about that, but she wondered if somehow God had not gotten a foothold into Lord Devlin early in life to make him so passionate toward others.

"Nicole, I do understand what you say, that is why my proposal is so important to me. If it passes, I hope it will lead to the end of poaching. I am not naive enough to believe it will disappear completely, but it will make it easier to prosecute the criminals, knowing that is what they are."

She sensed his emotion as he spoke to her gently, and she could tell that he, too, had come to the realization that they must agree to disagree.

"My lord, I daresay you have never spent such a dull afternoon. I shall allow you to return me to my home so you may still have time to be back before the fashionable hour. I hope you will do so with a more companionable lady."

He teased her. "I am quite reconciled, my sweet. Once I make a commitment, I accept the weight of it. I should never show the least sign of impatience. How do you suppose I came to be the outrageous flirt you often call me?"

Nicole giggled at him, and he tweaked her chin. She was coming to love his endearments, knowing they were most improper. Then she found herself wanting too much for him to leave his hand on her jaw.

"Did you inherit your compassion for your fellow

man through the works of your father?" he asked. Nicole was quiet for a long moment, and he berated himself for bringing up the painful subject. They both spoke at the same time.

"I am sorry. I should not have trespassed…"

"My father was…"

"Manners dictate that I defer to you, my lady, but I do not wish to distress you again, so let us speak of other matters."

"It is quite all right, I promise you, my lord. I am afraid I still miss him very much, so I sometimes get emotional when I speak of him. You will think me a watering pot! But it does not mean I do not *wish* to speak of him, I assure you. Indeed, there are times when I absolutely *need* to talk about him, yet my mother and Chelsea are not inclined to do so. Therefore, if you truly wish it, I would be happy to tell you about him."

"I admit to being curious. It seems to have been an unusually strong bond. And to own the truth, I hope it will tell me more about your uniqueness which I can explain in no other way!"

"You exaggerate, my lord!" Nicole smiled. "I am not uncommon in the least, and you think to turn me up sweet by talking about him. Very well, I will add to your vanity by allowing outright that your ploy has worked on me."

She leaned back against the wooden bench slabs and her impish manner left her. "I do not believe you are as inexperienced in such familial ties as you proclaim. You speak of your grandmother in quite the same affectionate manner as I do of my father. It is all the same type of love, and it pleases me to see a man with such respect for his family. It is a very attractive quality, my lord." She blushed; she must guard her wretched tongue.

"I am never prepared for your compliments, Nicole! They are not at all frippery or superficial. I believe I shall have to make my mental list into a written one. It will be titled 'Ways to Please Lady Nicole Beaumont,' and I shall keep it on hand at all times when my ego needs a boost!"

"You are talking nonsense, my lord." Nicole blushed again at the thought that he might seriously wish to discover what pleased her.

"How quickly things can change. I have been set down! We will turn the conversation back to your father and I will refrain from interruptions."

Quietly she began to talk, and he had to lean down to hear her. "As I told you once before, I believe my father would have had a great fondness for you. In addition to being a man of great morals and loyalty, he also enjoyed laughter and teased me often. I have spoken to you of his nature before, so I am not sure exactly what you wish to know."

Devlin hesitated, knowing part of his curiosity could cause her pain. He had experienced such a disappointing relationship with his own father that he wished to hear about one so special. "I should like to know about your relationship with him."

Nicole did not hesitate, as she knew she would not be able to talk at all if she allowed her emotions to run amok. "We had a very special regard for each other. I wish that Chelsea had been older before he died so she, too, could have felt his extraordinary love. His devotion to God and his fellow man was inspiring. I believe he was much esteemed in return.

"When I was old enough, he made sure he instilled in me a true compassion for others by helping to meet their needs. It worked very well—too well, in fact. I am afraid I have even come to see the division of our classes as a bad thing. The rich get no less sick than the poor, and charity needs to be more giving of self and time than a few alms on Sunday morning." Very thoughtfully she added, "He would have loved your speech yesterday."

She began to chew on her lower lip, trying to put her next thought into words.

"When he became ill, we thought it was influenza. I never dreamed he would succumb to it. Mama kept Chelsea away from the sickroom, as she was so young. Since I had been helping with the sick in the parish she let me nurse him."

"We had the most fascinating conversations. I think it was only due to the fact that he was confined to his bed. Usually we were so busy, we had no time for lengthy discussions. But during those last few weeks, we had a chance to talk of many things."

A tear slid slowly down Nicole's cheek, but she *would* finish. "He seemed to feel the need to release the burdens he suffered, verbally. He knew he was forgiven by God, but he seemed to seek an inner peace. I reminded him of the tremendous good he had done, but I believe he felt it keenly that we should be without him."

"When he died, I thought I should pine away into nothing. He had taught me to rely on God's strength, and that is what brought me through."

She finally smiled; she had made it through the hardest part.

"Your strength and presence of mind during a trial is very…moving. Nicole, I think you should like my grandmother very much. It is almost as if she were sitting before me, telling me of her faith." He went on hurriedly, "Your father sounds like a very special man to me. I appreciate your candidness and willingness to talk about him." As he was now sure a discussion of the afterlife might ensue, he arose and pulled her up with him.

Walking back to the carriage, he teased her. "As London's most accomplished flirt, I cannot possibly allow you to be low upon our return. I must keep up appearances, you know." He handed her into his vehicle and directed his coachman to her home.

"In order to keep my reputation with the ladies intact, I must ask you to put arguments over poachers and sad recollections from your mind. Indeed, I shall be quite selfish and remind you of the pleasure we look forward to on the morrow when we attend the theater."

Nicole laughed at him. "I believe I have discovered the secret to your success, sir. You make sure to leave us laughing!"

He also laughed. "No, you quite mistake the matter, my dear. It is rather the trick of discovering the lady's

innermost longings, then offering them to her. Other
ladies do not hesitate to inform me of what pleases
them. You, however, are as tight lipped as any foreign
spy. Once you revealed your weakness for music, I immediately gained the upper hand!"

"I will keep that in mind, my lord."

Nicole was introspective on the drive home. She
wanted to replay the conversation between them that
afternoon over and over in her head. He had talked to
her, and listened to her, as an equal. Though he had not
changed his mind, he had allowed her to have opinions
of her own and had not treated her as a vapid female.
Even her father had seldom had the time for such debate
as had passed between her and Devlin that day, and she
was intoxicated by it—there was no other word for it.

Nicole had told Toby she wanted to find out Lord
Devlin's mettle, what he was made of. Over the past
two days, his character had been made crystal clear,
and she could no longer deny the racing of her pulse
and the beating of her heart when she thought of him.

It had been an absolutely perfect day.

Chapter Six

Lord Devlin sent a note the next morning saying that he had invited an old family friend, General Overton, to join them at the opera. He also mentioned that Lord and Lady Hampton, his personal friends, would be in his box. They would take separate carriages so as not to crush the ladies.

Nicole was excited about attending the opera with Devlin. She admitted to herself that she thought about him way too often. He had shown her so many facets of his character, but only small glimpses.

But Nicole was not thinking of his character this night. She was too nervous about attending the famed Drury Lane Theatre. As much as she loved music and had always dreamed of visiting the acclaimed playhouse, going with Lord Devlin rendered it an almost harrowing experience. She did not lament the fact that she could not see the performers; the music would be enough. The crowds would probably cause her some panic unless she could keep Toby with her, but she had no idea if that was even permissible. Her mother had chided her once again for not telling Lord Devlin the truth, but Nicole did not want to ruin this night.

She almost wished that it was *not* Devlin taking them to the opera, as she knew he would more than likely be a distraction. Yet after the recent time spent in his company, she could not imagine sharing the experience for the first time with anyone *but* him.

Concern was also uppermost in her thoughts at meeting the Hamptons when she was so nervous. He spoke of them sometimes, always with respect and caring, so she knew they must be special people in his life.

Her thoughts once again turned to Lord Devlin. *Lord, I know You are not a God of confusion...then why am I so confused?* she prayed. She believed she had discovered God's plan for her life through the accident. If God was giving her an opportunity to be more like Him, she could accept that. A friendship with Devlin was a purpose that had a meaning that aligned with His plan. Yet that same friendship had evolved so quickly that it made her second-guess His purpose, something she had not faced before. Shaking off her disturbed thoughts, she knew she could determine nothing tonight so she said a quick prayer and left it to God.

Her first hurdle of the evening had been what to wear. She had spared little concern for her appearance since coming to London, but tonight was special. She told Stella that she thought everyone was very elegant at the opera, and she needed to look her best.

Stella immediately pulled out a green velvet dress Nicole had never worn. "C'mon missy, it's time this green dress seen the light o' day." Her mother had urged her to purchase it several weeks ago, hoping Nicole would develop an interest in making her visit a success.

"Stella, we purchased that as a ball gown," she reminded her maid. Her mother had intimated it was eminently suitable for the opera, but it would have shown to its best advantage in a twirling dance under sparkling lights. But Nicole had not worn it to any balls she'd attended. Truth be told, she had avoided the gown, as she much preferred to remain as secluded as possible at those austere events.

The dress was unlike the Empire gowns so commonly in fashion. Indeed, when they had entered the Bond Street shop, the very french Madame Suzette had taken one look at Nicole and exclaimed, "Enfin! Finally! I have found the figure of an *Inglese* who can do my creation proud!" The modiste had designed it for one of her regular patrons, but once it had been made, the "imbecile" thought it too unusual and refused to purchase it. Nicole's mother and the Frenchwoman had agreed, and been adamant that it be bought for Nicole. "Eet is *parfait,* oh how do you say it, perfect for you. You have zee so small waist. Oui, zee dark green color will complement your dark eyes and *splendide* hair color."

The gown *was* exquisite, but the modiste's previous client had the right of it. It was unusual as well. Both women seemed to notice Nicole's hesitation as they described it to her, so they began to enumerate its advantages. "Zee velvet and lace," she cooed. "How zee gentlemen love zee velvet and lace!" Nicole had laughed to herself as she considered how little *that* meant to her, but in the end her mother would not hear of giving it up.

As Nicole dressed that evening *she* could feel the singularity of the gown just by the way it fit. It was emerald velvet with long sleeves that came to a point over the backs of her hands with an extension of lace.

It had an extremely unusual décolletage design. The bodice was cut in a low sweetheart-shaped neckline, the velvet creating a deep V down to her waist. From the tight waist, the skirt flared with yards and yards of deep green velvet to the floor.

Madame Suzette had been right about one thing—the lace was exquisite. Beautiful Irish lace was bunched perfectly in the V of the sweetheart bodice, keeping the low neckline modest. It became at once innocent and alluring due to the illusion of skin that was visible through it. That same lace trimmed the high-necked velvet behind her head.

At the lowest tip of the V in the front, where the bodice met her waist, was another tight gathering of lace that spread wider and wider to the hem. By the time the lace reached the bottom of the gown, the panel was almost a foot wide. It presented an hourglass of lace from the width of her shoulders into the tight waist, then wide again where the hem brushed the floor. It enhanced her figure in the most elegant way, they told her.

Her mother had insisted on the purchase of an emerald-green velvet ribbon to wear as a choker around her neck, and to ornament her hair. Chelsea applauded the end result. Nicole hoped it was perfect for the opera.

Her heart even wished it were striking, that Lord Devlin would be proud of her, but she would settle for appropriate tonight. Indeed, she resigned herself to accept whatever response it would garner.

Nicole had decided her hair must be changed as befitted the evening, so Stella had pulled her thick tresses back loosely off her face, tying it with a green ribbon at the top. With the heated curling tongs, Stella made cascading ringlets that hung down the back of her head. The ribbon and lace hung through the curls to complement the matching one around her throat. To finish her coiffure, Stella pulled a few curled wisps of hair around her face.

As she finished her toilette, Lady Beaumont knocked at the door to view the finished effect. The silence was deafening until Chelsea applauded once again and exclaimed, "Nick, you are a princess, a fairy princess!"

Nicole turned toward the doorway and spread her arms wide. "Well, Mama, will I do tonight?" She was mostly teasing, but still needed that bit of reassurance that she would meet the expectations as one of Lord Devlin's party.

"Oh, Nicky," her mother cried, "I do not think I can bear it."

Nicole heard her sobs as she ran scurrying from the room.

The silence once again seemed interminable. Finally, it was Chelsea who came to life as she hugged her older sister. "Nick, you know how she is. She wants so badly for you to be happy that sometimes it makes her *unhappy*. You truly look so beautiful that I think every man in London will fall in love with you tonight. Only that makes her unhappy, too, because you will not let any of them love you. Couldn't you try, Nick?"

Nicole was very quiet for a moment while attempting to control her emotions. Then she hugged her sister tightly, so much so that Chelsea squealed as the air rushed out of her. "You, my little imp, are a very special treasure. You must never forget that." Trying to be cheerful, she swiped at a tear on her cheek and teased Chelsea. "You know, for a moment, when Mama was as silent as the grave, I thought I might be wearing my petticoat on the outside!" When Chelsea giggled, Nicole sent her on her way, saying, "Now do not wait up tonight. I promise I will tell you all about it in the morning. No falling asleep on my settee, understood?"

"Oh, very well, Nick." She ran for the door, and as she was pulling it closed behind her, she said, "I love you, Nicky."

"I love you, too, darling," Nicole whispered to the air.

Immediately another knock sounded on her door, and Toby entered to escort her downstairs. Nicole thanked Stella and took the fan she was pushing into her hand. "You don't need to stay up. I can undress myself tonight."

Toby took her arm and told her she looked "very charming." He even teased her by asking if she was "planning to pop the eyes out any one particular gent, or did she intend to rattle all the gentlemen as a whole?"

She laughed and thanked him. He told her that her mother and Lord Devlin were waiting for her in the foyer, yet she stopped him before they went more than a few feet.

"Toby," she said, "before we go downstairs, I would like to talk to you about something. I want to ask you a favor. But please do not laugh at me or berate me. I assure you I am already quite embarrassed." She sighed and lowered her voice, then began again, "Toby, when you walk down a street and you notice a woman, what are your thoughts?"

Toby felt himself blush for the first time in many years. "I don't understand, Lady Nick."

"Yes, you do, Toby. I mean *what* comes to your mind? Do you think, 'Oh she is a beauty,' or, 'I would hate to have to go home to her each night,' or even, 'That one has a nice face but needs to eat less sweets'? I mean, what do you *think?*"

Toby was palpably uncomfortable. "Well, missy, I guess sometimes I thinks about things like that, but what 'as that got to do with a favor?"

Nicole decided this was important enough to keep trying.

"I want to know what Lord Devlin is thinking when he sees me tonight." Now she could feel herself blushing! *Please forgive my vanity this once, Lord!*

There were times her blindness caused her significant embarrassment. "Knowing *your* thoughts as a man looking at a woman, would that not help you to know the thoughts of Lord Devlin?"

Toby's response was instantaneous. "'Cor, Lady Nick, I don't look at no gentlewomen and 'ave those thoughts! Maybe *real* gentlemen don't even 'ave those thoughts! 'ow am I gonna know?"

Nicole was losing the battle, but kept fighting. "Toby, I am quite sure men are men, whether lords or servants. I realize you may not be able to tell what Lord Devlin is thinking. There may not be time before we are bundled into the carriage. *But,* if you *can* read a look of pleasure or disdain or just nothingness, will you tell me? I have no way to get into a man's head, and as I cannot see it for myself, I thought…"

"'Cor, why won't you jest tell the man? I don't think 'e's nothing like Doc…'e ain't like the others."

She ignored him. "Oh, I know that he will *say.* 'You look charming, Lady Nicole,' just as you did. But I hoped that, as a man, you might be able to tell by his expression what he was *really* thinking. I shall make it easy for you, I promise. As we walk down the stairs, I shall be completely engrossed in conversation with you. You, of course, will be watching his expressions. You may then lean over and tell me of his reaction."

"Lady Nick, I don't know what I'll be able to tell, but if I sees something that I recognize as a look I might give, I'll be 'appy to describe it to you." He felt her smile before he saw it. "But if I may be so bold, you do not need that 'igh and mighty lord's approval. We as knows you thinks you're right pretty no matter what you're wearing."

Her heart swelled and her countenance stilled. "Thank you, Toby," she said quietly. "Not only for the compliment but for reminding me that it is what is on the inside of a person that is important." They began to move together, years of being side by side making their gaits match easily. "Will you forget I even mentioned such folly? I shall remember to value the compliments of my family as I should." She finished, "Forgive me, Toby. I was just…afraid that if Lord Devlin appears as handsome as I expect he will, that I might disappoint him in some way."

Descending the first few steps, Toby chuckled. "Lady Nick, I don't know as 'ow I'd even be able to read 'is lordship's mind about you. I'll admit with that full black get up 'e wears and that pitch-dark 'air, 'e will 'ave all the ladies sighing. But God's 'onest truth, you will be the prettiest one there. I s'pose everyone else will be right jealous."

"Toby, you are a very good friend to me. I do not think I can ever repay you for all the years I owe you, but I hope you know you have become very important to me. Taking into consideration your tendency to exaggerate, *and* your decided partiality—" she smiled "—I believe that is the most beautiful compliment I have ever heard! Now I suppose we must go down before they decide to leave me behind."

Continuing their descent, Nicole could hear her mother and Lord Devlin speaking at the bottom of the steps. Her grip on Toby's arm tightened, and she shushed him as he began to chuckle. "What is it, Toby?"

"Lady Nick, I may not be no expert on reading minds, but 'is lordship just looked up at you and dropped 'is gloves."

Nicole's brows furrowed in question. "I do not understand. What does that mean to a man?"

"It's like this, 'e 'ears us coming downstairs, 'e looks up and does the dangdest double take you ever saw. Then 'is gloves just kind of fell to the floor like 'e didn't even realize 'e was ever 'olding them. You could probably catch flies the way his mouth is 'anging open!"

"Toby…" Nicole reproached. Her heart had begun to pound as she realized Toby had granted her ridiculous request. It pounded even more that he thought Devlin was pleased.

"Lady Nick, if I'm lying may my Ma be struck dead by lightning. There ain't no need to read that man's mind, 'e knows 'e is seeing a very special sight."

"Thank you, Toby," she whispered from the bottom of her heart.

As they reached the bottom of the stairs, Nicole's mother immediately hugged her. Lady Beaumont leaned close and whispered, "I am so sorry I ran out earlier, my dear, but you looked so beautiful I could not even speak." Then louder she said, "Darling Nicky, when I saw you dressed, I knew you needed my emerald and diamond brooch as the finishing touch to your toilette. Will you wear it? We can pin it in the center of your choker, and it will be just enough to dazzle without taking anything away from my beautiful daughter."

She hugged her mother, "Oh, thank you, Mama, for everything!"

Nicole heard Lord Devlin clear his throat. She turned to him and he took her bare hand in his and raised it to his lips. He held it there longer than was proper, and it sent glowing slivers that went all the way to her heart.

He lowered her hand from his lips, but continued

holding on to it, whispering, "I apologize for my bare hands. I must have left my gloves in the carriage. I could not wait one more moment to greet you."

She felt herself blush, but to cover the sound of her beating heart, she chuckled as she said, "I believe you dropped your gloves on the floor. I am afraid I made you wait too long."

As he bent to retrieve the offending articles, she teased him. "My lord, all of the women in London must think it very unfair of you to outshine them when you invite them out!"

While he turned her away from him to place her cloak around her shoulders, he whispered earnestly into her ear, "I do not particularly care what the other women in London think. I find I care only for the opinion of one woman tonight, and she stands before me. I take umbrage at your compliment, my lady. Not even the noonday sun beaming on the heather of the moors in Ireland could outshine you."

Each compliment he gave moved her more than the last. She felt the whole world disappear in her effort to listen to his whispers in her ear. She only hoped he could not hear the pounding of her heart.

If only he were not such an expert with women, she thought. He made her feel so…special, and she did not know how to handle it. She assumed he addressed all women in such a way and did not wish him to think she had changed her intentions of friendship. She laughed his compliments away. "I think it is safe to say your reputation as a flirt remains intact, my lord."

His sigh told her immediately that she had said the wrong thing.

He turned her back to face him and took her arm. "I think we had better go in order to miss the crush. We can relax with refreshments in the box before the music begins. General Overton and the Hamptons will be meeting us there."

Heavenly Father, I am in over my head. I confess this situation is all of my making. You never would have had it so. I ask Your forgiveness, Lord, and that You would guide me onto or back to the path You want for me.

Nicole's prayer was uttered in earnest, but she could only will her heart to match the words.

Chapter Seven

Nicole's first visit to the theater was magical...and miserable. There was no other description for it.

It began quite well. Devlin was very thoughtful, and planned their arrival early to avoid the crush. Those wishing to see what others were wearing, and wishing to be seen in turn, were always fashionably late. He remembered her particular fear of crowds and went out of his way to be sure of her comfort. She truly appreciated his solicitousness; he put her needs before anything else, without even knowing why. Would he have only felt awkward if he had known the truth?

Despite their early arrival, the number of waiting carriages was overwhelming. There was even a frightening moment when Lord Devlin stepped down from their coach. A man on horseback, apparently out of control, nearly ran Devlin down. Had Toby not been there to push him out of harm's way, he might have been seriously injured. The ladies were aghast at the near miss, but Lord Devlin made light of the episode, then tried to hurry them into the famous auditorium.

In the end, Devlin and Nicole did not have as much time to themselves as planned. Devlin's other guests arrived very soon after, just as happy to avoid the throng downstairs. As Lord Devlin introduced his guests, it was discovered that General Overton was an old admirer of Lady Beaumont, so the party began very merrily.

Nicole was enchanted with each of Lord Devlin's friends, and she felt an instant affinity with Lady Hampton. The gentlemen had placed the three ladies in the front seats of the box, and conversation between them was easy and pleasant.

Lady Hampton was nothing if not straightforward. "I am so charmed to finally meet you, Lady Nicole. Dev has told Peter much about you. I confess I find it very intriguing that he would do so about a woman he had known such a short time." Nicole blushed and Lady Hampton quickly apologized. "My wretched tongue! Please forgive me if I have embarrassed you. Hampton constantly scolds me for saying exactly what is on my mind. But you must know that he was not gossiping about you. We both enjoy sharing the events of the day, and he mentioned your friendship with Devlin. He and Devlin are such old friends. I sometimes feel like Dev is the brother I never had. Is it not funny? I felt such an immediate rapport with you as well!"

Lady Hampton finally drew breath, and then laughed at herself. "In the event you are wondering, Hampton also reminds me if I do not pause midsentence, others do not comprehend one out of ten words I say." She purposely took a deep breath, then continued her conversation with a wink and at a much slower pace.

"Hampton says that you and Devlin have become great friends. I was hopeful that you and I might do so as well. You must call me Beth and I will call you Nicole, and we may begin as we intend to go on."

Nicole laughed at this confusing and charming discourse, and was greatly pleased with Beth. She made her feel quite welcome and seemed just the sort of friend Nicole would have chosen. She instinctively felt that if Beth knew about her condition, she would have been one of the few to stand by her. That always sealed her feelings for people and she said, "I have no problem with you speaking your mind. I am afraid I have the tendency myself. But you may notice that people close to me usually forgo the formal Nicole and call me Nick or Nicky. Please feel free to do so."

"I dare any human alive to look at you in that gown and call you Nick!" She laughed as Nicole blushed and recalled how she felt when Devlin tenderly asked if she would permit him to call her Nicole. Oh dear, her heart was not cooperating at all!

Lords Hampton and Devlin stood in the back of the box for the half hour before the opera was to start. Peter did not hesitate to act the abused friend upon seeing Nicole for the first time. "You old dog! You said there was a *slight* physical attraction, but you purposely did not tell me she was a diamond of the first water! You will have every young buck in London in this box before the night is over."

"She does not have an interest in any of the 'young bucks,' and I do not think I care for the admiration in *your* voice! It is a very good thing I know what a happily married man you are, or I might have had to plant you a facer." He spoke in jest to his friend, but was a little unnerved at how quickly he became her protector.

"This gets better and better, Dev. 'We are just friends,' indeed! I am excessively diverted, old man. You are as jealous as can be, even when it is only the General who addresses her. The reason you want to spend all your time with her is because you are in love with her!"

"Heaven spare me from friends who want me to become leg shackled. Do not be ridiculous, Peter. You know my views on marriage, and you certainly know my history when it comes to love. I only prefer not to spend the intermission tossing a crowd of unwanted simpering fops and dandies out on their ears. If you knew her better, you would know I speak for the lady, as well."

"That, old boy, is exactly my plan. To *get* to know her better." He hesitated a moment then asked, "Can I ask you who brought the giant manservant posted outside the box door? I…um…heard he came with you."

"That is one story I have not been able to fathom as of yet, but I certainly intend to. It has to do with an accident she had at some point not long ago, and she never goes out without him. No, no, do not ask me any more questions. I do not know anything about the accident either. But I shall persevere, I assure you."

"Well, I am off to charm the ladies in the front while

you fight off the swains back here. Thanks for inviting us. This is going to be much more interesting than I had hoped!" He chuckled as Devlin scowled at him.

The two ladies found no shortage of conversation, and Nicole was enjoying herself immensely. Lord Hampton's voice interrupted their chatter. "I thought to get a jump on the hoards of men that will soon be forming, but I see that it is my wife who has been before me."

Nicole blushed but smiled. "How do you do, my lord? I am Nicole Beaumont, Nicky if you like." She invited him to join them. "Your wife is such a treasure. I vow I do not know how you can endure ever being parted from her."

He let out an exaggerated sigh. "Indeed, Lady Nicole, short intervals are all I can bear."

Though he teased, there was such tenderness in his voice that it caused an unsought pang of envy in Nicole's heart.

At that moment the orchestra began to tune up, and all thoughts of conversation flew from Nicole's head. She felt the three men settle in the chairs behind her, but once the opera began she was mesmerized and had no inclination to hear anything else. Several times she leaned back in her chair, eyes closed, letting the music invade her soul. Many times in church she felt she could happily discard the sermon and spend the entire time worshipping through hymns.

The emotional conviction of the arias brought her to tears. She felt a tap on her shoulder as Lord Devlin closed her hand around his handkerchief. She was so entrenched in the music she did not even stop to think that he must have been watching her instead of listening to the song.

Heaven help me, thought Devlin! As he watched her close her eyes and feel the music, he was reminded of the evening she had made him use his sense of smell on her garden terrace. He had the intense desire to follow her lead again. He had been to the opera too many times to count, yet he had never enjoyed one so much. Could Peter be right? Was it because he was with her? Were they merely friends—or *was* he falling in love with her?

He was beginning to feel a determined closeness each time he was with her. What concerned him more, however, was the *need* he was experiencing when he was *not* with her. He could not remember a time when he had gone to such lengths to please a woman. He gave up any pretext of enjoying the opera. He just wanted to watch her.

Lady Nicole aroused his desire to protect her. He could no longer deny looking forward to being with her. With no bark upon it, he just enjoyed spending time in her company. There was no denying there was a physical attraction as well, at least on his part, but she was a beautiful woman. Where was the mystery in that? He ran his hands through his hair, wondering what in the world he should do.

At intermission he leaned forward to ask Nicole if she would like to take a turn in the grand hallway. Before he could even speak, her subtle fragrance wafted over him. Once again this sense of smell surprised him. But the immediate tension in her body told him he had made an error.

"If you do not mind, my lord, I should rather remain where I am," she whispered. "Crowds are a particular trial for me, and I would rather avoid them, if possible. To own the truth, I do not as yet wish to let go of the beautiful music I have just heard." She was a little too cheerful as she begged him to feel free to accompany his friends. "I shall be perfectly content," she said, and meant it.

"I cannot regret your desire to avoid a crushing crowd…it is how I met you. I told you that night that you had bewitched me. And you know I am never wrong."

Her face flushed at his compliment.

"You know, that blush is so enchanting," he murmured close to her ear, "I am beginning to contemplate ways to bring it about." Her face flamed, but he just pinched her chin, saying, "But I shall give over now and ask if I may get you a glass of punch before the second act starts."

"I would appreciate that greatly, my lord."

Lady Hampton chose to stay in the box as her husband accompanied Lord Devlin to get refreshments.

Nicole felt a little uneasy. "Please do not feel you must remain with me, Lady Hamp… I mean, Beth. I am sure you would rather be strolling with your charming husband than sitting here with me. I am truly fine and will not mind a few quiet moments."

"Oh dear, would you *prefer* to be alone?" At the shake of Nicole's head she continued, "Nicole, I am probably saying more than I should, but I do not want you to feel bothered by the stares of Lady Robinson in the box across from us."

Nicole laughed at the irony of it and said, "I feel very stupid. I have been so caught up in the music that I never noticed that I was being stared at. Does she have some particular reason for staring at me?"

"You have not noticed that you were being stared at?" Beth asked incredulously. "Good heavens, Nicole, either you are a tremendous liar or the most modest woman I have ever met! Every *man* turns to look at you at least once or twice a minute hoping you will take notice of him. Every *woman* looks at you in that gown and wishes to see you boiled in oil. Lady Robinson, well, we shall not worry our heads about her."

"No, please tell me."

With a perplexed look, Beth said, "I thought Hampton said you had been in London the entire Season?"

"I *have* been in London all the while," responded Nicole. "I must admit, however, that I did not wish to come, so I have made no push to seek new friendships. I can see I made a mistake, or I might have known you much sooner."

"Oh, you are a love! But even if you had not been officially introduced to me, I expect I should have noticed you at balls and soirees and such. What are you avoiding *besides* people?"

Nicole almost winced as she realized this woman was much more sensitive to the feelings of others than anyone else she had met in London. Nicole nearly decided to cast her fate to the wind and share her problems with this special lady. But she stopped herself. Instead she ignored Beth's pointed question. "I believe we have gotten away from the subject of Lady Robinson. I now admit to a great deal of curiosity at her stare."

"Oh dear, it is another thing I have said without thinking! It is too late now, however, and if you are staying for the rest of the Season, there is no way you can escape her. She has been setting her cap for Dev these five years or more. She has been staring daggers at you all night. Please do not let her distress you. Dev has absolutely no interest in that direction and has been trying to avoid her at all costs."

"Beth," Nicole said hesitantly, "Lord Devlin is free to show interest in whomever he wishes. We are friends and Lady Robinson has nothing to fear from me."

"My dear Nicole, I hope we too shall become fast friends. I should like to be able to share your company throughout our remaining time in London…but I think I would like to start by being honest with you. Dev may think that you and he are only friends, but I saw the way he watched you tonight, and I believe he is fast on his way to falling in love with you."

She continued in a grave voice, "I think you need to be prepared for that because when the realization comes, it will not be easy on him. Suffice it to say Dev has been hurt in most of his relationships, and has vowed he will never be hurt again. Once he discovers he is in love with you, he may overreact. He may do his best to fight his feelings so as to remain unscathed. But in doing so, *you* may be hurt by *his* actions. It is time enough that he had some happiness in his life."

Fortunately for Nicole, the shock she did not think she could hide went largely unnoticed as several gentlemen appeared to pay their respects.

Lords Hampton and Devlin returned very soon after and sent the visitors out in a rare twig. The second act had just started, but Nicole could not remember a single chord when it was over. She had been so distracted by Beth's assumptions about Lord Devlin falling in love with her that she could concentrate on nothing else. Surely Beth was wrong. She knew they had a unique relationship for the times, but love?

Before her accident, there'd been no doubt she knew the characteristics she wanted in a husband. He would love God as much as she did. He would want a simple life in the country, eagerly helping others. Did Lord Devlin's feelings about the returning soldiers qualify as such? No! The man she pictured, before her accident, would definitely *not* be an expert with women. All of this, however, was moot, as her accident had changed everything. Beth was surely wrong!

Nicole was completely distracted during the second act, unable to concentrate any longer on the beautiful music around her. Suddenly Lord Devlin's voice sounded in her ear as he leaned forward and asked if she and her mother would like to avoid the mass exodus and leave before the farce.

Nicole acquiesced immediately, but General Overton and the Hamptons offered to escort her mother home.

Nicole would now be in just such a situation as she was trying to avoid. She did not wish…she could not ride home with him alone. She must have time to think.

Lord Devlin draped Nicole's wrap over her shoulder while she profusely apologized for causing so much trouble. Had she known her mother had wanted to stay, she would have waited.

He whispered that she should stop worrying; he, too, would appreciate the early departure.

Oh, Nicole thought, this was dreadful! During the length of the entire second act she had wondered how she would spend the rest of their time in London avoiding this charismatic man. She could never have him fall in love with her…even if she realized she was on the way to falling in love with him.

As they walked to his carriage, she sought to change his flirtatious mood. "I do not suppose this early departure has anything to do with the discouragement this might cause Lady Robinson, my lord?"

She could hear the frustration in his voice when he replied testily, "Nicole, I cannot fathom why you keep trying to turn simple compliments into other than what they are. Let me assure you that Lady Robinson plays no part in any of my thoughts or actions."

Nicole closed her eyes for one second. She had only made the situation worse, as he was now trying to convince her that she alone was his reason for wishing to leave. She quickly invented one more excuse and called to Toby as he began to climb up on the box. "Toby, that cold may get worse if you ride up there at this hour. We would not mind if you rode inside with us. Mama is not coming until later, so you will not crowd us."

Imitating someone with a cold, he sniffled out, "Not to worry, Lady Nick. You know I'm a tough one. I'll be fine up 'ere with John Coachman."

Lord Devlin helped Nicole into the carriage then climbed in and sat on the seat opposite her. She kept her face turned toward the window as the coach began to move. The silence was deafening. She jumped when he asked her, "Did you not enjoy the opera?"

"Oh, my lord, how remiss I have been! The music and the play were the most wonderful I have ever heard. I thank you heartily for escorting us tonight."

"I see," he said, sounding wounded. "You enjoyed it so much that you are now back to 'my lording' me at every turn. Have I done something to offend you, Nicole?"

"My lord, I mean, Devlin, what would make you think such a thing? Of course you have not offended me. I fear I am a little tired and do not have much by way of conversation tonight. It is I who should be apologizing to you."

Devlin relaxed a bit in the candlelit carriage. Nicole, however, was very close to tears and wished she were alone with her thoughts.

"I am happy to hear I have not offended you. I am also happy to hear your apology, though I do not think you know how *you* offended *me*. May I be so bold as to admit that you did offend me earlier this evening?"

He reached across for her hand. "Do not worry, sweetheart, it was not such a grievous offense, just one

I felt I had to point out. It seems to me that either you do not take compliments well, or you truly do not believe someone sincere when they give them to you. Of course it may be that you only doubt *my* compliments, since your comments seem to indicate you think me flirting with you."

This was getting worse, Nicole agonized. All she wanted was to avoid him, and they were sitting in a carriage alone discussing compliments and flirting! She gently pulled her hand free and placed it in her lap. "I am afraid I do not know to what you are referring, my lord."

"I think, *my lady,* that you do. You accused me of flirting with you in the foyer of your home when I gave you a very sincere compliment."

Nicole determined to turn this into banter rather than a full-blown discussion. She had never minded his flirting before, so she must pretend Beth's words had never been uttered.

She smiled a little tensely. "Sir, you cannot blame me for suspecting your charm when we have already determined your reputation as a flirt is commonplace!" She had wished to sound teasing, but was distinctly aware he was not laughing. She dug her hole deeper. "I am forever hearing upon someone's lips how the clothing makes the man, and now I see it applies to women as well. I have not received as many compliments in the whole of the Season as I have tonight in Madame Suzette's gown. She will be thrilled, but I should be happier if gentlemen would be honest and admit they admire the dress and not the woman wearing it.

"Why must everyone in London place so much importance upon a pretty face? There is also too much significance put on clothing and…and…capabilities. It is the inside of a person that is essential." She was being unfair, as she remembered how much she'd wanted her appearance tonight to please him. And she could hear the anger in her own words by the time she reached the end of her speech. Good heavens, why had she turned it into such a tirade?

The silence hung in the air thickly, and she was afraid she would no longer be able to hold back her tears. It was so quiet she could hear the trickling fountain in the small park on Berkeley Square. Knowing herself near home, she felt it safe to say, "I apologize, my lord. As I said, I am a little overtired tonight, and you already know about my lamentable temper. We should never have entertained such a silly topic. Before we get home I would like to thank you for my first night at the opera."

The horses slowed to a stop, but before she could turn to step down, Lord Devlin grabbed both of her hands and demanded she give him her full attention. "I am going to make you eat those words someday, Nicole. My compliment had nothing to do with the gown you are wearing. It *was* based on the entire person you are—your beauty and your inner qualities. I felt quite fortunate to be escorting you tonight, and I intend to spend the remainder of the Season teaching you how to tell the difference between Spanish coin, flirting and a sincere compliment…and being able to accept the last. Good night, Nicole."

As she stepped from the coach, her only thought was *what a horror of a coil!*

She got little sleep that night. After tossing and turning into every position possible, she decided what she needed to do. She knew her mother would not hear of leaving London before the Season's end, so she determined she must end her relationship with Lord Devlin, whatever that relationship might be. She wondered at the ache in her heart as she became resolved.

Since her accident two years ago, Nicole had given up on the idea of love. After Michael, she was certain no one would want her, and she was equally certain she would never trust enough to love again. She knew her blindness made her undesirable as a wife, and she vowed she would never be a burden to any man, so she had accepted her fate and committed herself to her faith, her home and her family.

Her mother had counseled her not to compare her experience with Michael to other men she might meet. But she could not help it. She no longer loved Michael, but when he had come to take the position as doctor on their estate, she'd been charmed. He was so different from the men she had grown up with; he was mature and caring and he loved God. They'd grown close as she'd helped him get to know his patients, and it had not been long before she'd been sure she was in love with him. When he had asked her to marry him, it had seemed the most natural thing in the world to tell him yes.

Now, however, all her well-laid plans were crumbling. *Lord, did I go against Your plan by agreeing to this trip? Should I have remained resolved despite Mama's pleas?* She was afraid she had let Lord Devlin invade that sturdy wall Michael had helped to build, and to be honest, she could no longer claim it was invaded in friendship. Nicole was determined to prevent further assault on her feelings before her battered heart could be completely broken.

Lady Hampton had made Nicole afraid she was no different from any other flighty woman who fell in love with a handsome face and charming manners! She knew she had never felt like this before, not even with Michael. She had not even known it *could* be like this.

But she must sever the connection. She could not actually believe Beth's assertions that Lord Devlin loved or was more interested in her, but, were it true, he would dissemble as soon as he knew the truth about her. And should a miracle occur and he prove her unworthy assumptions false, she could still never be a burden to such a man. Especially one she cared for so much.

As dawn broke through the windows of her room, Nicole came to the decision that she must protect him as well as herself. She would not allow their feelings or attraction or mutual affection—or whatever it was—to go any further.

Chapter Eight

While thoughts of avoiding Lord Devlin continued to occupy her mind, a quick knock sounded upon her door only seconds before Chelsea was in the room and on her bed with one quick leap. She was bouncing up and down in excitement.

"I have carried a missive upstairs for you that just arrived," she said, waving it all about her head. "But I will only give it to you *after* you tell me how you liked the opera!"

"Ah, it is to be blackmail this morning, I see," said Nicole, trying to rally her tormented spirits. "May I at least inquire who the missive is from before I decide whether to give in to your demands?"

Chelsea looked at the back of the beautiful ivory vellum and read out, with her nose very high in the air, "Lady Elizabeth Hampton," in her most haughty voice.

Nicole knew a moment of dread *and* a moment of excitement at what Beth could have to say, but she did not want Chelsea to read her thoughts. "That is enough, young lady. Lady Beth is a very nice person and not in the least starched up. I met her last night at the theater."

"So you liked Lord Devlin's friends and had a pleasant time?" Chelsea asked with a hopeful plea.

Nicole put on her best smile and said, "Yes, love, we had a splendid time, and the music was beautiful." Her voice changed to a conspiratorial whisper. "Mama even met an old beau, but you must not tell her I told you so."

"But what did Lord Devlin think of your gown? It was the most beautiful dress I have ever seen. Do you think I will be able to wear it when I make my comeout?" Chelsea ended with a sigh, as if that time were a thousand years away.

Nicole flinched as she remembered her outburst in the carriage last night and said, "Chelsea, the dress was a success, but you will be special in your own way when it is time for your Season. You will not need to depend upon a gown.

"Darling, it is I who got caught up for a moment in the vanity that I have been complaining about in others. We constantly turn our noses up at Lord Stokes for vanity over *his* attire. I know I am vain enough to want to look nice, but I do not want people to know me by my clothes." Her voice changed to a haunting whisper. "You know Father would never have wanted it so."

Nicole could tell she had dampened Chelsea's spirits, but she knew she had made her point, so she ended her recital in an indulgent confession. "To own the truth, I have never had so many compliments in my life!" She pushed herself up, leaning back against her pillows.

"Now why do you not read the missive before Stella arrives with my chocolate? That is, of course, assuming I have met the blackmail conditions!"

As she tore the vellum, Chelsea grumbled, "It is very short, what a disappointment."

Nicole breathed easier as she realized a short note was not a disappointment to her. "It would help if you would read it aloud, love!" Nicole said.

"All right, I'm reading, I'm reading…

'Dear Nicole,
I pray you will do me the honor of having tea
with me today. I so enjoyed meeting you last
evening. I have cleared my schedule in the ar-
rogant hope you would not refuse me. I would
like to get better acquainted. I will send my
carriage for you at eleven o'clock, unless I hear
otherwise. Be assured I shall not take no for
an answer!
Your friend
Beth'"

Oh dear, thought Nicole, *should I go?* What if Beth talked again of her suspicions regarding Lord Devlin? Determinedly she decided it would be the perfect time to reiterate her stand. Yes, she *would* go, and her spirits were immediately lifted.

"Chelsea, you see how your prayers are still being answered? I have met another friend in London, and I like her very much. You and Mama cannot say I am not being a gadabout now!" Nicole sat up straighter in bed as she heard her abigail knock on the door.

"Stella, I am to have tea with Lady Hampton this morning." Nicole started chewing on her lip. "Do you know what I should wear?" She turned her head in the direction of Chelsea, and covered her mouth with her hand in surprise! They both laughed aloud at how closely the question had come, following her lecture to Chelsea only moments ago.

"Is it to be a party, Miss Nick?" asked Stella.

"No, it will just be the two of us," she said and then added, "It does not have to be anything special, Stella, I am resolved to dress as dowdily as I did before!"

Chelsea's laughter echoed down the hall.

Toby led Nicole into the Hamptons' townhouse, and Beth rushed to meet her in the foyer. "I am so glad you have come, even though I gave you no other option!"

They both laughed, and Beth put her arm around Nicole's waist as soon as the butler took her wrap. "As it is such a beautiful day, I thought we might take our tea on the veranda. If you would prefer to remain indoors, however, I am quite agreeable."

Nicole said, smiling, "The veranda would be wonderful. I am always out of doors at home and much prefer it to a drawing room." She faltered a little, then added, "If you would be so kind as to have your butler tell Toby where we are, I would appreciate it."

Lady Hampton leaned in close to Nicole's ear. "You *must* tell me about your manservant," whispered Beth. "Indeed, he intimidates me so!" She drew a short breath. "He is so large and obviously more than a foot-man to you. Well, I am at it again, am I not? I am acting as if you have known me for years and will tell me ev-erything about yourself, even though we have only just met. You must not mind me, and you must stop me if I get too forward."

During this fast-paced speech, Beth led Nicole to a comfortable lounge chair with soft padding. Nicole heard Beth settle in on her right with a small table in between for the tea tray.

She smiled tenderly and said, "Beth, the only time I will ever stop you is to make you slow down!" Then, as she became more serious, she twisted the hands previ-ously resting peacefully in her lap. "Yes, Toby is more than a servant to me. I am sure you have heard by now that I was in an accident a few years ago." She blushed as she talked, not knowing what Beth was thinking. "Toby is always with me…since then." She was quiet for a moment and felt Beth's eyes on her. "If you do not mind, I would rather not talk about the accident quite yet. I would much rather spend an afternoon getting to know *you*."

Beth leaned over and squeezed her hands. "My dear girl, we can talk about anything you like. It is amaz-ing to me how there are people that you just know are going to be special to you. I felt that when we met last night."

The butler interrupted with the tea tray. While she prepared two cups of tea, Lady Hampton spoke of the beautiful lawns spreading out before them and why she loved to sit exactly where they were. When they both settled in again, Beth continued as if the interruption had never occurred. "I so much wanted to see you today!"

Both relaxed comfortably with their shoes off and their feet tucked up under them like little girls. They laughed at the picture they must present. They imitated the outraged expressions of old governesses and the patronesses of Almack's, could they see them so!

Beth sipped her tea. "You know, I was quite serious when I said I knew instantly we would become fast friends. I think God provides us with the special people we need just at the right moment." Nicole heard the slight questioning in Beth's voice. The *ton* had little use for God, and she knew it was a risk for Beth to discuss it with someone she barely knew.

Emotion gripped Nicole, and the rattle of her teacup was the only indication of its intensity.

Beth quickly took the dainty porcelain cup from Nicole's shaking hands. "I did not mean to upset you, dear. You must not worry, I do not intend to push myself upon you. I understand that most people are not so easily attached and I often…"

Nicole broke into this speech with a sound that was one part laughter and one part sob. "Beth, please stop. I promise you have not upset me. I…" She stopped, eyes pooled with tears, now openly portraying how her heart was touched. She turned her face upward to feel the sun's warmth before she spoke. "I feel you will think me all silly sensibility, but I was afraid to hope you would desire a close connection so quickly. And I have yet to meet another soul who *mentioned* God, much less believed He has provided all they have! It has made me miss my home so much. I have felt isolated and lonely here, and I hoped that this agreeable feeling I had toward you would be just what I needed." She wiped at the tears on her cheeks, then sought to regain her composure.

"You *have* been lonely, have you not?" Beth asked tenderly. "I thought you must have been very solitary when in London since so many of the gentlemen in the box last night asked for introductions to you. To own the truth, I felt some of that was what you wished for."

Nicole admonished her through a few lingering tears. "You, my lady, are too knowing by half!" *Dear Lord, thank you for this day and this new friend,* she prayed silently before she went on. "Mama thought it would be good for me to come to London. We are to see a renowned doctor while we are here, but Mama wanted me to take the opportunity to meet new people as well." She became more forthright. "But I am not good at meeting new people. I miss my home and I have found no one until now with whom I felt the least bit comfortable." She would have liked to add, *excepting Lord Devlin,* but she did not wish to discuss him.

The discerning woman sitting next to her, however, had other ideas. "What about Dev?" She knew she had caught Nicole off guard the previous night with talk of love, and she hoped to remedy that.

Nicole determined it was time to clarify the relationship between her and Lord Devlin. She only prayed she could explain it rationally.

"Lord Devlin is definitely the exception," she said.

"I consider him a special friend, indeed. At first I never knew when he was teasing me or flirting with me. It did not seem a relationship that other men and women shared in London. But I have seen enough now to know that it is *not* normal. It is very strange having the most sought-after bachelor in London as a friend!

"I am not explaining this very well." Nicole gave a frustrated sigh. "He has been all that is truly kind and amiable, but I think he enjoys me because I am no threat to his bachelorhood."

Nicole knew Lord Devlin held a special place in Beth's heart, so she wished to be as honest as possible. "You have known him longer, of course, but he seems to me to be the first *real* man I have met in London. He talks about serious issues instead of putting on airs to impress the rest of Society. That may be because he knows he does not *have* to put on airs with me. I hope that is true."

She knew she must completely empty her budget if she was to convince her new friend she was serious. "He is also very funny, and I think his humor is more meaningful than many of his other characteristics. He laughs with me, he laughs at me and, most importantly, he is not above laughing at himself. I know I tell you nothing you do not already know."

She was rambling like a silly schoolgirl, and she determined to get to her point. "What I do *not* know is why God brought him into my life at just this time." She was reflective for a moment. "I suppose He knew I needed Lord Devlin in the same way He knew I would need you. I have been so very disillusioned by the people I have met in London.

"The difference, however, between you and Lord Devlin is that the friendship he and I share cannot go any further, especially once the Season is over." She hoped she made Beth realize that she *had* accepted Devlin as a rare friend. But she could not leave an opening for Beth's hope of making a match between them.

Lady Hampton, too, set down her teacup. "Nicole, I know I shocked you last night, and I am very sorry. I have been worried that I might have given you a disgust of me." At Nicole's immediate protest, Beth interrupted, "But I want us to be totally honest with each other, and I have not changed my opinion. I truly believe if he is not already in love with you, he soon will be." There was a pregnant pause. "Nicole, I would not see him hurt again."

"Beth," Nicole said, emphasizing every word, "I would never knowingly hurt him." She paused, feeling God's quiet conviction even as she spoke the words. She was not telling him about her sight, knowing her secret might cause him pain, but she brushed if off, doubting that the information would be anything of lasting import to him.

"You must own the truth," Nicole continued. "You only like us both so much that you *want* it to be so. Much more than it *is* so. Lord Devlin and I have been honest with each other about avoiding marriage, and we have even discussed how very strange our relationship is in light of our genders." She put the finishing touches on Beth's hopes. "Indeed, dear lady, I could not imagine it being anything more because he has no relationship with God. It is just too important to me, as are my home and my duties."

"Oh, Nicky, you are going to be so good for me! But before we leave the subject of Dev, may I explain two things?" Nicole started to shake her head, but Beth knew these things would not cause Nicole any more pain.

"First of all, I love him like a brother, that is why I am concerned for him. But, secondly, do not rule faith and love out of his life. Devlin seldom speaks of his family, except in sarcasm, so I know his parents gave him little affection. But he utterly adores his grandmother. She is one of God's most faithful servants, and has always been a major presence for good in his life. She gave him all her love, and he in turn values that love above all else. He may disdain love all he likes, but he understands the emotion well enough.

"He also has Hampton and me as an example. I hope that does not sound arrogant. Dev would never admit it now, but I know he had a difficult time accepting that Peter and I were great friends before we married. He assumed I was only trying to get my claws into him. He is honest enough to admit that Peter did fall in love with me and was not tricked into marriage. And he would certainly agree that our love is real and well worth the having. Dev has truly had reasons to become cynical about love, but though he may scorn it, he knows that it does exist. He has not yet realized, as we have, that love is not something we can control."

"You have the right of it, Beth." Nicole sighed. "But

we *can* control our response to it. There can be no more than friendship between us."

Lady Hampton seemed to accept the futility of further discussion at the present and let go of the subject. "Very well, that is enough about Lord Devlin. Why do you not tell me about yourself?"

They spent a lovely afternoon sharing stories of their childhoods, and Nicole knew she had found a true friend. She realized she must put that faith to the test, and trust Beth with the story of her accident. She waited patiently for an opening.

"What I cannot understand," Lady Beth said at one point, "is how you got to be three and twenty and still remain unwed. If the men of Cheltenham are so immune to *your* charms, I am glad *I* did not grow up there! The men in London, however, are not so immune, it would seem."

Nicole took a deep breath and said a silent prayer in preparation for what was to follow. She had dreaded its arrival, but now she felt a freedom in complete honesty. "I *was* engaged once," Nicole began. "He is a doctor on our estate. We fell in love and prepared for what I thought was God's plan for us to serve others. I was happy with Michael, but happier still that I would continue to be close enough to our home to help my mother. It seemed quite perfect at the time but…we called it off."

"Nicole!" Beth gasped. "I am so sorry. I did not know. You do not have to talk of this if you do not wish to. We will have plenty of time to get to know each other's skeletons."

"No," Nicole said with downcast eyes, "I think I do finally wish to talk about it. You are the one person I feel I *can* talk to about it. You see, in truth, *he* broke it off." At Beth's distressed groan, she added, "You must not blame him. Indeed, I do not. It was after the accident and…" she paused, not believing the truth was finally to come out "…I do not think he could have handled it. You see, Beth, in the accident, I…"

Suddenly the veranda doors pushed open, and Lords Hampton and Devlin walked through them. "Beth, my darling wife, you will never guess who I found! Poor Dev was wandering the streets alone and dejected, so I invited him to luncheon."

Both women hurriedly lowered their feet to the floor and reddened, one in embarrassment, one in anger. As he saw Nicole, Lord Hampton apologized profusely. Nicole was shaking from the disastrous timing of it all and from Lord Devlin's appearance. Why did his presence always seem to affect her so? She gathered her poise enough to say, "Lord Hampton, this *is* your house! You are certainly allowed to come in it any time you please without apology."

Lord Devlin froze into inaction. The drive home from the opera the night before had been a disaster, and he could see that Peter had intruded on a matter of import between Beth and Nicole. There was nothing for it, however, it was too late to go back now. "Good afternoon, ladies," he said as he kissed each one's hand. He noticed Nicole kept her eyes bent on the ground beneath her feet. All he got from her was a murmured "My lord."

"Beth, I have been trying to tell this husband of yours that I was going to have luncheon at my club. He would not take no for an answer. I apologize for intruding like this."

Both women realized that they could not get the moment back, even had the two men left on the instant. "Of course, Peter did right, Dev. We would be delighted if you would join us. I was about to ask Lady Nicole to join us, as well. Perhaps you may both help me persuade her."

Nicole finally jerked her head up. "No!" she ejected, and then apologized for her outburst. "I really cannot remain, Beth. I have already been away longer than I planned, and I am promised to Mama for this afternoon. Thank you so much for the tea and visit. If you would just ring for Toby, I will leave the three of you to enjoy your luncheon."

The two women chatted quietly of the opera the night before, Nicole feeling an eternity pass waiting for Toby to arrive. The butler finally announced that her servant was waiting for her in the hall.

Beth took her waist and walked her into the house as Nicole bid the gentlemen good day.

"Nicole, I am ever so sorry," Beth whispered. "Peter was supposed to be gone all day, I promise you. I would never have put you in such a situation had I known he was to be home."

Nicole turned in the foyer and hugged Beth closely. "I know that, dear friend. I truly do thank you for inviting me today and for the special bond we have formed through our faith. Perhaps you can visit me soon and we could enjoy another happy afternoon like this one."

Toby then led her out into the waiting carriage, and the ride home was unusually quiet. She had almost gotten the truth out, and while she wanted *Beth* to know, she knew in her heart she was not ready for Lord Devlin to know. That was not the way she wanted him to find out.

Maybe she was not meant to tell Beth that day. That was how she must look at it. But God had given her a new friend, and one she thought she could count on for life.

Nicole thought about that afternoon long into the evening. Her thoughts were actually centered more on Lord Devlin. Beth had been honest and expressed herself confidently; in her opinion Devlin was either in love with her or on his way to being so. That was what concerned her now.

She viewed him so differently since she had heard his speech. The attraction had been subtle when he'd flirted before, and she had appreciated his humor as she had seen in no other. But his feelings *that* day had been real and important to him. They had never shared anything of significant import before then. And since he had just come from giving his speech, it would be likely they would talk about it, not because he had developed a tendre for her, but because they both felt so strongly about the issue. They were aware that their relationship as friends would take a little time to get used to.

The problem now was that she knew this *was* a man

she could love. She did not want to. There were too many differences, too many obstacles, especially since the accident. She also admitted to herself that this did not fit into God's plan for her life. She had taken so long to come to grips with His purpose; she could not allow this test to weaken her resolve.

Devlin could be effective and help people by his involvement with the government, but she would be a hindrance to him here in London. She knew she was really only useful at home where she could help her own people. It was, of course, on a much smaller scale, but it was all her world would allow.

Even if he did have the same affections for her that she had begun to feel for him, she could not bear the pain if he rejected her once he knew all about her. And she was sure, unlike Beth, that he *would* reject her as too much of a burden. Look at his feelings on marriage! If he dreaded being married, how would he feel being married to her? She would be a ball and chain that he would have to drag around his world. Tears sprang to her eyes even at the thought. His friends would only gape and wonder at his strange blind wife.

How she wished her father were alive. He was so wise; she had always felt that she could talk to him about anything. Even this, she knew, would have caused her no qualms to discuss with him. His compassion for others extended first and foremost to his family, and no problem was too big or too personal to discuss and pray over.

She surmised what he would wish her to do in this instance. He would tell her to stop pretending, to be herself—open and honest with everyone. Honesty prevented words and actions from coming back to haunt you. And she had lived her life that way, until her mother had insisted upon coming to London. She had feared facing Society openly, so had concealed the details of her disability despite her ethics. And the hypocrisy haunted her each time she complained of the superficial populace around her. She suspected her father would have understood, but she knew that he would never condone her actions.

She would go through the rest of their time in London avoiding Lord Devlin. Beginning on the morrow, she and Chelsea would visit all the sights in London. They should exploit this once-in-a-lifetime opportunity at all events, should they not? Then she would go back home to her real life.

Nicole kept her promise to Chelsea. The two of them, and Toby, of course, filled the following week with sightseeing. Each landmark excited Chelsea and everything seemed more wonderful sharing it through the heart of a child.

When she returned home each day there were often flowers from Devlin, always roses, and twice he had called while she was out. Her mother was getting impatient with her for avoiding his calls and using exhaustion as an excuse to cry off evening engagements. And though she missed Devlin terribly, even more than she could have imagined, she must adhere to her plan not to see him any longer.

There had also been a note from Beth, apologizing

yet again. She responded immediately, bidding her not to worry in the least. Nicole explained she was occupied with her little sister, but hoped they would meet again soon.

If her nights were lonely and sad, she vowed no one would know it in the light of day.

Chapter Nine

"Nicky, I am fully aware you never wished to come to London, and I have truly appreciated *most* of the effort you have made to please me. However, I desire your attendance this last week." Lady Beaumont confronted her daughter with severity. "I wish you to go to Lady Freemont's musicale, to the alfresco luncheon dear Albinia is hosting and, most importantly, to Mrs. Stouffer's ball with me tonight. Mrs. Stouffer has been a friend of mine since we were young girls. I want to go to her daughter's betrothal ball, and I wish you to accompany me. Our meeting with the doctor is nearly upon us, and then we will go back home. Will you do this for me?"

Conscience tugged at Nicole's heart. "Yes, Mama, of course I will. I *have* been avoiding some entertainments lately, but I have grown so bored with them. Chelsea was a good excuse at first, but we have truly had a splendid time each day. I am a sad trial to you, Mama," Nicole said, trying to tease her mother back into good humor. But it seemed real anger fueled her mother's words. She imagined her mother was aware that Lord Devlin was somehow involved. Fortunately, she was not using him in her entreaties to get Nicole to attend tonight. "I will be ready, Mama."

Balls were of little interest to Nicole any longer. Before her accident they had been one of her greatest pleasures, but attending them now only seemed frustrating and futile. She had always believed her love of dancing was a natural extension of her passion for music. But one could not dance when one was blind.

Before coming to Town, she had invented a ruse which proved quite successful and allowed her to suffer through balls with little anguish. Her mother had begrudgingly agreed to grant Nicole the advantage of appearing early, to avoid the crowded receiving lines. Upon their arrival Nicole would accompany her mother to where the dowagers congregated. She would then choose a seat as isolated as possible, where she would remain unobtrusive but could enjoy the festivities through the gossip of the supreme matrons. Many rooms had potted ferns that provided a most ideal hiding place!

Nicole's mother abhorred her tactics, but as it was one of Nicole's stipulations for attending at all, she had given in. She had not given up, however, and often brought young gentlemen over, trying to outwit her contrary daughter.

Upon seeing her, most men wandered over to her, and they never failed to ask her to dance but she had determined long ago to say she did not dance and thank them prettily. Some asked if they could sit out the dance with her, but all she had to do was begin expressing her opinion on the shocking state of London's orphanages or the mistreatment of underage chimney sweeps and they soon took themselves off, looking for more interesting game. So she would sit quietly, enjoy the music and get through an evening with little fuss.

The only time she had deviated from that plan had been at the Swathmore ball. Only see what a simple walk on the terrace had done! She had met the man who *was* interested in her conversation and who shared many of her opinions. But he had turned her world upside down in the process. No, her original plan would be perfect tonight, and she intended to stand firm.

She heard the musicians tuning up for a country reel and smiled at the lively tune, always having enjoyed the invigorating steps. She even began to hum along when *his* voice interrupted.

"Lady Beaumont, what a pleasure to see you here tonight. I have been sorry to miss you when I called."

"Lord Devlin," Nicole's mother said as she bowed her head. "How delightful it is to see you." Her mother preened just a little among the dowagers. "I so enjoyed the opera, and Nicky has done nothing but hum the strains of several arias all week."

Nicole did not raise her face and knew an impulse to pretend she had not heard her mother. However, his extensive experience showed only the most proper of manners. "I am, of course, charmed as well to see you, Lady Nicole. I was about to ask if you were in attendance tonight."

"Good evening, Lord Devlin," she said, turning her head this way and that, pretending to watch the dancers.

"Would you do me the honor of taking a turn about the room with me? We might better view the dancers." He was not going to speak his mind while trying to dance with her!

"I am sure, my lord," she said, trying to sound light-hearted, "you would be much better occupied dancing the reel yourself rather than strolling the outskirts of the dance floor."

"I assure *you,* my lady," his voice was almost menacing as his teeth clenched, "I would enjoy nothing more than your company."

"Oh, for heaven's sake," interrupted old Lady Brachurst, "walk with the young fellow so we can go about our business." The other dowagers tittered at the virago's outburst, but Nicole blushed as she realized others had been listening to their conversation.

She stood, and decided she now knew how one must feel on the long walk to the guillotine!

She allowed him to put her hand in the crook of his arm. He laid his own atop hers, as if afraid she would not stay with him. They walked for some time without speaking, and she could feel various emotions emanating from him. He was angry with her, she knew from his subdued silence. His stillness indicated he was suppressing bewilderment. Most importantly, she felt his hurt, and that almost unnerved her.

"Is that why I have never encountered you in London, because I have not stalked the decorous greenery? I shall endeavor to remember to look there first in the future." He was not teasing; his voice was tight and filled with feeling.

"My lord, I do not dance. It has always seemed silly for me to sit on the sidelines as if waiting for a partner. It only makes hostesses force some unfortunate gentleman to sit out a dance he would rather not. It is as simple as that. There is no need to be angry."

"No need to be angry," he ejected, more in pain than in anger. Several heads turned their way so he lowered his voice, but not his cynicism. "You have politely repaid me for an evening at the opera by avoiding me at every turn, and you think I have no right to be angry?"

Nicole's temper flared when he spoke, as if she should be at his beck and call. But it burned out quickly, because she knew there was truth in his words. "If you must know, I have been taking my sister to visit London's sites. I promised it to her when the London trip was planned."

Suddenly she felt the wind go out of his sails and knew she would now get questions that would hurt. She dreaded wounding him and wished he had stayed in an angry frame of mind. That hurt them both less.

"Do you have any concept what I have been through this week? I have racked my brain trying to figure out how I have offended you. I have relived that night at the opera and the carriage ride home a thousand times, trying to recall something I did to turn you away from me. I almost gave up when you dashed out of the Hamptons' at the mere sight of me.

"But when I saw your mother here tonight, again

without you, I was prepared to break into your home, handcuff Toby and get you to tell me what I had done."

She could not tell him she knew exactly how he felt. She only knew in her heart that she had missed him more each day, but she would not and could not tell him that.

He paused and in a low voice asked, "Nicole, I thought we had become close. Has your regard for me changed?"

This side of him touched her heart. Beside her stood a man she had come to love—in what fashion she was not entirely sure. But he was not too proud to express the feelings and pain in his heart. Only it was like to break hers. Why must he always do something that made it even easier to care for him?

Could she tell this man the truth? Mama pressed her daily to give up the secret. But would he still care for her despite her failings? He seemed to have so much compassion. No, it would only hurt him. He would have to make a choice of acceptance or rejection, and she could not bear it if this man outright rejected her.

"Devlin, I am sorry I put you to so much trouble this week. I promise you did nothing to offend me. In fact, I told you I would treasure that evening for the rest of my life. I truly have been taking Chelsea around London. I realized that sweet little girl has spent much of her time alone while Mama and I have been out and about. I wanted her to remember this trip as well."

He did not say anything so she felt he expected more. "By the end of the day I was too tired to go the soirees Mama had committed us to. I sent you several notes to thank you for your flowers. I had no idea you would worry so. I am truly sorry if I hurt you. I hope you know I would never wish to do so."

This was all wrong, Devlin knew it. She was apologizing and making it all sound quite ordinary, but she was not telling him the entire truth. And she had not answered the most important question he put to her: had her feelings for him changed? Perhaps they had. She *had* been avoiding him, but he could not discern why. He had never before been lonely when it came to women. Yet he missed her so much it scared him. Had she not missed him?

An idea struck him that could account for her actions without meaning she did not wish his company. If Peter had been hounding *him* about love and marriage, perhaps Lady Beth had been filling Nicole's head with the same. Could she have panicked in distress?

Whatever the problem, Devlin became calm enough to realize he was not going to obtain any answers in the middle of a crowded ballroom. Instead he took her completely off guard and asked, "Why do you not dance?"

"It is a long story, my lord," she evaded. "And no, you do not have time to hear it now."

The ensemble began the strains of a waltz. He understood now that when she closed her eyes it meant she was stirred to her very heart.

Devlin was so in tune with her now, he felt the feelings she was holding back. Perhaps he could use that to his advantage. "You must know how to dance, sweetheart. Music is too deep in your soul. Besides," he whispered, "you look quite healthy to me. Dance this waltz with me."

"No!" she burst out without thinking. As she lowered her voice she said, "It would not be proper. For more than two months I have refused to dance with any other gentleman and have been making poor inane dandies sit out dances with me. How should it look if I suddenly danced with a wealthy and unattached earl? Gossip, which you so aptly explained to me the night we met, would run rampant.

"I am sorry, but I do not dance. Now, for heaven's sake, please take me back to Mama and go dance with someone who *wants* to dance with you!"

He laughed at her temper. "There's my girl! You want to dance with me, and you will not admit it."

They had strolled near the doors to the outside balcony, and he led her out into the clear night rather than back to her mother. The cool breeze reminded him of the night they'd met. She seemed nervous and confused, something she had never been with him before.

She tried once again. "Lord Devlin, listen closely, I am not going to dance with you…"

"Shush," he whispered. "We are out here alone. No one will see you dancing for the first time this Season. That also means no one will see if you make a misstep or two. I will be holding you in my arms, guiding you every step of the way. It will soon come back to you."

For a moment Devlin tried to justify his feelings by their seclusion on yet another moonlit terrace. But something inside would not allow it to be so. It was… romantic, and he could not recall ever using that word before. He did not understand how such a simple thing had turned into such an amazing experience, but quickly lost all interest in analyzing it.

Before she could protest, he placed his hand on her waist and lifted her free arm to his shoulder. He took her other hand tenderly and held it against his chest, and she knew it was most improper, even for a waltz. He began to move her in the steps. She was stiff and unyielding.

He whispered in her ear, "Close your eyes and feel the music as you did at the opera. Rely on your other senses as you taught me on your terrace. The waltz will come back to you soon enough." Devlin's movements were minimal to give her time to relax. He whispered again, "Now admit that you *do* want to dance with me."

His old ways of flirting did make her relax for a moment, forgetting her scruples.

Her trust was now completely in him; he would never know how much so since she could not see, only follow. She leaned her cheek against his lapel and let the strains of the waltz overtake her completely. The reasons the dowagers shunned the waltz was now eminently clear to Nicole. They danced so closely she did not even have to think about her steps; she need only let him lead. It was the most intimate moment she had ever had with a man, including the chaste kisses she had experienced from her betrothed.

Nicole had not forgotten how to waltz, but she knew *this* was the way it was meant to be danced. She wanted the musicians to play forever. He was whispering gentle and teasing words in her ear about moonlit terraces. She forgot her mother, her secret, her fear of crowds and just let herself bask in this one dance that she would store away, in minute detail, for the rest of her life.

As the music ended, they stopped dancing. However, she could not let go. Her head rested still against his shoulder, and his arm circled her waist. She was so afraid of breaking the spell that she could not bring herself to end the moment.

With his finger lightly under her chin, Devlin raised her lowered face to his. Her eyes were still closed. She wished more than ever that she could see. She wanted just one glimpse of his face to read his thoughts and to have that memory until the day she died. He slowly lowered his head; she could feel it in his shoulders. She could no more stop him from leaning down to kiss her than she could stop breathing.

She stiffened a little when his lips touched hers. How could she have ever imagined just that light touch would move her so? She knew she had never felt so when Michael had kissed her. She slowly relaxed and automatically moved her hand, the one on his shoulder, around to the back of his neck to touch the hair that her mother thought "a little too long to be fashionable."

When he finally lifted his head, she opened her eyes and they were filled with tears, but she smiled and he relaxed. Suddenly she lifted her hand from his neck and placed it on his cheek. She closed her eyes again and softly rubbed his cheek and jawline. When she gently touched his lips with her hand, he sighed and the moment was broken. She began to pull away from him.

"I am sorry, Nicole," he said. "I did not mean to frighten you. Your touch moved me."

She fought the yearning to stay where she was. "We must go in. There will be talk. I am afraid Mama may be worried. I know Toby certainly is."

"Do you expect me to just let you walk back in there as if nothing has happened? We must talk, Nicole. You know that, do you not? I cannot allow you to start avoiding me again." His voice intensified. "I cannot."

"You are right, Devlin, we do need to talk. I have many things I wish to tell you, but not tonight on a moonlit terrace. It must be in the harsh light of day with our heads clear of waltzes and…kisses." She flushed as she finished; she had never spoken so to a man.

"Will you ride with me tomorrow?" he asked hurriedly. "We could go to Richmond Park. It would take us more than an hour. We could have luncheon at a small inn I frequent there."

Nicole knew a ride was out of the question for the morrow, and it caused her some impatience. But after tomorrow, she promised herself, after she told him the whole truth, she could ride with him anytime. She only hoped he would still want to.

"If you do not mind, I should prefer it if we went in your curricle so we could talk more easily. I have much to tell you."

"Very well, a curricle then, but if you 'my lord' me one more time, I shall not be answerable for my actions."

She smiled as he intended, but he did not want her to go. "Nicole, may I kiss you again?"

She turned her face away in answer. She should never have allowed the first one, but she was calmer now and called on God's strength. "I think we should go back inside."

He took her arm with a sigh and escorted her back to her mother.

Chapter Ten

Nicole awoke the next morning happier than she had ever been in her life. She was finally going to tell Devlin the truth. She was awake much of the night remembering his words, his arms, his kiss, and she blushed at the way he made her feel. Her inherent fears rose several times as she thought about how she would tell him. How would he respond to her truth?

She also knew that she *had* fallen in love with him. It was no longer just a thought, and it was no longer just friendship. She thought him her best friend, but that meant so much more in the light of her love. This was the love her mother had described when she told of giving up her former life for Nicole's father.

Nicole knew it was not the same for Devlin. He had made his feelings clear about love and marriage. She knew they could be nothing more than friends and that there would be no more of the intimacy they had shared last night. But if he still wanted her in his life after her revelation, she vowed that would be more than enough. Something had happened to her on that terrace. She felt she could trust him with all her heart, and she could not wait to have everything out in the open. She was not absolutely sure how he would take the news, but she knew that she wanted to tell him. She prayed he would understand.

Nicole got out of bed and knelt on the floor beside it, folding her hands before her. "Lord, You have sent Lord Devlin to me for some purpose, and I thank You for the opportunity to share the truth about my life with him. I have come to love him, Father, but I know that his love is not part of Your plan for me. Perhaps Your purpose is that he will come to know You better through me, and so I ask…"

The door to her room burst open and Chelsea ran in and jumped on her bed, talking a mile a minute. "Nick, you promised to tell me every detail of last night's ball. You must tell…" Her bouncing stopped. "Oh dear, I have interrupted your prayers. I am sorry!"

Rising, Nicole smiled serenely. "I was just about done. It was a perfectly lovely night, minx. I even danced, if you can credit that, but I do not have time to tell you the rest now. I am sorry, goose. Lord Devlin is coming to take me to Richmond Park. I promise I shall tell you all about it later, at dinner perhaps?"

"You are going to Richmond Park? I have heard *famous* things about Richmond Park. Are you sure you would not like an opportunity to further the education of your little sister? Lord Devlin likes me very much, you know. He may truly want me to join you!"

"I am sorry, love, this time I must have his full attention. Would you help me pick out a gown instead?"

Chelsea, for once, obeyed her sister without question and stopped bouncing on the bed. Tears choked her next question. "Oh, Nicky, did something wonderful happen with Lord Devlin? *Do* fairy tales really happen for people like us?"

Nicole hugged Chelsea but spoke seriously. "Chelsea, this is not a fairy tale. We do not even need to hope in fairy tales when we have our Heavenly Father always available to us. Own up to it, puss, many good things have happened to us." She let her sister go with a kiss on the top of the head. "Please ring the bell for Stella, love. I told you it was a wonderful evening, but you must not take it for more than that. I haven't the time to tell you now, but you could help me begin to dress until Stella arrives."

The Beaumont ladies were waiting in the drawing room when Lord Devlin was announced. Chelsea and Nicole had chosen a new peach gown with a straw chip hat that made Nicole appear as fresh as the whole outdoors.

He entered and greeted Lady Beaumont, but his eyes gazed intensely at Nicole.

He had spent the most harrowing night. He thought he might be falling in love with her, yet it felt nothing like the emotion he had experienced with his wife. He had been so infatuated with Vivian that his professions of love now seemed ridiculous. This was not a blind passion based on outer beauty. He already admired, nay loved, Nicole's inner qualities. But last night had made him believe he had finally found real love—an intense physical and emotional need based on the mental attraction they had previously shared.

He needed to see if her response to him last night had meant the same to her. He needed to tell her about his first wife and why it had killed any desire for another marriage. And he needed to find out why she was so adamantly against the idea. Her plan to take care of her family and home could not be cast in stone, could it? He *would* get his answers today!

"Excuse me, my lord, but while you have been gawking at my sister, you missed my new curtsey," Chelsea pouted adeptly.

"Chelsea, please guard your tongue," moaned a resigned Lady Beaumont.

Devlin shook himself out of his reverie and pinched her cheek. "Chelsea, is that you? I was on the verge of asking to be introduced to the young lady who was so quiet and reserved, and looked so beautiful this morning!"

She scowled, and then giggled at the easy manner he displayed.

"Enough, Sprite! I have a surprise for Nicole out in the front, and if you wish to see it you must get your cloak."

"You have brought a surprise? Oh, Nicky, a surprise for you! How big is it?" Chelsea could not keep her exuberance leashed as they moved toward the front door.

Devlin took Nicole's arm and whispered, "I know you preferred we go in my curricle, but I wanted to give you a pleasure you have missed. You've spoken of missing Solomon so much. I wished to erase it from your mind."

On the instant Nicole feared the surprise. Why had she not anticipated his kindness? She must calm herself; it may yet turn into nothing. Yet tension gripped her as her mind seemed to stop functioning. Inside she screamed at herself, trying to divert the approaching tragedy. This could not happen here in front of everyone. *No, please, Lord, not this way.*

"Devlin," she spoke, pulling back against his arm, resisting his forward movement. "I need to speak to you right away, *before* we go outside." The screech from Chelsea stopped her in terror.

"Nicky, she is the most beautiful horse I have ever seen. She will make you want to retire old Solomon when we get home."

Nicole went rigid on Devlin's arm as he leaned over once again to whisper in her ear. "I know you did not plan to ride today, but I saw her and could not resist. She is only on loan, so if you do not like her, feel free to say so, but she seemed perfect for you."

Nicole's panic had taken complete hold and she began to tremble, needing to invent an excuse immediately but unable to make a sound.

Chelsea's next comment made her freeze in shock.

"Nicky, she is chestnut and will perfectly match your russet riding habit. She has four white feet, but you must not call her something silly like Socks. She is too beautiful for that. Toby, don't *you* think she's beautiful?"

Nicole covered her face and tried to pull away from

Devlin. She leaned on the hall table as Chelsea continued her description. No, no, this was not how she wanted him to know. She wanted to start from the beginning and tell him the entire tale gradually.

His viselike grip on her arm kept her from decamping, and he spun her around to face him, anger and questions emanating from him.

"Nicole? Why is your sister describing every detail of a horse standing only a few feet in front of you?" When she made no comment, he barked an order. "Look at me, Nicole, what is it?"

"I c-cannot," she stuttered through streaming tears. "I c-cannot look at you." She kept her head lowered and said the last part in a whisper. "I cannot see you. I can see almost nothing at all."

A deadly silence shrouded the hall.

"No, no…" He shook his head in disbelief, rubbing his hands over his eyes. "You are *blind?*" As the weight of his question bore down upon her, he could no longer control his temper or his words. "You have been keeping this from me all this time? How *could* you hide such a thing?" He let go of her arm and began an agitated pacing. He finally stopped and ran his fingers through his hair. She could feel him brush against her as he turned to continue his tirade.

He came to a halt. "You have taken great pains to do so, have you not? You have practiced this deception to perfection." His voice conveyed his emotions with each accusation. "You have been lying and pretending, making fools of us all for months. Is that your idea of friendship? *Was* this ever a friendship, or was last night to trick me into marriage? I think I begin to see. Blind country belles do not make a splash in London. They do not catch rich earls as husbands! Not even those as beautiful as you. Unless of course, they pretend they are *not* blind. I have been such a fool. I fell right into the trap, didn't I?

"This explains everything…not riding, your fear of crowds, not dancing and Toby—how could I forget Toby?" He stopped and covered his eyes. "What it does not explain is your talk of loyalty and honesty and truth." He was pacing, clenching his teeth in anger. He had been duped by his first wife and now he had done it again.

"Devlin, please, it was nothing like that. Please let me explain…"

All Devlin could think of was that he had spent so much time with her and had been too stupid to see the truth. But worse, she had not told him. It never occurred to him to consider any other reason for her behavior. And his anger made him overly hard. "When *did* you plan to tell me, Nicole? Were you waiting for a proposal?" He growled in frustration. "What a fool I have been."

Suddenly Chelsea ran in from the doorway. She had heard Lord Devlin's furious words and was distressed. She ran to Nicole and hugged her, sobbing hysterically. "Nicky, I am so sorry, I thought you told him. I thought he knew and that is why you were so happy this morning. It is always my treat to describe things to you. This is my fault. You must make him understand." She ran to Lord Devlin. "Please, sir, I am to blame. It is not as you said. Do not be mad at Nick."

"Is this, too, a ploy, Lady Nicole? Have you even used this innocent child in this entrapment?" His question began with complete surprise and ended with loathing. "Good day, Lady Nicole."

Nicole knew she would never forget those horrifying words if she lived to be ninety.

Surviving this day took one of the most Herculean efforts Nicole would ever make. All she wanted to do was run to her room and never come out.

After Lord Devlin left, Chelsea was almost inconsolable. If she could only explain more, Chelsea kept crying. He did not understand and she could fix it, she promised. But Nicole knew it could never be fixed. She tried to cheer Chelsea by telling her everything would be fine.

Chelsea went to her room much agitated, and it was a long while before her governess could quiet her tears.

But Chelsea had been nothing compared to her mother. Lady Beaumont had not yet left the drawing room, but had, of course, heard every horrid word. Her silence was the scariest part. Nicole might have handled her mother better had she had a bout of hysterics, but her mother's withdrawal was almost too much to bear.

"Mama, I am sorry." Nicole was emotionally drained, and it sounded in her words. "You were right all along. I should not have hidden it. I have made a terrible mistake. I need to go home, Mama. I need to try to get my life back to normal somehow, and I cannot stay in London. This is the second time I have lost a man I loved. Only I do not know how I am going to survive it this time. The one thing I do know is that I cannot do it here."

Lady Beaumont responded in a deathly quiet voice. "There is no need to ask, Nicole. As soon as the rest of London hears about this, we would need to leave anyway. Unfortunately, we decided to consult with Dr. Morrison at the end of our stay. Therefore, we must remain through tomorrow." As Nicole began to protest, her mother lost patience with her. "No, Nicole. We will not leave without accomplishing the most important reason we came."

Nicole felt her mother's anger quickly fade. Since her accident two years before, Nicole had opposed every attempt she'd made to offer compassion. Quietly she spoke again. "Despite all that has happened, love, I have not forgotten our prayer for you to see again. We may pack this evening and leave at first light on Tuesday. But tomorrow we will see the doctor."

Lady Beaumont rose to leave the room but stopped abruptly. "Nicole, I had hoped and prayed that time would convince you that you are no less precious in our sight, and that vulnerability was not something to be avoided at all costs. But you have remained stubborn and hidden behind your facade of strength. I know that I am guilty of pressing this visit on you.

"I also know you need comfort right now, and how I long to give it to you. I know you are going through indescribable pain. If your father were here, you would let him comfort you. He always did. But your pain is also breaking my heart. I have loved you so much since the day you were born, and only wanted what was best for you. I made you come to London, and I will have to live with that mistake and hope you will come to forgive me."

She heaved a despairing sigh. "I think Lord Devlin was falling in love with you, yet you could not seem to trust your heart to him. I know all that you have been through and I have suffered every pain with you—maybe more, because you cannot know what it is like to watch your child suffer. But I thought this time you had come to care for someone enough to let him show you that his love was sufficient to overcome your obstacles.

"As your mother I want so very much to help you, but, as usual, I sense your need to be alone. I am smart enough to know that the comfort I want to give you probably would not help, in any event. Your independence has always been an enigma to me, but if you need me, I will be here for you." With that Nicole's mother walked out of the room.

That was all she could take. Nicole could face no more and she ran to her room in tears. She cried for hours—for her father, for her family and mostly for the mistake she knew would haunt her for the rest of her life. She finally cried herself to sleep.

Nicole awoke late into the night. The house was completely quiet. Could it all have been a nightmare? *Oh, please, God, let it have been a nightmare.* But she knew it was not when she realized she was still in her clothes from this afternoon. What should she do? All she could think of was Devlin. She was almost glad she could not see, not well enough to see his face in any event, knowing the look of hatred that must have been there. At least she would not have to remember *that* the rest of her life.

Lord Devlin had not deserved her distrust, and she knew she had hurt him. She could not leave things as they were. The least she could do now was apologize, explain and leave his life forever. She had never been a coward, but she knew in time she could convince herself it was unnecessary. So she must see him now. He was probably at his club relating the terrible deception she had perpetrated on the *ton,* but she would go to his home and wait for him. It was more than improper—it was social suicide—but she had no thought of anything or anyone but Devlin.

She got up and brushed and pulled her hair back in a ribbon. There was no point in changing: she could not do it by herself and she would be wearing a cloak, in any event.

Nicole knocked on Toby's door across the hall and waited as she heard muffled curses as he shuffled to his door. When it opened, the shock in his voice was apparent. "Miss Nick, I mean Lady Nick, what is it? Is something wrong?" He looked at his pocket watch on the dresser. "It's two o'clock in the morning!" He had been outside when Lord Devlin had started his tirade, and Nicole could only imagine the restraint he had used. She was glad he had known to stay with Chelsea.

"Shush, Toby. I need you to go with me to Lord Devlin's. I need to talk to him before we leave London, and

I believe this is the only time I should be allowed to approach his home."

Panic caused Toby to stutter as he coaxed her back to her own room. "N-no, m-y lady. Uh, I know a little more 'bout gentlemen than you do, and now is *not* the time to be trying to explain anything. Give 'im some time to cool down, and we can try to set things aright tomorrow."

"Toby, I mean to leave here in ten minutes with or without you. Now, if you are coming, get dressed and I will meet you in the foyer. Do not worry about a carriage. We will take a hackney so we do not have to wake the stable boys."

"Miss Nick, this is crazy…" he began, but at her look of agony he said, "I'm going, I'm going."

Toby did his best to put a halt to her plan during the ride to Lord Devlin's house. He told her *if* his lordship was home, and *if* his lordship was awake, he would be in no mood to hold a rational conversation with a delicate female.

Nicole just patted his hand like he was some child who did not understand. "Do not worry, Toby, I am not trying to change things. I know it is too late for that. I just want a chance to explain, to apologize and to ask him to forgive me."

The pounding on his door at two-thirty in the morning finally broke through Devlin's haze of sleep and brandy. "What is that racket?" he muttered as he heard his butler scramble through the foyer and unbolt the door. The sound of a feminine voice registered some-

where in the recesses of his brain, but he could not reconcile that to the pounding.

Devlin *was* drunk. He had always been able to hold
his liquor, but an entire afternoon of downing one
brandy after another had left his head pounding almost
as loudly as the front door.

Grant entered the library softly and said in the most
surprised voice Devlin had ever heard from his butler,
"My lord, there is a young lady here. Lady Nicole Beaumont. She says she will not leave until she has spoken
to you."

"Tell her to go away, and do not disturb me again."

Apparently Nicole had bidden Toby to follow the
abashed butler to the library. They heard Devlin's order,
but they pushed past the butler into the room. "I will not
go away, my lord, until I have spoken to you. Please let me
have my say, then you will never have to see me again."

"If that is what it will take that I may never set eyes
on you again, have your say and go."

Toby led her to a high-back chair near Devlin, but
she did not sit. He wondered if she needed the strength
of that chair to face him.

Nicole took a breath, beginning to speak, but was
again interrupted by Devlin's slurred words. "You may
be able to tell, madame, that I am in no condition to
behave with decorum or carry on an intelligent conversation. Indeed, I probably will not remember this even
happened, so this is an exercise in futility. You have had
your fun, you have duped an earl and while you did *not*
get the hoped-for marriage proposal, there's always the
Bath Season."

* * *

Nicole had not realized the hatred she had aroused in him and every minute now was breaking her resolve, her calm and her heart. "No!" she shouted. "My lord, I came to London as a promise to my mother. When my father died and I began working on the estate, she used to berate me for trying to fill the void my father left with work. I told you that she tried several times to convince me to come, but I always refused. When I had my accident…lost my sight, it took me a while to get my life back to some sort of normalcy. But with my family's help and Toby's loyalty, I pulled through. However, my mother now had the added impetus of seeing a London doctor to persuade me to come. I finally agreed."

Once she started, Nicole found she could not seem to stop, even for a breath. She was not sure he was listening, but she had to finish this. "I only agreed on the promise that we would keep my loss of sight a secret as long as possible so people would not feel awkward around us. Mother was opposed to such a plan, but I was adamant and with Toby's help I learned to deal with most situations quite normally. My sole purpose for this trip was to allow Mama and Chelsea their share of some of Town's enjoyment, and to submit to one more doctor's exam to help them accept the inevitable."

She choked on the thought. "I never put myself forward or openly lied to the *ton*. If you remember, you never even noticed me until we met on the Swathmore terrace a full two months after the Season started!"

She knew she had to keep going. Obviously it was to

be her one and only opportunity. "That night on the terrace was a mistake. I know that now. I should have left you immediately, but it had been so long since someone had conversed with me without embarrassment or sympathy. It was a lapse in judgment on my part, and I apologize. I never thought to see you again. When I did, I justified my continued silence by reminding myself that our visit was almost at an end. I was sure you would not even remember me.

"When we became friends, I should have told you. Again, I made a grievous error. My whole family liked you and pleaded with me to tell you, but I found my fears had changed. I knew if you rejected…I knew if you rejected me, I would never be happy again. I never intended to lie to you or to hurt you, and I am sorry if I have embarrassed you. I told you from the start that I had no interest in marriage. I was not trying to trap you into it. Can you please try to understand and forgive me? I have asked for God's forgiveness, now I ask for yours."

"I find it rather ironic that you have the audacity to bring your God into this. Did you ask Him to forgive your deceit, or did you ask Him to forgive you for getting caught?"

Nicole flinched as if he had landed her a physical blow.

"Are you finished?" Devlin asked so coldly that it felt like a winter wind had come through the room.

At the undisguised anger in his tone, Nicole slowly closed her eyes in defeated resignation. "Yes, my lord," she said quietly. "I just wanted you to know the truth before we left London."

"Toby?" Devlin asked from his chair, never once turning around. "I know you are hovering somewhere, ready to pounce upon me should I decide to do physical harm to your mistress. Get her out of here and do not bring her back."

Nicole sobbed quietly most of the way home—the kind of sobbing that came from total defeat. When they drew near the townhouse, she wiped her nose and said, "Toby, I am sorry for all I have put you through. You have seen me at my worst, and I would not blame you if you left. I will always be in your debt, and I will never forget you or stop loving you."

"I ain't leaving, Lady Nick, and you know it. I told you 'e would be in no state of mind to be listening to this tonight, but you 'ave a stubborn streak a mile wide. If you want to try to talk to 'im again, I'll take you back. But it will 'ave to be when 'e ain't so drunk, and if 'e sputters off like 'e did tonight, I'll darken 'is daylights!"

"Do not worry, Toby, I am not going back. I have made a terrible mess of it all. He will never forgive me, and he will never believe anything I have ever told him." Tears began to stream down her face and she added, "He will never believe a word I have ever told him about God. I knew that was God's purpose in giving him to me for a little while, and I was found wanting."

How had it turned out this way? She thought if she went to him—explained it to him—he would understand. She had always feared that he could not cope with her blindness. Now she knew. To her, hiding the blindness had been a sin of omission. To him, it was a lie. And that lie had destroyed everything.

Nicole wanted to convince him that their friendship was real. Their like-mindedness had been a real bond. But she had failed miserably, and there was no hope of a reconciliation…or forgiveness. The tears flowed freely down her cheeks.

And back at Devlin's townhouse, Jared DeVale cried as he had not since he was a boy.

Chapter Eleven

As Nicole sat with her mother in Dr. Morrison's office the following morning, despair almost entirely engulfed her. She would never forget Lord Devlin's angry words or the conviction of her perfidy in his voice as he sent her from his sight forever.

Her thoughts were forcibly interrupted by a man's voice, getting louder as he neared her chair. "Good morning, ladies. I must apologize for keeping you waiting."

Nicole did not know what to expect of the highly recommended physician. After the accident two years before, Nicole had visited several doctors. Michael admitted at the outset that he was no expert in her particular injury, and even urged her to seek other medical advice. His contacts had been numerous, and he had accompanied her to those visits to hear the prognosis of each one.

What always surprised her were the hurried examinations and quick assertions that nothing further could be done. She did not expect miracles from mere men, but she was inclined to believe doctors a gifted breed with an intense desire to help others.

What she discovered during her many consultations was exactly the opposite. The more renowned the man's reputation, the more egotistical the man. If they could diagnose your malady instantly, they were heroes and given their due accolades. Should they be unable to quickly cure your complaint, it was somehow due to your own weakness or should never have been referred to them at all.

Nicole had become very disenchanted with the medical profession, and she bade Michael never to become so impervious to the problems of others. Then she realized that it was she who put them on pedestals to begin with. She had fancied them all called by God to devote their lives to their hippocratic oath. She had not been naive enough to believe a patient could always be cured. Yet she had somehow expected that bedside manner and compassion were a natural part of the gift. She had even come to look forward to the time when she and Michael were married and were a team. Though only Michael could impart his medical findings, she thought she had enough heartfelt compassion for others to encourage and minister to those he was helping.

The previous letdowns came unwillingly to Nicole's mind, and she had to push back her impatience to leave this office unexamined. She just wished to be left alone. But Dr. Morrison's next words caused guilt to override her former bitterness.

"I prefer to spend as much time as I possibly can on a patient's initial consultation. While that provides me much-needed information, it often causes my scheduling to fall dreadfully behind." His words were spoken with such candor that Nicole felt a release of tension.

As he shook hands and traded amenities with her mother, Nicole had an inclination to laugh at herself. Had she not learned as near as yesterday that she had no ability to judge another's character? She had been misjudging others consistently, even as far back as Michael.

But the doctor was soon before her, raising her hand in his, making her forget for a moment the debacle she had created with Devlin. He led her and her mother into a different room that smelled of his sandalwood cologne, well-worn leather and permanent traces of cheroot. The unpretentious scents calmed her. She suddenly pictured a graying man in his late fifties, much like her father—caring, wise and committed. She began to thaw.

He moved away from her, and she could tell by the sound that he had seated himself behind his desk. "I have not had the pleasure of working with Dr. Gibson since our service on the continent, but I am proud that he would suggest I might succeed where he could not."

Nicole did not tell this polite man *her* opinion of the cold and calculating Dr. Gibson, but was glad that her mother had taken his referral to heart. She only hoped this doctor's polite words about his colleague were an indication of his kindness and not another telltale sign of the "brotherhood" of the profession. She would certainly not allow her hopes to rise, but her instinct told her that Dr. Morrison would leave no stone unturned in his search for answers. She must remember God's constant presence in even the smallest details of her life.

The doctor was speaking again in a calm, gentle manner. "I should like to start at the beginning and hear as much as I may before we do an actual exam."

Nicole proceeded to relate the events that transpired on the day of her accident in a concise, intelligent manner. She heard his pen scratching frantically as she spoke. He uttered not a word until she had nearly reached the end of her recital.

"Excuse me, my lady. I want to be sure I understand you. You are not in total darkness, is that correct?"

"Yes, Dr. Morrison. I *was* totally blind for a short period of time, a few weeks, I believe, while it was assumed there was some sort of swelling or temporary damage. When I suddenly was able to tell light from darkness, we hoped my problems seeing were due to the bump on the head, and there was no actual injury to the eyes. But that is the best it has ever gotten. If I am staring in the direction of a sunlit window and someone should cross in front of it, I can perceive that. But there is little else I could tell you. Whether that someone was inside or outside, or whether it was a man or woman, I would not know. Of course, at night, unless I am in a brightly candlelit room, I cannot even tell that much."

"That was quite excellent, young lady. I can see I shall have a cooperative arrangement with you from the start."

Nicole sobered but did not return to her previous state of anxiety. She waited patiently for his first question. She wished sincerely that she could see the doctor's face so she could gauge his expressions. But for now she knew she must wait.

"I believe that is a very good beginning. Lady Beaumont, if you would kindly help your daughter into my examining room, I may begin to study the area of Lady Nicole's injury."

They returned to his office after the intensive exam. The waiting was always the worst part, Nicole thought. In the past this was where the doctors had always come and affirmed that the damage was permanent, and she would feel her heart break just a little more. And after yesterday she was not sure her poor heart could stand such another wound. Tears filled her eyes as her thoughts turned to the dreadful scenes with Devlin. Fortunately for her sanity, Dr. Morrison came back into the room before she made a complete fool of herself.

Nicole found her emotions very close to the surface, not out of fear but due to the sincerity in the man's voice. She realized she had finally met the physician whose goal *was* to help each of his patients. For that she would not make the job of telling her the inevitable any harder for him.

"Dr. Morrison, please do not fret so. That your news is the same as that of the others in no way reflects the very different experience this has been for me. You are not God that I would expect you to wave a hand and heal me. I *do* have the hope of God one day doing just that. Insofar as doctors are concerned, all I ever truly wished for was a caring attempt to solve the problem. You have more than amply met my wishes."

He was a little stunned. "I would not have you leave here believing I can give you any answer for the good or bad, this day. If that has been your experience with my esteemed associates, I can only apologize on their behalf.

"It appears to me, at first blush, that your case involves at least one other area besides your eyes. Traumas to the head are *not* in my area of expertise, so I can in no way make a complete medical determination based on my examination alone. A bruise or blow to the area of the brain that tells the eyes what to do could just as easily have caused your blindness. I should like the opportunity to discuss your case with a number of my confederates, whose abilities in these other areas would allow us to combine our data for a more complete diagnosis."

He sighed. "Lady Nicole, I would not mislead you. I have no proof at this time that your injury is reversible. I do not claim any power above the other physicians you have seen. I have not, however, done a complete evaluation of the information you have given me today. I believe some of my colleagues have failed you in making a final determination at the point of examination, but it does not follow that their diagnoses were wrong."

Nicole could do no more than send a silent prayer to God thanking Him for leading her to this understanding and considerate man. She leaned forward and turned her head to be as close to face-to-face with him as possible. "Dr. Morrison, I thank you from the bottom of my heart. I could ask no more of anyone."

After the brief interruption of the doctor visit, Nicole's severe heartache returned with a vengeance. As she awaited the loading of their trunks onto the departing carriage, she had never felt so torn. She wanted more than anything to be going home, but she had no desire to leave knowing Lord Devlin thought so little of her.

She had sent Toby on a few final errands and was beginning to get concerned at his continued absence. Waiting for him brought her a mixture of pain and hope. She thought she could have made Devlin understand. She had tried so hard to explain it to him last night. She knew the pain that she would never see him again. What a mess she had made of her life.

In another quarter of London, Lord Devlin was in a towering rage. How dare that upstart servant come to his home and upbraid him as if he were a grubby schoolboy!

As he was checking the cinch on Orion's saddle, he heard footsteps behind him and saw several stable boys look past his shoulder. Devlin turned and saw Toby standing there, proud as a duke, blocking his way.

"What are you doing here? Go back to your mistress and stay away from this house. I have warned you once, Toby. This is the last time."

The look of disdain, almost hatred, on the earl's face would have cowed a lesser man. "My lord, I come to 'ave a few words with you. We are leaving London today, but I plan to give you a piece of my mind before I go. There's nothing or nobody gonna stop me. Now I can say what I 'ave to say right 'ere in front of all your men, but I'd like it better if we could go off alone. That empty paddock would suit me jest fine."

The earl fumed. "Since I do not give a hang about what would suit you, I am afraid you are wasting your time. You stupid fool, do you know who I am? I could have you sent to Newgate for speaking to me this way."

"Yes Sir, I 'spose you could. But I plan to 'ave words with you, like it or not. This ain't got anything to do with your rank or mine, it's jest man to man."

Devlin had to admit a grudging respect for the servant, but his anger would not allow a softening toward him. "Very well, Toby. I have no specific complaint with you so the sooner you have your say, the sooner I can see the last of you." Devlin called for one of the stable hands to hold Orion, and he walked toward the paddock with Toby. When they reached the fence he turned and said, "Say your piece."

"First off, my lord, I know that we *do* owe you thanks for not letting the London tabbies get a whiff of this. It 'as saved my ladies much embarrassment. And I knew you wouldn't be in no condition to 'ave Lady Nick come see you the other night, but I couldn't stop her. I'm willing to give credit where it's due."

"Great guns, man! Do you want me to thank you for recognizing good breeding? To be honest with you, with the deceit you have been associated with, I suppose I should be surprised you do recognize it."

The punch that knocked Lord Devlin to the ground was the hardest he had ever felt. And he had sparred with Gentleman Jackson himself! He put his hand to his jaw, sure it was broken, and began to rise to his feet. "Why, you…"

"Look, *your lordship,* I tried being nice. You can beat me to within an inch of my life, *after I 've my say.* Those ladies got no other menfolk to protect their 'onor, and I swear, even if I go to prison, I'll knock you down again if you say anything else like that."

Devlin rubbed his bruised jaw. "Do not flatter yourself. You will not catch me unawares again. Just say what you have to say and go."

Toby took off his hat and began to twist the offending article in his hands. "You were in a pretty bad way the other night when Miss, I mean, Lady Nick came to see you. I don't know if you remember any of what she said…"

"I was drunk, but I heard every word. If you have come to repeat the story, you might as well go." Devlin was quickly regretting his decision to hear the servant out. All he wanted was this reminder of the woman he could not get out of his head, to go away.

"What you 'eard wasn't even 'alf the story. That's what I'm 'ere to tell you…the whole truth. It ain't short and it ain't pretty, so don't think you can just shake me off. I ain't never gabbed on any of my ladies before and even this don't set right with me. I don't always speak proper when I'm nervous, but I ain't leaving 'til you know the truth."

"Then get on with it, man." Devlin was beginning to feel an impatience to know what was so important that this man would risk his freedom to come here.

"I always listened when Miss Nicky would be telling everybody about 'er Pa and what a special man 'e was. Well, 'e was a good man, to be sure—to 'is family and servants and them that belonged to his estate. But he wasn't a saint. Most times 'is 'ead was stuck in a book or 'e was riding 'is land. But 'e was much more interested in *them* than in doing much work. While he *listened* to everybody's problems, it was Miss Nicky who done fixed them. She was different. The man just weren't a doer."

Devlin feigned a yawn. "This is all very fascinating, Toby, but I have no interest in your story. I agreed to let you have your say, but I am not reliving her childhood again. I have been down that road once, so maybe you had better go."

"No!" Toby shouted in exasperation. "That's my point exactly. You ain't never 'eard 'er *real* story. You've only 'eard it the way she tells it."

Devlin ran his hands through his hair in frustration.

"When my lord, God rest 'is soul, 'eard all the estate problems, Miss Nicky did all the work. She took baskets to the sick and 'ungry. Miss Nicky decided to meet with the owner of the parish living. She even took to learning doctoring so she could fix some of their ills. She believed Providence meant 'er to be a servant to other folks.

"Lady B let Miss Nicky do it all because it was easier than fighting it. Lady B's upbringing was as a highborn lady in London. She tried to turn Miss Nick into one of them frippery misses. But seeing as 'ow Lady B 'ad given up town ways, she knew she'd 'ave a 'ard time convincing Miss Nick. It wasn't all 'er fault. Miss Nicky was stubborn and wouldn't think or say anything bad 'bout 'er father. She just went 'bout making what 'e said 'appen."

Toby looked past the earl as he spoke, remembering each detail. "She even started a school for the littlest ones that wasn't old enough to work the fields yet. She taught it 'erself."

Devlin remembered Nicole telling him her parents had worked for schools for the children, but she never told him she was the one who had made it happen. He turned back to Toby's words.

"...but guess who got all the credit? The Earl, that's who. I don't 'ave nothing to say against the man. All I want is for someone to know the truth 'bout Miss Nicky after all these years."

Devlin was surprised at much of this. He thought he knew Nicole well enough to know she would care for others and would work hard at helping them, but he had envisioned a different picture of her father from what she had told him.

This was crazy! He was back to believing in the "saintly" Nicole after one sad story from a servant who worshipped the ground she walked on! No, he must remember the lying woman he now knew she was. He knew if he kept listening he would regret his harshness to her, and he was not ready to give up his injured heart.

"I am sorry, Toby. I have heard enough and I have to go. I can see your loyalty to your mistress, and commend you for it. But I neither care nor have the time to listen to any more."

Toby rose to his full six feet four inches and stared at

Lord Devlin. "I told you that neither of us would leave 'ere until I said my piece, and I meant it. I realize you probably wanna darken my daylights, and if it makes you feel better to go a round of fisticuffs, I'm willing. But I'm still saying my piece. I also realize you could call your lads to throw me out on my duff, but if I 'ave to remind you that I saved your 'ide on the trip to the opry to get you to listen to me, I will. If you don't owe this time to Lady Nick, then *I'm* calling in your IOU."

Devlin clenched his teeth in anger. "Knowing your mistress, I should not be surprised you would stoop to blackmail." As Toby started toward him with fists raised, Lord Devlin held up his hand and said, "No, do not hit me again, just get on with it and leave me be."

"You don't even deserve to 'ear the truth, but I promised myself she wouldn't leave London with anyone thinking 'er a liar, so I'm gonna finish.

"After taking all the responsibility for making the tenants useful, Miss Nicky's Pa died. I can try to explain 'til I'm blue in the face what 'er father meant to 'er, but unless you knew that child, then you wouldn't understand. Lady B was weeping and fainting, always ending up laid down on 'er bed. Miss Chelsea was jest a little mite and 'er world was falling apart. So Miss Nicky jest 'eld it all together for the family and the servants. This seventeen-year-old girl was as devastated by 'er Pa's death as anyone could be. But she couldn't go grieve, she couldn't lie down on the bed crying, she jest 'andled it all. The new earl didn't waste no time taking 'is rightful place at the 'all, so Lady Nick had to move part and parcel to the dowager house."

By now Toby was angry and did nothing to conceal it. "You know the one time I saw 'er crack, your lordship? I found 'er and Solomon after they 'ad been missing a couple of 'ours. She was on the terrace setting in the dark. I could tell she'd been crying and she says to me, 'Toby, will it ever be the same, will it ever be 'ome? Can it be 'ome without 'im?' That was it, the only time. The rest of the time she was too busy *making* it 'ome to worry 'bout it." Toby took out his handkerchief and wiped it across his nose, then quickly put it away.

Devlin could see the whole picture in his mind, Nicole as a very young lady with all the responsibility of the world on her shoulders. Toby had heard her crying for the past that she would never have back. It did not help that it brought back the same feelings he had often had as a boy when the sadness and loneliness of his world came upon him. But Toby had not finished.

"...she *made* everything right. She worked with Beaufort's estate manager to begin gettin' the 'ouse in shape. You know what she found? The man had been robbing the estate and her Pa blind. She booted 'im out and began managing 'er own self. She set workmen to make the 'ouse cheerful for her mother. Then she began to work with the parish vicar more.

"That was when she caught Ben Thatcher poaching on the estate. The man 'ad come back from the war without 'is left arm and 'e couldn't find work. She sat 'im down and talked to 'im about 'is family and 'is skills, and ended up asking 'im if 'e would 'elp 'r manage the small property that came with the dowager house. And between the two of them, it became a 'ome."

So that was how she knew all about the soldiers coming home maimed and with no work prospects, Devlin thought. And that was why she fought against criminal punishment for those men. By George! She had *lived* his speech!

Toby's voice became jeering as he went on. "One day one of the youngsters took sick with some disease Lady Nick couldn't fix. When the child died she took it personal-like and began advertising for a doctor. Ain't no small towns got their own doctor and the new earl didn't want no part of it, but it didn't matter none to Lady Nick. She would make sure no more lives would be wasted 'cause of it. That's when Mr. Perry was hired. Doc was a young, strapping man with lots of book learning. He weren't married either.

"By now Lady Nick was nineteen and, as you well know, pretty as a picture. She 'ad the gift of making each person she was a talkin' to feel like they were the most 'portant person on earth. Doc Perry did the only natural thing, 'e asked 'er to marry 'im. They got engaged and she was 'appier than I seen 'er in a long time. I think she saw a way to go on with the life she 'ad with 'er Pa."

So there *was* a man at home. Well, of course there was, he thought, his jaw clenching. She *was* all those things Toby described, when she wanted to be. The pang of jealousy that hit him in the chest knocked him for a loop. Was that the broken engagement she had spoken of? He must not think of her with another man.

But what did it matter anyway? He had no interest in her now. He wondered if the doctor had been killed in the accident. Perhaps that was her reason for saying she would never marry. What in the world was taking the man so long to get on with the story?

"Lady Nick was taking a step down to marry Doc Perry. Fact is, even though we all thought 'im too starched up, we knew if she married 'im she'd still be close to home and we was that selfish. She believed marrying Doc Perry was God's plan for 'er life. I believe 'e was…well, I guess it ain't my business to tell what I thought."

Toby sounded as if he was choosing his words carefully. "Then *it* 'appened. We were in the stables when someone came a-yelling that a tenant cottage was on fire. We all hurried to get there, but Lady Nick was on Solomon and beat us all to it. Missus Brown was a-crying outside the burning building. She screamed that 'er tyke Jenny were still inside. The smoke was so thick she couldn't get to 'er. Lady Nick put a blanket under a pump, put it over 'er 'ead and runs into that building. I was jest getting there. I can remember thinking that she was the stupidest…and bravest girl I ever laid eyes on.

"We all tried to run in after 'er but the smoke was too thick. Some of us waited at the doorway opening, and some of us went to see if we could get in another way. We saw 'er 'eading back toward us with Jenny in 'er arms. Lady Nick 'ad wrapped the little girl in the wet blanket, leaving nothing to cover 'erself. All at once we 'eard a beam in the ceiling split. I will never forget that cracking sound as long as I live. The fiery pile fell atop Miss Nicky and knocked 'er down. We didn't care 'bout no smoke after that, we jest ran in and grabbed them both."

Tears were streaming down Toby's face in his agitation, and Devlin could not have moved an inch if his own house had been on fire.

"Since Jenny 'ad been wrapped in the blanket, she came through all right, but one of the beams 'it Missy on the 'ead. I carried 'er over to a tree jest as Doc Perry came. She wasn't moving. The Doc said she was jest unconscious and 'e used them smelly salts to bring 'er around. She kept a-coughing and coughing but wanted to know if little Jenny was safe. When we told her she was, tears ran down her face and she thanked God as she lay there on the ground.

"We was all wondering if she was all right. When Doc said nothing was broken or burned too bad, we praised the angels for keeping our lady safe. But when the Doc asked 'er 'ow she felt, she whispered, as quiet as a mouse, 'I cannot see.'

"The rest of the story is mostly too 'ard to imagine lessen you were there. According to the Doc, since she wasn't burned and since she come 'round pretty easy, the 'eat from the fire must 'ave swelled something in 'er eyes. Doc said 'e didn't know if it could be cured or not. Why in the world 'ad we brought the man as doctor if 'e couldn't 'elp our girl?"

Toby was staring off into the distance; reliving it in his mind. The sadness he felt was palpable.

"It was the last straw. After losing 'er father and

'aving to leave 'er 'ome, Miss Nick almost gave up. The blindness jest broke 'er spirit. She didn't ask God why, but she didn't know if 'e could possibly give 'er enough strength to fight this battle. She stayed to 'er room mostly. She was able to deal with the family, but she was afraid of the outdoors because she knew it wasn't safe no more.

"She 'ealed quick enough on the outside, but we worried 'bout 'er insides. We were glad she 'ad Doc Perry to get 'er through it, but as time went by, 'e didn't come round much anymore." Toby's jaw clenched. "We knew 'e were busy without Miss Nicky's 'elp, but hang it all, he shoulda made time for 'er."

The level of emotion between the two men had run the full gamut. Toby knew he had to get this last part out. "Finally, on top of everything else, Doc broke the engagement. Said 'e was sorry but 'is wife needed to be 'elping 'is doctoring. And if she couldn't see, then…"

The silence was deafening.

He continued in a deceptively mild voice. "I think I could 'ave killed a man that day. And I think the only thing that stopped me was that she would never 'ave forgiven me. She needed 'im and 'e jest let 'er go. So I 'ad to settle for the 'ate 'e was gonna face from the townsfolk when they 'eard about it."

Devlin had no words and did not know how long the new silence between them lasted. He sat on the ground and covered his head in his hands, trying to fight the emotion he was feeling. Anger, pain and sadness all merged together as he realized no human could have listened to her story untouched. Nicole was so much more than he had even imagined. He thought he might break down in front of Toby, and it no longer mattered.

In almost a whisper he asked, "What happened then, Toby?"

"She let 'im go. She told everybody she couldn't be a burden to such a needed man. She made 'im the good one, then slowly closed 'er 'eart. She not only lost that worthless doctor, she watched God's will go with 'im. We all watched as she withered away.

"Then one day little Chelsea snuck into 'er room and laid up there on the bed beside 'er. She seemed so small, but she understood our worry and she did the only thing a child knows to do. She told Missy that she didn't care that she couldn't see. She told 'er she would tell 'er 'bout anything she wanted to know about. And as the little girl's tears fell, she begged Miss Nick not to leave 'er, too.

"Our prayers were answered that day. Lady Nick's love for other people, especially 'er family, broke through 'er own misery. She started the long climb back. She memorized every piece of furniture in 'er room, then in the whole 'ouse. She wouldn't leave it 'til she could get anywhere she wanted by counting steps. She didn't want to disturb anyone else. She said she realized God's plan for 'er 'ad always been to 'elp those around 'er, jest not married to the Doc. She wouldn't be a burden to 'im. She even offered to keep 'elping him!

"Outside was 'arder but that's when *our* agreement started up. Outside she wasn't safe unless someone was close enough to 'elp 'er. She said we would be partners." The pride in his voice was unmistakable.

"Riding was the 'ardest because Solomon 'ad to be on a lead. She 'ated that, after all 'er freedom, but she accepted it and slow-like got as involved on the estate as she was before. And after almost two years of the 'ardest work I've ever seen any person do, she started to live again." He stepped away from the fence he had been leaning on and put on his hat. "I'm jest 'bout done, your lordship. Do you want me to finish?"

"Go on, Toby."

"Lady B was so proud of Miss Nick as she pulled 'erself up by the bootstraps and moved on again. She figgered it was time for them to enjoy a spell in London. Lady Nick pleaded and begged not to go. She didn't want the staring, the stumbles, the awkward times—any of it. She tried to explain what a trial it would be for 'er. Lady B couldn't see that, so she made Missy feel guilty. She said that she and Chelsea deserved some time away, but since they couldn't leave Miss Nick, they wouldn't be able to go.

"Lady B told 'er 'bout a fancy doctor in London who might be able to 'elp 'er. She 'ated seeing new doctors, but she said yes for Lady B."

Toby let out a sigh. "Lady B thought she was doing the right thing for Miss Nick, but she jest couldn't understand how the pain and fear of new places affected Missy. I'm jest a servant…never claimed to 'ave much in my brain box, but even I knew that. When Miss Nick agreed, it was only if they tried to keep 'er blindness a secret. She wanted people to treat 'er normal-like. She promised she would practice until it would be nigh impossible to tell, and she promised to 'ave me with 'er all the time. To give Lady B credit, she never wanted to go along with that. She knew if it got out it would make things look worse, but it was the only way Lady Nick would agree.

"That's the story, your lordship. She never came looking for no 'usband or title. She never wanted to come at all. She came to please someone else, like she always does. She even tried to avoid you after that first party where you met. She felt you were too smart to fool for long."

Toby's eyes pierced Devlin's with accusation and malice. "But you know what she told me when I gave 'er a piece of my mind for going out on that terrace alone that night? She told me it was the first time since the accident she felt like 'er old self. The one and only time she felt that way because you talked normal to 'er. You got mad at 'er when you were mad, and she said you even flirted with 'er some. She forgot 'ow that felt. She thought God provided you to lift 'er spirits. The longer it went on the 'arder it was for 'er. She thought she'd cause you 'urt so she tried to avoid you." His voice rose in anger. "Folks jest don't seem to understand that she can't abide anyone suffering! But once again she's the one ended up 'urt, and I for one don't see 'ow much more that little girl can take."

Devlin could not move. He had judged her against every other woman he had known and assumed the worst. He had accused her of misdeeds she had never committed. When he thought Toby was to keep *him* in line, the servant was protecting her from harm. He had made a total fool out of himself, and he was more confused than ever.

He thought back over times that now seemed so clear to him, but mostly showed him his own failings. When he had kissed her and she had touched his face, had she been trying to "see" him? How could he not know?

He was paralyzed with emotion and did not know what to do. Would she see him again? Could they talk this over? Should he leave her alone, or would that cause her more pain? If he did leave her, he knew it would be at the sake of losing a woman he had truly come to care about. Why did she not trust him enough to tell him? Did she not know how *that* would hurt him? They had become so close that he would not have changed his feelings toward her because she could not see. Would he? No, he knew he would not. *He* would have been her "Toby."

Great guns, he had forgotten all about Toby.

Without looking up, he said, "Toby, I am sorry. I am sorry you had to come here today, and I am sorry you had to knock me down to say what you had to say. Most of all I am sorry for the hurt I have caused your mistress. I hope you can convince her to see me again so I can apologize to her." He looked up, hoping to see a sign of encouragement in Toby's eyes.

But Toby was gone.

Chapter Twelve

Devlin sent a missive to his grandmother requesting permission to visit her for a few days. For a fortnight he had kept up appearances; he was seen at all of his usual haunts. Inevitably each night found him home early, reliving every moment with Nicole and wondering a thousand times how he had missed the signs of her blindness.

He had seen how important Nicole's faith was to her. It had apparently sustained her through many trials. Yet she did not use that same faith in connection with him. His own recriminations stopped him; by his own actions he had proved her right not to trust him.

He knew that had he left his stable immediately after Toby had opened his eyes that day, he could have reached Berkeley Square before the Beaumonts left London. Yet he did not go. His own insecurities stopped him. Suppose Nicole now turned her back on him. He deserved it, but he did not think he could bear it. Was that how she felt the many times she wanted to tell him? He had made a muddle of everything.

In the end he justified letting her go by telling himself that nothing he could say would make up for his actions. He conveniently put aside the noble and forgiving character Toby had described, assuming this was one thing she could never excuse.

Devlin further questioned the relationship itself. He had come to care for her—as more than a friend. The heart-stopping kiss shared on a moonlit terrace had proven that. Yet her secret had come out before they'd the opportunity to explore those new feelings.

Perhaps all the kiss had meant to her was the belief that she could trust him with her secret. Should he go to her and make amends? Would she assume a deeper meaning? Would he? What in the world was wrong with him? This woman had changed everything, and he could not figure it out.

He decided that he needed time to consider the matter further. He knew his grandmother's house would be a safe haven for him as he deliberated his next move. He would invite Peter down for some hunting and spend time with the people closest to him, even as he agonized over the fact that Nicole topped that list. She had carved a niche into his life that would prove difficult to remove.

The Beaumonts left London and returned to the Dowager House at Beaufort soon after the doctor visit. Nicole tried to keep her spirits up in front of the others but it was the hardest thing she had ever done, considering the times she felt her heart breaking in pain. She had secretly convinced herself that her explanation to Lord Devlin that late night at his home would wipe away his anger and disgust. She'd imagined he would come and see her before she left Town. She had asked for his forgiveness and had explained the reasoning behind her duplicity. Nicole had harbored the inner hope that it would be enough.

She must now face the sad truth. It was not her subterfuge which had angered him, or he would have accepted her apology. Her blindness had given him a disgust of her, and somehow that hurt more than all the rest.

The problem facing her now was getting over Lord Devlin and that kiss. Though she had eventually put Michael out of her mind, she could not expect that experience to help her now. Even the waltz they had shared on the moonlit terrace had aroused more emotion in her than anything she had ever felt with Michael.

Nicole finally called on the strength that had gotten her through hardship before, and settled back into her routine at home. She had discovered the heartache that deviating from God's plan could bring. She would do so no longer.

If she spent her nights in tears and self-recriminations, only she and the Lord knew it.

When Devlin arrived at his grandmother's, her health was the first subject he broached.

"I am feeling more the thing, Jared. I believe that last attack of influenza knocked me about a bit. I had done better to mind the doctor's instructions." She paused shortly before chiding him. "But had I been one hundred times worse, I would very soon have joined *you* in London. I should like to know if there is any truth to the rumors I have been hearing. I have never condoned setting up innocents as flirts, yet from the stories I have heard…"

Devlin cut her short. "Gossipmongers—I abhor them."

"Jared, calm yourself. I do not listen to idle gossip and you know it. But I have been receiving notes and missives from some of my London friends, and I certainly hope I know which ones to take seriously and which to ignore. My living outside of London has never kept me from the latest *on-dits*. You pointed that out yourself the last time you were here. So if you thought your doings would not reach my ears, your intelligence has dulled somewhat since I saw you last."

"Madame, I cannot imagine what you have heard, but there has been nothing to upset you so. I had not even planned on mentioning the matter to you, but should you like to talk about it we certainly can…*after* I have settled in and *after* you have rested."

"Take heed, Jared. I will not be put off. I have heard too many worrisome accounts that have cut up my peace." In a gentler voice she said, "Jared, you are more important to me than my own son. I am glad you came here to see me. I will be glad to see Lord Hampton as well. But I am not so foolish as to believe you just happened to need a visit on the heels of this affair in London."

He could see the situation called for delicate handling. "I shall make you a pact. If you promise to go rest awhile now, we will meet again at dinner, and we may spend the evening catching up. I know you keep country hours, so I will meet you here at six to take you to dinner." He turned to walk out of the drawing room but stopped at the door. "Thank you for letting me come stay with you, ma'am. I have missed you and your wisdom very much lately."

When they met at dinner Devlin gave his grand-mother a rehearsed, and much edited, account of his dealings with Nicole.

"Jared, I may be five and seventy years old, but I am not in my dotage. There is more to the story than this. I am afraid I heard you were actively pursuing this woman more than anyone could remember in a long time."

Devlin cursed his luck as he realized she would not accept his light explanation, but he was not prepared to share more. "Grandmother, I will admit to seeking peace here to try to sort out the confusion in my mind. You are correct, there is more to the incident than I have related, but more than that, I cannot say now." He saw the look of determination on her face and smiled sadly. "I am not avoiding you, I promise. I just need to come to some conclusions on my own. I have not lied to you, ma'am. I had a very special friendship with Lady Nicole. We enjoyed each other's company, but there was no breach of promise and no compromise of her reputation. It is complicated. It is confusing—indeed, some of it is nothing less than unbelievable, but I am not ready to discuss it. Can you understand that? I am not trying to shut you out. It is just not the time."

"Jared, I appreciate your honesty, but pray consider that *sometimes* talking things out with someone, especially someone you can trust, *helps* you work it out in your mind. If or when you need that, I vow I will always be available to you."

Devlin knew he had gotten off easy and so spent the next few days hunting with Peter. Evenings were quiet, with reading or cards.

On their final evening together, Peter and Lady Augusta were debating the pleasures to be had at Vauxhall Gardens. Devlin silently sat reading one of the London newspapers. Lord Hampton interrupted both his hostess and his friend with his usual aplomb. "Speaking of London, old boy, if I leave here without the address of the Beaumont chit, Beth will have my head. Seems they forged an everlasting bond, and she has been after me an age to get it from you. She was not aware they were to leave London so soon and wants to invite the girl to Hampton Court for a few weeks."

The silence that descended was foreboding, and as Lord Hampton looked confused, he added, "I am sorry, have I said something amiss? You know I am ever one for putting my foot in my mouth…"

Lady Augusta spoke up. "No, young man, you said nothing wrong. You have, however, broached a subject my grandson has been trying to avoid since he arrived here. And if his distraction these past few days is any indication, he has been very unsuccessful at it."

"Great guns, Grandmother! I told you that I am

always fodder for the tittle tattlers of the *ton*. I was not courting Nicole Beaumont." His face was flushed, but he apologized under his breath for his language.

"I have to admit, old man," Peter replied, candidly, "I thought you had serious designs on the girl. Beth could talk of nothing but the two of you smelling of April and May."

Lady Augusta and Lord Hampton jumped unexpectedly as Devlin slammed his newspaper onto a table and began to pace the room. "It seems you two will not be satisfied until I tell you the whole of it. No matter that I have tried to make you understand this is not a topic I wish to discuss."

"Darling," his grandmother said. "It is quite obvious you have not conquered your demons on your own. We love you and want to help you. Is that not why you came here?"

"Very well, I shall endeavor to satisfy your curiosity, but on my oath, if one word of what I say goes out of this room, I will never forgive either of you. This is my business and my business alone. Do I make myself understood?"

The two waited as he paced the length of the room then went to lean against the mantle, staring into the fire.

"You are right, Peter, I did like Lady Nicole a great deal. I told myself I found the same friendship you had often touted with Beth. I found a real friend, who happened to be a female. But what I have related to you, Grandmother, is also true. There was no courtship. I will admit that as the weeks passed, my feelings became quite confused. Lady Nicole was as interesting and smart as any man of my acquaintance, and a pleasure to be with. I will also go so far as to say I had begun to be extremely attracted to her. But neither of us wanted marriage, and we were both open about that. I began by enjoying her friendship, as I think she enjoyed mine, but I confess I had no clear thoughts as to how such a relationship could continue. It was not as if I could invite her to go hunting with me at the end of the Season! You must see my dilemma?"

His eyes never left the fire and as he began to speak, it appeared he was explaining it to himself rather than to his listeners. "She was quite an enigma to me. When I met her, the Season was all but over. She had been in Town the entire time, yet I had never seen her before. When we discussed her past, she led me to believe it was quite mundane. Yet something in her air indicated a life much more than ordinary. I cannot explain it any better than that. I was intrigued."

Devlin finally walked away from the fire and went to stare out the window. He continued talking, his back to them. "Do you know what she did? I mentioned to her that I had a speech to give in Parliament a few days before we attended the opera." His voice continued in an awed tone with his next words. "She came to hear it. I know of no other woman of my acquaintance who would have cared a jot to hear the speech, much less forego an afternoon of festivities to do so. And when I think of…" His voice trailed off as if he could not finish. He just ran his hands through his hair.

"But that night after the opera, Peter, she began to

avoid me. You know that evening was quite pleasurable for us all. I could not understand the change in her. When we met again at your house the next day, you must have noticed she could not quit the place soon enough.

"Then one evening I attended a ball, and discovered her sitting among the dowagers with her mother." He began to speak as if thinking out loud. "I suppose that is why I never saw her during the Season. She purposely hid there." He shook his head to clear it.

"To make a long story short, I confronted her that night. I took her onto the terrace, lost my temper in my attempt to get answers, and then quite irrationally offended her. Deciding it was not the place to air grievances, she agreed to explain her actions to me the next day and we left quite…in charity with each other." Devlin did not feel the need to mention the kiss they shared, yet it was much on his mind. "We arranged to meet the following day for a drive to Richmond Park."

He finally came back and sat down in the chair he had recently vacated, which faced both Peter and his grandmother. "The rest of the story will show you what a truly despicable man I have become."

Both of his listeners gasped in surprise, and then began denials.

He held up his hand to stop their defense of him. "I am not proud of it. I came here to see if I could conquer my doubts, mayhap justify my actions, but the more I think on it the more I curse them." He stopped there and drifted off into his own thoughts.

Lady Augusta kept a calm voice and said, "Just tell us what happened."

"Very well, I hope you may feel the same when you know the whole of it. We had ended the evening on such good terms that I wished it to continue. She had often mentioned the pleasure she had in riding, so I decided to surprise her with a horse for our outing instead of the constraints of the carriage. I truly thought she would be overjoyed with my plan. Needless to say, the surprise was an utter failure." He paused again and put his head in his hands for a moment, as if the remembrance of that day caused him physical pain. "You see, she could not see my surprise. I took her to the front steps, and as her sister began describing the horse in detail to her it all became quiet clear. Nicole Beaumont is blind."

"Blind!" yelped Lord Hampton. "That is not possible. We spent that whole evening at the opera and I would have known. We all would have known. How could she have attended your speech in Parliament and danced at balls?"

"I quite agree with you in theory, Peter, but we did *not* see." Devlin harrumphed sarcastically at his own irony.

"She did not dance at any of the balls. She did go to Parliament and to the theater, but she had become quite adept at hiding her disability. Do you remember her strange servant, Toby? He guided her through those situations. I met her on a dark terrace, and after talking to her for some time with no suspicion, it never occurred to me after. We always take our ladies' arms and lead them, you know. There was never any reason to suspect."

"Oh, Jared, the shock you must have suffered. I am so sorry. And that poor girl—I do not imagine she intended you to discover it in such a manner," his grandmother said, feeling for them both.

"It is a pity none of your sympathy occurred to *me* in that instant, Grandmother. Indeed, I did not see her as a figure for sympathy at all. My own feelings became tantamount to anything else, and I realize now that I must be the arrogant brute she once thought me. I only saw a woman who had lied, not only to all of London, but especially to me. In fact, I felt completely betrayed.

"I saw a woman who talked only of loyalty and honesty and concern for others, pulling a hoax on Society. I saw a woman like all other women, who would do anything to hide her flaws to get a rich and titled husband." His voice lowered to a whisper as he finished. "And I saw a woman who could not trust me with the most important facet of her life."

"Jared," his grandmother cried as she moved her Bath chair to where he sat. "You cannot blame yourself for those feelings. The shock of it all must have been overwhelming."

"No, love, I suppose the *feelings* were somewhat natural to an arrogant earl, but that I *said* all of those things to her in front of her entire household was inexcusable."

"Jared, you did not?" Her voice was no more than an agonized whisper, surprise causing the question to come tumbling out.

"Yes, Grandmother, I did. I accused her of every vice imaginable in front of her family and her servants. I acted out a Cheltenham tragedy in the foyer of her home like a common simpleton. And do you know what? That night at two in the morning, when I was feeling deuced sorry for myself *and* doing some very heavy drinking, *she* came to my house to apologize to *me*. She tried to explain. You were correct, Grandmother. She had planned to tell me on our drive that day. She tried to make amends to *me!* Did I let her? No, I told her I could never believe anything she ever said again and told her to get out of my house."

Peter was angry with his friend. "Jared, I have been here with you these three days, and you never once intimated any of this."

Devlin jumped out of his chair and went back to the fireplace. He spat the words out coldly. "Do you think I am proud of this, Peter? Having to tell the two of you at all is the hardest thing I have ever done." An evil sneer entered Devlin's expression as he continued. "I am afraid, my friend, you will think that a small thing when I tell you what happened next. You have every right to be angry."

Lady Augusta interrupted the two men. "Jared," she said quietly, "do you know *why* Peter is angry with you for keeping this from him? He knows how you must have been suffering, yet you did not trust him enough to be your friend. You should know him well enough to know that he would think no less of you because of what happened. You could have counted on his support. Can you not see that you have just done to Peter what

Lady Nicole did to you? You have hurt him with your assumption that he would think less of you, the same anger you feel that your young woman, more special to you than any other, has feared your reaction to the truth."

"Grandmother, I appreciate your attempt to see me innocent. However, you do not yet know the half of it." Devlin proceeded to tell them about Toby's visit, and finally he told them he could have reached her before she left London, but did not. "Still want to make me out a hero, Madame?"

"Jared, when you told Lady Nicole about Vivian and why you are avoiding marriage, did she appear disappointed?"

"Great guns! I never told her about Vivian. What did that have to do with anything?" He was taking much of this out on the person he loved most, but he could not help it.

She was quiet again. "You expected total honesty from her, but that was not required of you?"

"You put my first marriage on equal footing with being *blind?*" he asked in stupefied indignation.

"Oh, Jared, you will not understand. Think beyond your own hurt for the moment. And do not think I regard your pain lightly. This is a horrible experience any way you look at it. But yes, I would assume the two equal in some respects. You believe your first marriage is no one else's concern, and even now get tired of the gossipmongers when they remember it. Lady Nicole got tired of people treating her differently. Therefore, she took that information out of their hands. I do not see much difference."

"As I said, Grandmother, I knew you would not be proud of me. But you *would* hear it, so you cannot beat me up any more than I already have."

"No, my dear, but I can try to make you see that mayhap it never *was* a matter of trust. You did not tell her about Vivian, but it was not because you did not trust her. It was because you did not want special or different treatment because of it."

He watched as her tears fell freely. "And now you are overtired because of me." He raised her hand to his lips.

Lady Augusta dabbed her eyes. "I gather that means conversation is at an end for tonight, so I will leave you gentlemen to your brandy. Jared, could you and I continue this conversation in the morning? I am not asking that you marry the girl or even resume your friendship, but you do see that you must apologize to her and end the hurt feelings between you, do you not?"

"Grandmother, I love you. Even after one of the worst things I have ever done in my life, it appears you are not going to cast me to my fate. But Peter and I are leaving in the morning as planned. I believe this night *has* helped me. It has made me realize that I made a mull of things, lost a good friend and learned a great deal about myself in the process. And much of what I learned I do not like. But I have come to the conclusion that there is no proper way to undo this tragedy, and I shall try to forget it and move on. There is nothing else I can do, except consider your recommendation to apologize. But then it is over."

He mumbled one more sentence, but she heard him and it broke her heart. "Then I shall try to change the pride and arrogance I have apparently grown unforgivably comfortable with."

Lady Augusta sighed in resignation as he pushed her Bath chair out of the room, then kissed her cheek. "Good night, Peter," she said over her shoulder before he closed the door and wheeled her to her chambers.

"My darling boy," she said to her grandson when they were alone, "if you think I shall let things rest as they are then you are in for a rude awakening. You do not yet understand the God who works in mysterious ways. He decides when it is over."

"Nicky, the post has brought you *two* letters this morning!" The surprise in her mother's voice was evident as they sat down to breakfast. She also knew her mother was using any means possible to help her forget about the debacle in London.

Nicole's heart felt one second of anticipation, a secret longing that Devlin had written to her. Her mother's next words dashed those hopes.

"One is franked by Lord Hampton. I assume it is from his lovely wife." But Lady Beaumont could not keep the excitement out of her voice as she picked up the next missive. "The other is a sealed envelope with a crest upon it. It is there on the left side of your plate. I thought at first it might be from Lord Devlin, but I do not recognize the frank. I cannot imagine who it is from."

"Mama," Nicole sighed, "you know you shall have to read it to me in any event. You could have opened it at your convenience."

"Upon my honor, that was uncalled for, Nicole." Her mother bristled with hurt feelings. "You know very well I only read what you ask me to, and only after you have been the first to receive it."

"I am sorry, Mama," Nicole apologized, despondently. "I only meant that you have my permission to open such correspondence as that." Lately she seemed to do and say the wrong thing at every turn.

These were the things Nicole hated most about being virtually blind. As soon as she got over the initial shock of losing her sight, Nicole had accepted her inability to live her life as she had been wont to do. Each day taught her that even the slightest, most commonplace of tasks were now beyond her power. She could not read her letters alone and savor the parts she wished. She could not snuggle before a fire with a good book. She could no longer read her Bible. The daily reminders sometimes seemed the hardest to bear.

Her mother had no other interest beyond the crested envelope, while Nicole should have loved nothing better than to find a quiet place in the garden to read the letter from Beth. She was torn when she thought about what the letter could contain. Truth be told, Nicole had often wondered what Beth had thought of the afternoon they had spent together. They had not met again before leaving London. Not counting Devlin, she thought Beth was the one person she would miss the most.

And she knew she would never again meet anyone like Devlin. She might secretly envision Devlin appearing and announcing his love for her, blindness not withstanding. And no matter how much pain she was in, had that miracle happened, it was still not God's plan for her life and she was now intent on doing His will.

A nudge from her mother brought Nicole back to the present and to the correspondence they were discussing. "Goodness, Nicky, you were a thousand miles away! Do you want to find out who this crested letter is from?"

"Yes, Mama, I am sorry. But do you mind reading the letter from Lady Hampton first? I suppose she has heard the news by now, and I need to know her feelings."

Her mother opened the note a little awkwardly, as always, doing a simple thing Nicole could not. Nicole knew her mother tried to understand her inner pain, having to hear a private letter read by another. She began to read.

> *"My dear, dear Nicky,*
> *I may call you that, now that you are not before me in that gorgeous velvet creation you were wearing the night of the opera! How I have missed you. Dare I hope you have missed me as well? I have begged Hampton a thousand times to obtain your direction for me. I have been longing to invite you to come visit me.*

"More seriously, darling, Peter just returned from a hunting trip with Jared at Lacey Court. He told me the whole story.'"

Nicky's mother interrupted with a sigh, saying she had known it would become the latest *on-dit* soon enough.

"'I daresay you must now think all of London is gossiping about you. Well, you must not think it. Jared broke down while visiting his grandmother and told them of his horrid actions. He has, of course, put them under oath never to breathe a word, but Jared knows that Peter tells me everything. I will not say much on this subject now, but you must not think the worst of Dev. I told you once before that as soon as he realized he was in love, he would fight the feeling or take an easy way out. I do not know whether he realizes yet or not, but Peter tells me this entire situation has confused him greatly, and since I am not supposed to reveal any other confidences I shall say no more on that subject. I only want you to try and remember what I told you about his past when you feel angriest at him.'"

Nicky was flushed and Lady Beaumont was embarrassed. "I am sorry, darling. I wish you could read this in private."

Nicole tried to set her mother's mind at ease. "Do

not fret, Mama. You know everything for the most part, and I will not hide things any longer."

Lady Beaumont read on.

"My dear girl, I think of you often. When I think what we all must have put you through as you attended the Season virtually blind, I cringe. You are the bravest woman I have ever met and I am very proud to know you.'"

Tears now welled in Nicole's eyes as she remembered her intuition that this woman would never have rejected her because of her disability. She listened closely as her mother continued.

"I wish you had been able to tell me. I realize now that you probably meant to that afternoon we spent together. I wish we had not been interrupted all the more now, because I can only imagine the burden you have been under. I truly do understand why you felt you could not reveal your secret. I have found that most in London are downright cruel in situations they do not understand. And when Devlin discovered the matter, it never occurred to him to consider your feelings, did it? I am even sorrier I didn't know then. Perhaps knowing you both as I do, I could have helped in some way.

My purpose in writing is actually to invite you to come and visit me for a few weeks. I know how involved you are in the management of your home, but could you not take a

*little time and come to stay with me? It is even
more important now as I have exciting news.
I am increasing! Oh dear, I promised Hampton
I would not tell a soul until he told his mother!
He will soon have me spending my days re-
clining on my couch if someone of sense does
not come. You must let me know what weeks
would be convenient for you, and I shall cancel
all engagements so we may relax and gossip to
our hearts' content. Please, oh, please, do come,
Nicole. I truly have missed you dearly.*

    *I must go now, as the frank on this letter will
probably give Hampton a case of the vapors.
Give my regards to your lovely mother, and
write soon to let me know when you can come.*
Love,
Beth'

"Well, dear, that was lovely. I liked her ever so much
when we met in London, and now I see that her manners quite match her personality. I think it would do you
a great deal of good to visit her. I hope you will consider it. Now do you wish me to open the other letter?"

Nicole nodded absentmindedly. Could she really visit
with Beth for a few weeks? That would be the perfect
remedy for her melancholy. She could be totally honest
with Beth and express some of the things weighing
heavily upon her heart. She was trying so hard to be
cheerful for everyone. If she could talk her feelings out,
perhaps it would be easier to get on with her life. Yes!
She would go…

A screech from her mother brought her abruptly out of her reverie. "My goodness, gracious, what can this mean?"

"What is it, Mama? Tell me quickly!"

"It is an invitation. It is an invitation from Lady Augusta DeVale. She requests that you and I visit her for the weekend at Lacey Court. Goodness, what can she want with us after all that happened in London? It will not do. We must, of course, decline."

"Lady Augusta?" Nicole's mind could not seem to get past the name. "I do not understand. I... Oh dear... his grandmother!"

"Of course it is his grandmother, Nicky! The dowager countess, Lady Augusta."

"Why does she want us to visit, do you suppose?" Nicky asked. She wondered, after Beth's letter, how Devlin's grandmother would have reacted to hearing her story. "We will not know unless we go. When does it ask us to come?"

"My stars, Nicky, you cannot possibly be in favor of this! We do not need the aggravation, my love. You have finally settled back in here, and I will not have this all dredged up again. You need time to heal. We will make up some excuse."

Nicole laughed a little nervously. "Mama, you know if we have learned anything from all of this, it is to be open and honest. If Lord Devlin's grandmother has heard that I have mistreated her grandson and she wishes to give me a piece of her mind, then I owe her that. Yes, Mama, we will definitely accept this invitation." Nicole almost had to laugh despite her fear. It seemed so long ago that she had once doubted his grandmother had even existed!

Chapter Thirteen

Nicole and her mother *had* accepted Lady Augusta's invitation, and they were to leave at first light the next morning. It was a journey Nicole could not easily anticipate, despite her brave words to her mother upon receipt of the missive. She would rely on God's Word: *I know the thoughts I think for you, saith the Lord, thoughts of peace, and not evil, to give you an expected end.* He would take care of her through every circumstance as it would prepare her for *His* expected end.

As the coach neared Beckenham, Nicole's doubts began to resurface, making her question her decision to come. The necessity of apologizing to Lord Devlin's grandmother remained, but the hidden purpose Nicole's mother suspected had begun to take hold in Nicole's imagination as well. Could Lady Augusta have been so angry that she sent for Devlin? Would he be there, too? She thought she could hold her own with his grandmother, but she was not yet strong enough to face him. The two of them would be an indomitable force should they wish to take her to task for the deception she'd perpetrated on Society. Nicole no longer cared what Society thought of her, but Lord Devlin was another matter.

She prayed her worst fear might not be realized. *Please, God, do not let him be there.* She only wanted to put their time together out of her mind and move on with her life. She hoped this summons from his closest living relative might help her obtain that goal.

The butler came forward and took their cloaks. He spoke to them in a respectful voice, easing Nicole's mind somewhat. "I am Higgins. Her ladyship awaits you in the morning room. If you will follow me, I will take you to her."

He led them into an inviting drawing room. As they passed by him into the sunny chamber, he announced, "Lady Beaumont and Lady Nicole, Madame." Higgins bowed and backed out of the apartment, closing the double doors behind him.

Lady Beaumont led Nicole to the fireplace where a very distinguished woman sat in a Bath chair.

The austere lady spoke first. "Forgive me, please, for not greeting you at the door. I am afraid being tied to this chair keeps me from welcoming my guests as I should like. I am Augusta DeVale, and I am very pleased you accepted my invitation."

Nicole often lamented the loss of her sight, but there had only been two occasions when she would have given a king's ransom to have it back for a moment. The first was on the terrace where Devlin had kissed her so tenderly. The second was now. She would love to see the features of the woman so special to him that he had mentioned her at their first meeting. More importantly, she wanted to read the feelings she knew must be evident.

Lady Beaumont said all that was proper, still quite anxious as to why they had been summoned. Then Lady Augusta spoke again. "I am sure you are tired from your trip. I have had your things taken up to your rooms. I thought you might like to refresh yourselves, even nap, for a few hours. We may then meet again here for tea. I am afraid I myself must resort to afternoon rests more often than not, so you must not feel uneasy. Please take as much time as you wish."

Lady Beaumont agreed a rest would be the very thing, then asked the question she had worried over since the invitation had arrived. "Have you invited a large party for the weekend, my lady?" Nicole did not realize how very tense she had been until Lady Augusta spoke and lifted a great weight from her heart.

"No, Lady Beaumont. Since I have been confined to my chair I much prefer small intimate parties rather than grand *affaires*. I hope I did not mislead you in my invitation. We shall be quiet, I am afraid. There will only be one other guest attending, but she has already arrived and is resting. She will join us for tea and I think you will enjoy her company." Tugging the bell pull near her chair, her kind dismissal followed. "I will have Higgins escort you to your rooms."

It seemed Lady Augusta's speech was not yet finished. "Lady Nicole," she said, as Nicky's mother was leading her to the door, "I understand you have a special servant you keep with you at all times. I have made arrangements for him to be roomed near you."

Nicole's voice betrayed none of the nervousness she felt. "Thank you very much, Lady Augusta. Though Toby is not as necessary to me when Mama is near, I appreciate your consideration."

Lady Augusta continued, somewhat impressed. "I have found that as we learn to deal with life's inconveniences, we begin to accept whatever means God makes available that allows us to feel triumphant over them."

Nicole's head jerked around to where she could see the outline of the sitting woman in front of the ceiling-to-floor windows. She was surprised at the veiled hint of understanding from someone she had expected to be so formidable, but did not feel confident enough to delve further into her meaning. She was also surprised to hear the dowager talk about God. Beth had intimated Devlin knew about God from his grandmother. Was it a real relationship with the Lord, or just the common use of His name so often heard upon the lips of Society? She thanked Lady Augusta again and left the room with her mother. Toby escorted them both up to their rooms behind the butler.

Nicole discovered herself too restless to sleep. Stella had been unpacking her trunks, so she decided she needed fresh air to clear her head. Knocking lightly on the door across from her own, she asked Toby if he would take a walk with her. They found a gravel path that wound through immaculate lawns and gardens leading to a bridge-covered river, and she imagined the beauty and setting Toby described to her. She could not, however, enjoy the serenity. She had the rest of the weekend to face and it weighed heavily on her mind. She and Toby walked back to the house in silence.

The time had come. Nicole and her mother would spend the evening with Lady Augusta, not knowing what to expect.

Her mother tried to assure her with normalcy. "You have a special gift, love, of making simplicity look elegant. Indeed, you look regal."

"Thank you, Mama, but I fear you are somewhat biased." She smiled and kissed her mother's cheek. Nicole took the fan Stella was placing in her hand but could not hold back her anxious question. "Now that we have met Lord Devlin's grandmother, do you still believe we are to be castigated?"

"I am not sure that ingenious old lady is not up to something, but she was all that was polite earlier. I am resolved to do as your father always advised and give her the benefit of the doubt. Lady Augusta is a presence, to be sure, but she certainly did not seem intent on making us uncomfortable. Indeed, quite the contrary I would say. We must take encouragement from that and face the music. Just remember, you will not be alone, and I remember a thing or two about handling myself among my peers!" She reached for Nicky's arm and began to lead her toward the doorway. "I think we had better go down now."

"Thank you, Mama." Nicole *was* heartened by her mother's words, but she could not help feeling a bit apprehensive. Obviously, Lady Augusta was aware of her blindness. Beth Hampton had already informed her of that. Nicole's angst derived from wonder at Lady Augusta's graciousness to them. Why had she summoned them here?

Toby escorted mother and daughter to the bottom of the stairs where Higgins then led them to a different drawing room, one set off the dining room. As they entered the smaller parlor, Nicole's mother gasped, left Nicole's side and ran across the room exclaiming, "Amy, is it you? Is it really you?"

Nicole stood perfectly still until she heard Lady Augusta's voice from close to her arm. "There is a sofa approximately two feet to your left if you would like to sit down, my dear. I had not expected the reunion would be quite as emotional as this."

Nicole thanked Lady Augusta with heartfelt gratitude after feeling quite desolate at being abandoned in a room she had never been in before. But she also realized from Lady Augusta's comment that the additional invitee had been a calculated inclusion for the occupation of her mother. Any good hostess would provide companionable partners for their guests, but this was a bit too contrived to be a coincidence. She could not concentrate on the significance of it, as her mother rushed immediately back to her side.

"Nicky, darling, I am ever so sorry. I should never have run off from you like that. What will these ladies think of me? But, dear child, you will never believe who is here! You must remember hearing me speak of my dearest friend, Amy? She is properly Mrs. Amelia Davenport now, but she was always my Amy. I have not seen her since your father and I married. Oh, Lady Augusta, this is indeed a wonderful surprise!"

"When I heard Amelia was visiting the neighborhood, I thought you might like to meet again. When you both had your come-out, everyone in London knew the Bradford and Chesdon chits were the belles of the Season." Lady Augusta leaned closer to Nicole and sighed. "It appears you will be obliged to keep me company most of this weekend, my dear." Then louder she said, "Why do we not go in to dinner? I am sure you must be famished."

Higgins arrived to push Lady Augusta's chair and Toby escorted Nicole. The two old friends were arm in arm and already quite oblivious to their surroundings. Nicole's suspicions were confirmed that Lady Augusta had obtained her sole attention quite by design. She would soon get her chance to take the upstart who had hurt her grandson down a peg or two. Nicole had no complaint with this; as someone who liked being in control, she appreciated a smart woman who could regulate events to her liking. And Lady Augusta had the decency to keep it between the two of them when she might have made quite a show of it to the uppermost peers of London.

Dinner was an informal affair with Lady Beaumont and Mrs. Davenport exchanging remembrances from their pasts. Time flew by quickly, and the ladies had a very pleasant evening all in all, while Nicky waited on tenterhooks.

Devlin's grandmother arranged the rest of the evening as Nicole expected. "I have planned no activity tonight, knowing you might like to retire early after your journeys. Tomorrow we shall be free to visit as long as we like. Breakfast will be served whenever you rise. We may relax in the drawing room at the back of the house. I spend much time there for the warmth of the sun." She tugged on the bell pull. "I will have Higgins take you up now. Good night, ladies. I shall look forward to the morrow."

Nicole thought she would lie awake all night. The suspense was beginning to wear on her, but she very soon fell asleep and did not wake until Stella brought her chocolate. She knew it was much too early for the others to be about, so she quickly dressed in a lavender day gown with a high ruffled collar, hoping she and Toby could enjoy a solitary breakfast.

He escorted her to the breakfast room, but paused in the doorway. He led her to the table and as he pushed in her chair, he said, "Good morning, Lady Augusta." He bowed out of the room with a quiet "Ma'am."

Nicole froze in shock. She stammered, "I… You… I did not realize anyone else would be down so early, my lady." She felt awkward and alone. She specifically avoided situations without her mother or Toby, and Toby could not properly breakfast in the presence of Lady Augusta.

The silence seemed to stretch on forever while the servant fixed her plate and poured her tea. Since losing her eyesight, Nicole had never felt so intimidated. Her anger began to rise as she felt more and more like a mouse whose tail was caught under the cat's paw. As the cat would torture its prey before the kill, it appeared

Lady Augusta would get additional satisfaction in Nicole's discomfort. Finally, the footman placed her food in front of her and Lady Augusta dismissed him. Nicole was not surprised. On the contrary, she was relieved. The time had finally come.

"Nicole, you seem flustered and from what I have heard, that is not a state in which you often find yourself. I must apologize for causing a guest such distress. I promise you it was never my intention. Once I realized my error, I could not leave the room without addressing you."

The cat was pawing the mouse in pleasure.

"You must feel free to breakfast in your room with your servants, if it is what you wish. I should have given those directions last night before I went to bed. I did not think of everything as I ought."

Nicole could only stammer in anger, "Lady Augusta... Ma'am, I beg your pardon, but your orchestration of each situation as far back as your invitation could only be to make us *un*comfortable. Do not fret, ma'am, I am glad we are finally coming to the point of this visit."

The woman she thought so austere laughed—not an evil laugh as Nicole expected, but one of surprised delight. "I should have known from Jared's description of you that you would speak your mind straight-out. Do you really wish for that tea and toast, or may we retire to my sunroom? I should like the opportunity to change your opinion of me."

"I, too, should rather get this over with, my lady."

Toby and Higgins appeared as if by magic at the

ring of the bell, and both ladies were soon ensconced in Lady Augusta's private sitting room.

"I do so wish you could see it, child. I think you would like all of the windows and the view of the pathway. Jared spoke of your love for the country and the outdoors."

"Lady Augusta," Nicole said determinedly, somewhat flustered at the veiled attempt to charm. "I should much prefer we cease the polite banter entirely. You obviously know all about me and, therefore, know all that happened in London. I readily admit to a gross error in judgment, and I deserve all of the things I am sure you wish to say to me. I shall not begrudge you your chance to berate me. That is something you deserve. I do want you to know, however, that I am heartily sorry for all of the pain I caused your family and mine." Nicole stopped, but only to draw breath. "I also appreciate the trouble you have taken to spare my mother's anguish. She has been in a wretched state, fearing further pain to all of us."

As her astonishment lessened, Lady Augusta shook her head and let out a sigh. "Well, that has cut me to the quick, has it not? I have just discovered that neither of us is as smart as we think we are."

"I am afraid I do not understand you, ma'am," Nicole said.

There was no mistaking the fact that Lady Augusta's voice was eminently serious as she asked, "Can you be telling me that you and your mother thought I brought you here to chastise you?" Without allowing a response from Nicole she hurried on. "More importantly, you came ready to accept it?" Shock finally registered in her voice. "You believed I planned to make you as uncomfortable as possible and that I would be pleased in your discomfort?"

More to herself than to Nicole she groaned, "Jared may have told me all about you, but I can only pray that you did not get this picture of me from him."

Nicole was immediately penitent. This fiasco was due to her folly, and she had no right to so address this woman, no matter her motives. "Ma'am, please let me assure you that Lord Devlin has spoken of you in only the highest regard. It has been quite evident that he loves you above anyone else."

"Yet you still believed I intended you malice in inviting you here!" It was a statement, not a question.

"My lady, I assumed you wished to ring a peal over me because I had hurt someone you love. And yes, I meant to accept it out of respect for that love. At the very least, you have every right to call me to account. I believe I, too, would demand that satisfaction to protect a member of my family."

Lady Augusta moved her Bath chair in front of the sofa where Nicole was sitting. Lifting one of Nicole's hands, she explained, "I asked you here for several reasons, but none of them were to berate you *or* your mother. I admit to inviting Amelia so your mother would be occupied, but it was so I would be able to have you to myself, to get to know you, my dear. Alone we could do so with no need to follow Society's dictates of mere politeness. I told your mother I intended to talk to you about Jared, but accusing you was never part of the plan."

"Perhaps you would care to explain it to *me,* ma'am?" Nicole asked softly.

"I did hear about what happened in London, but I requested your visit so I could meet the woman my grandson let slip away because of such a trifling matter. It was certainly not to cause you any further humiliation than I fear he already has." As she finished, she deflated a little. "I cannot imagine what you must have been thinking of me last night and this morning."

Nicole sensed that Lady Augusta could use a little comforting, but at the moment she was too astonished to give it. "Trifling?" she said, taken aback. "I… You do not know… Ma'am, Lord Devlin was perfectly justified in his anger. If you know the whole of it, then you know it was I who was deceitful and I who was at fault."

"My dear child, I did not hear the story from gossips. Indeed, I can honestly say that I do not know how this escaped Society's notice. I heard your story from my grandson. I am well aware he enacted you a performance to rival Drury Lane, but I could not get him to see past the harsh words he said, so I sent for you. Jared knows nothing of your visit. I wished to make your acquaintance and hoped we could discover a way to mend matters."

Nicole was confused. "I vow I do not understand, my lady. If Lord Devlin told you the truth, why should you wish to reconcile us? You must know I behaved very badly."

"My dear girl, Jared did tell me the truth. He is too honest, however, to exempt himself from blame. You see, child, it was not his description of events that roused my curiosity." Her voice subtly changed. "My grandson has a reputation among the general populace as a proud, independent man—not vicious, but somewhat hardened. He is also quite able to accomplish whatever he sets out to achieve. Without boring you with his history, I can vouchsafe for his being somewhat severe, though in truth he feels things quite deeply.

"You see, I have never seen him so greatly disturbed. His inner turmoil made me wish to know the woman he was so tortured about hurting. Unfortunately, he was too willing to believe you would never forgive him. It made it easier for him to walk away from the situation…but not to forget it."

They talked easily after that, and Nicole was astonished by the luncheon bell, not realizing how long they had been closeted together. When Higgins and Toby knocked at the door, they found Nicole seated on the floor at the dowager's feet with tears in her eyes.

"I believe your mother and Mrs. Davenport planned to luncheon in the village. Would you care to join me in here, my dear, so we may be comfortable?" Lady Augusta asked. "You ate nothing at breakfast, so if you would rather eat in your room and come back to me, please feel free to tell me."

Later that afternoon, when the ladies had satisfactorily shared their luncheon *and* their heartfelt concerns, Lady Augusta turned quite serious. "You do love him, do you not, Nicole?"

If Nicole thought this dear woman would have believed her, she might have told one more lie to save her the pain to come. But remembering her new vow of complete honesty, she pushed down the desire that said if she told her no, Nicole might believe it herself.

The strength of her emotions could not be hidden, however, in her simple answer. "Yes, ma'am, I do. I love him with all my heart. But that has no bearing now. Even if he *could* forgive me, you must try and understand that we did not have a romantic attachment. He believed we were friends, as did I."

Nicole rested her head upon the dowager's knees and sighed. "Even were there to be no more animosity between us, there would only remain the original friendship. You yourself told me he was not very comfortable with that kind of relationship." She thought she could stay at the feet of this woman for a long while. This day had brought her as close to Lady Augusta as she had become that day with Beth Hampton, and she believed she had found another friend for life. *Lord, I am not worthy!*

She lifted her head, looking toward the light that had been so bright this morning but had lessened in the late afternoon. She felt Lady Augusta's intent to interrupt her so she continued, "But that is only part of the story. I know you and the Hamptons think he is in love with me. Should that be true, and should he forgive me, I would turn down his love. He is an important, intelligent and active man who needs a woman who can be an asset to him." A helpmeet, she thought. "He does not need someone he cannot take out in public without a… tether." Her voice cracked on the last.

The inner pain she thought to share openly with Beth was just as easily shared with Devlin's grandmother, and one lone tear trickled down her cheek. "I have seen many doctors, my lady, even Dr. Morrison in London. There is not much hope this is a temporary handicap. I shall have to deal with it for the rest of my life."

Lady Augusta seemed regal in defense of her grandson. "You say you love him, but you do not know him as well as you think you do if you believe it is your blindness that overpowers his thoughts." She went into great detail describing the care her grandson had shown her when she was confined to her wheelchair. "He loves me as a person, not my abilities."

"Ma'am…"

"Nicole, you were not the only one to hide an aspect of your life. Jared did not tell you, but he has been married before. She died five years ago."

Nicole sat bolt upright, a look of enlightenment crossing her face. "I see. He has not yet gotten over her death. That is why he avoids marriage." She spoke in subdued resignation. "He could have told me that."

"That is my point, Nicole. He berated you for not trusting him with the entire truth, yet he withheld important details of his life as well. You see, he had a wife who *was* an asset to him yet she did him much more harm than good. His marriage was a dismal failure arranged by an abusive father. Vivian lied to him and deceived him from the day he met her, so he lumped all women into that class…until you."

Nicole was no longer subdued. She became agitated, wringing her hands in dismay. "Pray say it is not so! Then *I* deceived him and convinced him he was right!" She buried her face in her hands. "I have so much more to answer for than I ever dreamed."

Lady Augusta took Nicole's face in her hands, treating her as if she could see her. "No, Nicole, you do not understand. You have changed everything for him. You have turned his world upside down and he wants it to be right side up. I always hoped he would meet someone like you—someone who could take away the pain of his lonely childhood, his unnatural parents and his unfaithful wife. Now that he has, he is using your misunderstanding as an excuse to walk away. But I saw his true feelings when he spoke of you. His emotions were so near the surface, and he usually keeps his feelings very safely hidden."

She tried to evoke the intensity of *his* words. "Even though he did not acknowledge it as love, he knew it was special. He was amazed at your intelligence, your wit and your bravery above all. He said he had found a new friend, but his understanding of such a relationship confused him. Truth to tell, when he found out about your blindness he was taken aback. But only at first, and I can see how it would do that. But you should have heard him speak of your courage in facing London without seeing, just to make your mother happy. Again, that is a type of giving he does not understand in someone else, though *he* has that quality in abundance.

"After he lost control and displayed his hurt in a fit of temper, *you* came to *him* to apologize. You see, my dear, that was extraordinary to him, and he did not know how to handle it. Finally, when Toby took him down a peg or two…"

"When Toby did *what?*" Nicole asked.

"Did you not know about that? I think your Toby a very special sort of man. He planted Jared a facer as well." She chuckled a little. "It seems Jared did not wish to be chastised by a servant when he had already reproached himself quite thoroughly. Toby took him to account anyway!"

She turned serious again. "Nicole, imagine his further confusion. Jared had certainly never seen a servant fight for his employer. It made him wonder even more what kind of person you were to incite such loyalty."

Nicole's eyes filled with tears.

"Why are you crying, darling girl?"

"Toby should never have risked his life for such a reason! Doing that could change nothing, and he could have been hanged. What a dreadful coil. How I will give him a piece of my mind…and another piece of my heart." The last was said almost in a whisper. "What havoc I have wrought," she continued as she pulled her handkerchief out of her sleeve, wiped her eyes and finished in resignation. "I suppose I should be very thankful that the consequences of my actions have been much less than they could have been, and that it is over before any more damage can be done."

"No!" Lady Augusta cried. "You must *not* declare it over. We must come up with a way to reconcile the two of you. Jared thinks it is easier to send you a note of apology! Can you imagine? A note of apology? He will leave things the way they are rather than risk his heart again."

At that, Nicole was reminded of Beth Hampton's prophetic letter. She told Nicole that when Devlin realized how deeply his heart was involved, he might take an easy way out to protect that scarred organ. But she must not dwell on that any longer.

"It is only because of his past," the dowager continued. "You do not fit his definition of a typical woman, but he is afraid to invest so much of himself, not because he does not want to but because there is a risk."

Nicole was quiet for a long time, then placed her hands on Lady Augusta's knees and rested her chin on them. "I am sorry, dear lady, but it *is* over. I meant what I said at the time about not being a burden and never marrying him. I know he is not in the plans God has for me."

Lady Augusta sounded startled at Nicole's mention of God, but she could not stop to think about it now. "But you love Jared." The words came out in forlorn desperation and tugged at Nicole's already damaged heart.

"Yes. I know what true love is because of Lord Devlin. And because I love him so much, I would not marry him. I know that true love is placing the best interest of others before your own happiness. I am sorry, dear lady. I hope you and I can be friends, but Lord Devlin is right—it is over, and that is for the best."

Nicole's mother and her friend returned, and private conversation was no longer to be had between her and Lady Augusta.

As they said good-night for the evening, Nicole heard the rising wind of an impending storm. Before she went upstairs, she asked Toby to take her to Lady Augusta's suite of rooms. She felt the need to be sure of her comfort.

"I am fine, dear. Indeed, I quite enjoy storms. God replenishes His creation in many different ways."

"Lady Augusta…?"

"Yes, my dear, I think you and I have much more in common than my headstrong grandson. Perhaps our bond in the Lord will keep us close until He calls me home."

Tears welled in Nicole's eyes, and she needed this woman to know how special she had become to her in so short a time. "We will be leaving in the morning, and I did not know if I would get a chance to tell you how much your belief and trust in me has meant. I know I have let people down because of my selfishness, but I have learned an important lesson about honesty that I will strive for each day. That you have treated me kindly will stay in my heart forever. Thank you." She kissed Lady Augusta's hand.

"Child, from Jared's description, I thought I would like you. I now know you are the woman who could make him happy, and it makes me melancholy to think of what you both may be throwing away. Do not worry, I am not going to give you another dressing-down but I, too, will think of you often and maybe you will come to see me again soon."

Nicole reached out to touch Lady Augusta's face. She wanted to feel the beauty of those lined and wizened features to remember for all time. "Good night, my lady, and God bless you."

The morning brought a continuing light drizzle and all four women were in rather low spirits at breakfast. They had each, for their own reasons, put off leaving as long as they could and were just pushing back their chairs when a man shaking a soaking greatcoat walked into the room. At his first words, Nicole froze in shock.

"Grandmother, I am sorry for barging in like this. I did not realize you had guests." He paused, handing his coat to the butler. "Higgins informed me... Nicole... What?"

Nicole recognized his voice the moment he spoke. Terror filled her heart. No, she thought in horror, this could not be happening. Panic caused her to stand too quickly, resulting only in the overturning of her chair.

Her eyes sought light as a thirsting man seeks water. She made out a grayish tint, and remembered the French doors. She lifted her skirt with one hand and extended the other until her palm touched the cool glass. A slight push with both hands caused the door to give way, allowing the irrational decision that took her out into the storm.

Chapter Fourteen

Nicole knew she must get out of the house. He was there, and once again, he must think the worst of her. He would naturally assume that she had instigated the meeting with his grandmother. It was too much for her to bear.

Even as she did it, Nicole knew how dangerous it was to leave the house without Toby. Yet fear of Devlin overrode her fear of facing the outdoors alone.

She and Toby had explored the grounds that first day, so she knew that by leaving through the French doors off the dining room she would be standing upon a veranda that led to the back grounds. She also remembered the pathway that led to the stream had been of gravel. If she could reach that pathway, she would at least know where she was. A fallen branch, a set of steps—anything could be a dangerous obstacle but she felt the least danger would be the way of the path. *Please God,* she prayed, *guide me to that path.*

All of these thoughts ran through Nicole's mind within seconds. She did not have time for more. It seemed her luck had run out with the arrival of Lord Devlin. But as she stepped off the last step of the veranda, her right foot grazed the small pebbles on the footpath. "Thank You, Lord," she mumbled, then lifted her skirts with one hand, and with the other arm outstretched before her began to move as quickly as she thought she could safely go.

She knew Toby would be after her soon, but she prayed that Devlin would be so disgusted he would not follow. Even as the thought came, she knew that he would help any woman in distress, whether he abhorred her or not. She must count on Toby to be before him.

She let out a small cry as she twisted her ankle on the uneven surface. She slowed to catch her breath but determinedly continued on toward the bridge. Once she knew she was near it, she hoped to seek a quiet haven to avoid discovery.

As she slowed and her breathing quieted, she heard the sound of the stream. She did not realize she had come so far, and by the sound of the rushing water, Nicole realized the rain from the previous night's storm must have raised its level and speed considerably.

The thought did not make her pause. She had no plan to leave the security of the footpath, so the stream presented no danger. She only needed to stay on this side of the bridge.

She came to a full stop and realized the spot where she stood was uneven, like the root of a tree might be underfoot. She stood steadily on her good ankle and tried to feel along the root with her strained foot. Despite the pain it caused her, it led her to the base of a huge tree. Sitting with her back against the gnarled bark, she began to catch her breath and collect her thoughts.

Now, adding insult to injury, it had started to rain again. Nicole felt wretched and began to cry. The branches overhead provided some protection, but she was soon drenched and disheartened. Her ankle was beginning to throb in earnest. Self-pity began to invade her thoughts, and she buried her head into her bended knees to fully succumb to the tears she had fought so hard to hold in. It seemed their entire London trip had left nothing but a trail of pain and sorrow, and she did not know how much more she could bear while trying to keep up appearances.

As the rain became heavier, she was not sure what to do. Nicole knew she could retrace her steps back to the house, but in this downpour it would be too easy to miss *sounds* of danger. She was also levelheaded enough to know that they were more than likely searching for her, and it would be prudent to stay in one place. But the thought that intruded her frantic mind the most was that Lord Devlin would only have another excuse to be angry with her.

Before Nicole could think anymore about what she should do, she detected the sound of approaching footsteps on the gravel path. The rain was down to a drizzle now, but the water rushing in the background made it difficult to be sure what she heard. She had determined to call out, hoping beyond hope it was Toby. She next heard booted feet run onto the bridge and stop. Whoever it was, they had not seen her.

Lord Devlin's voice was barely audible over the surging stream as he called her name. The decision as to whether she should try to make her way back to the house was taken out of her hands, and truth be told, she was more than a little glad to have been found...even by Devlin.

"I am over here," she called. "I have twisted my ankle." She cupped her hands to be heard over the storm. "I cannot go any farther."

She thought she heard his "thank God" as he came back in her direction, but with the wind howling, it could just as easily have been a curse.

Devlin began his tirade even before his boots left the bridge. "You little fool! What in the world do you mean by running off like that? You have scared the life out of..."

The cracking sound that cut him off midsentence made Nicole's heart stop. She heard a groan as if the wind had been knocked out of him. She screamed his name, now despising her blindness and desperately listening for any other sound. Without conscious thought, she rose up and began to hobble to where she had heard him call.

"Stop, Nicole. That is far enough."

"Nicole, if you have ever listened to anyone in your life, please listen to me now. Do not come any closer. I am well. The rushing water has..." He stopped, leaving Nicole in a state of terror.

"The water has apparently weakened the structure of the bridge," he finished the sentence in distressed breaths. "I have fallen through some of the unsound boards, but I am unhurt. I have my left arm crooked around a beam that seems strong enough for the present. But if the river keeps rising, the torrent will overtake the rest of the bridge before too long."

Devlin regretted the words the minute they were out of his mouth. He had probably put her in danger by saying so, and he could have bitten out his tongue. He knew she would never sit still while the river washed him away. "Do not worry!" he yelled. "We have an army of people out looking for you so help will be here soon." With a more secure grip for the moment, he noticed she was closer to him than before. "Confound it, Nicole! I am not jesting. I am not trying to be kind— just…stay…where…you…are. You are getting far too close to the stream's edge."

"What is it, Devlin?" she shouted. "Where are you hurt?"

It was an odd moment to come to such a thought, but Devlin's instinct was guilt at his meager understanding of the blind. All he knew was based on biased ignorance. He remembered her intensity while trying to identify smells. Her other senses must be quite heightened, and he realized she had *heard* something in his tone indicating an injury. This all ran through his mind in seconds, and he was able to cover his pain and reassure her.

"Do not worry, Nicole. It is not bad." He had determined to tell her as much of the truth as she needed to know so she would start listening to him. "When I fell through the bridge," he shouted, "I cut my hand on some jagged wood. The cold water should keep it clean, and already it has stopped bleeding."

It had begun to rain again, and she cried as she wiped damp hair from her forehead. "With water so forceful, you will not be able to hold on long with one hand."

Great guns! He had also forgotten how smart she was. "I am doing fine for the moment. Start yelling for help in case any of my grandmother's servants are close enough to hear you."

Nicole did as she was bid, but his ears perked up when he realized she had lowered herself to the ground and had inched even closer to him *and* the racing stream bed! He thought his heart would stop in his chest. "Nicole, I swear when we get out of this I will make you understand when I am serious about something. You need to hold perfectly still." He was angry at her lack of understanding.

"Jared, I cannot let you drown, whether you are angry at me or not. I have two perfectly strong hands and could help pull you from the water. You cannot do it by yourself." She grabbed his right hand and pulled it to her chest with all her might. "Do not worry. I can hear how close I am to the water. I will not fall in."

They were close enough now that there was no need to shout, but shout he did. "Nicole, will you please use that beautiful head God gave you and do as I say!"

He lowered his voice as much as he could and still have her hear him. "Listen to me and listen good. I admit your blindness is not the handicap I first thought it was. But there are some things you simply cannot tell. The water is moving so fast that it has not only weakened the bridge, but the banks on each side appear to be eroding very quickly. What I meant earlier was that I could hold on as long as the ground stays strong enough to keep the bridge in place. Even your slight weight could be what causes that bank to fall into the water—with you and me in it."

Devlin was scared. He was scared he would not be able to help her if things got any worse. "Nicole, I must try and make you understand. With only one hand, there is no way I could help you, should the ground give way. You must hold perfectly still until I tell you otherwise. Now let go of my hand so the both of us do not get pulled in together.

"And Nicole," he said in words that reached her heart as none other, "you must pray as hard as you have ever prayed that help gets here soon."

Nicole lowered her head to the wet ground, tears streaming down her face in the rain, and prayed aloud for God to save the man she loved more than life. "You must not let him die. He is just trying to rescue me, please God, please." She prayed harder. "He cannot die without knowing that I love him. I do not care what he feels for me any longer. Please, just keep him safe."

Suddenly a quiet, gentle voice began to speak from several yards away. "I don't know 'ow you two got into that mess…"

Nicole recognized Toby's voice and cried out in relief. "Thank You, Lord!" Her head quickly rose, muddied from the ground.

"…but you both, *especially you, Miss Nick,* need to

listen very close and do everything I tell you, exactly like I tell you. Do you understand?"

"Yes," they indicated while nodding their heads. Devlin realized speaking out loud suddenly seemed to be a danger and a waste of precious time.

"Good." Toby started speaking louder to override the water and the storm. "Listen now. I don't think I can come any closer. That embankment is jest 'bout ready to slip."

Devlin muttered "good man" under his breath.

"I've got your 'orse, sir, and several ropes. I think I may be able to pull you to safety. But I'm going to 'ave to ask you some questions to get the lay of the land. When you answer me, be as still and as calm as you can be."

Devlin had always resented Toby his closeness to Nicole. He had been jealous when he found out that Toby had become her eyes after her accident. But seeing his capability and the risks he was willing to take for his mistress made Devlin realize that he could not think of one of his personal friends he would rather have here trying to save their lives. Toby was calm and keeping their security first through a raging thunderstorm, and Devlin had never seen a servant with such presence of mind. Keeping his wits about him under this type of pressure assured Devlin that Toby was quite deserving of the trust Nicole placed in him.

"Now, Lady Nick, I'm gonna throw a circled piece of rope to both of you. You'll need to put it 'round your middles. But you 'ave to put it on you with as little movement as possible, or more ground may give way.

Do you think you kin? I will do everything I kin to make sure the rope lands close 'nough so that you won't 'ave to move to get it. If it takes more'n one throw, don't do anything. I'll try again." Devlin knew Toby was worried by his lapse in elocution.

"Toby, I think *I* can, but Lord Devlin has injured one of his hands and is holding on to the bridge with the other. I could not put the rope around me and hold on to him at the same time."

"Toby!" Lord Devlin yelled. "She is holding on to me unnecessarily. She will do as you say and let go of my arm to put the rope around her waist. Do not worry about that. But you may not be able to depend on your own strength to hold the other end of that rope. The water is too fast. Use Orion and tie the other end around his pommel."

"Good thinking, my lord," Toby barked out. "Now before we work on Miss Nicky, we need to 'ave the whole plan ready. I can try to pull 'er to safety first, but the movement might jest cause that bank to cave in. Your end of the bridge might go with it. I'm thinking we need to 'ave both of you tethered at the same time in case something 'appens we *ain't* planned on."

No matter that he was in a life-or-death situation, Devlin could not help but appreciate the servant's judgment. "I do not know where you got him, Nicole, but I will wager you do not pay him enough."

"Got any ideas?" he yelled back at Toby.

"When I throw the rope to you, *are* you going to be able to put it 'round yourself? If not, once I get the rope 'round Miss Nick, I could crawl on my belly and pray the Good Lord lets the bridge 'old 'til I tie it 'round you."

"No, Toby. That would just put another weight on the area and put you in danger, too. We need you too much right now, old man. If you throw me the rope, I will get it on me."

"Toby!" Nicole screamed over the pouring rain. "He cannot use his right hand, and his left arm must already be numb from the cold. Is there not some way I can help get his rope on?"

"No!" both men screamed at the same time. "Miss Nick, you don't seem to unnerstand how serious this is, and I swear if I was close 'nough I'd box your ears. I'm sorry to be disrespectful, but now's not the time for niceness. You *must* stay as still as you kin. Getting the rope 'round *you* is going to risk both your lives. Do you understand that? I am dead serious! We are doing our best, hang it, to keep us all alive, and we can't protect you if you won't listen."

"You definitely do not pay him enough," Devlin said, close to tears out of fear for her.

"Toby," Devlin yelled, "Nicole is probably right about my left arm being too numb, but the hand she is so desperately holding is only cut. I think I could use it long enough to get the rope around me."

Lightning flashed, and all three were silent for a moment.

"That's good news, sir! With all this lightning, we 'ave to get you two under cover as soon as we kin. I'm worried about pulling you both at the same time. There'll be more movement than I want, but we got a better chance of catching you both 'ere if we do it that way. Downstream may be even worse than this. What do ya think, sir?"

"Good man! That should do the trick. Count to three and get both those ropes over here at the same time. Neither of us will try to grab for them." He added an aside to Nicole. "Do you understand that, Nicole?" He said nothing further to her, expecting her complete co-operation. Then he returned to Toby. "You will need to throw them as closely as you possibly can to each one of us. Very slowly we will pull each rope near us and get it around us with as little movement as possible. Once the ropes are latched, we will let you know. Then you and Orion will need to begin to pull us free. As long as we are both secured, all we need to do is to wait until Orion pulls us. It may not even matter in which order." Devlin knew they had already said all of this, but he wanted to be sure each of them had heard the plan, had understood it, and would stick to it.

"My lord, I'm tying the ropes with slip knots and when I get 'em ready, I'll count three and throw." While they waited, Devlin sent up his first prayer to the God that his grandmother and Nicole depended upon. *God, if this does not work, let Toby use all his power to save Nicole and forget about me. Amen.* Nicole had talked to Him as a friend when she prayed. Devlin hoped God allowed that kind of friendship on a first attempt.

He, at least, had a chance to save himself if the bridge collapsed. He wanted to be sure that Toby knew that was what he wanted, but Nicole would protest such an order, and they could not afford to waste energy now. He must depend on Toby…and God.

The count of three came all too soon, and the two ropes landed on their clasped hands. Devlin watched as Nicole slowly lifted one rope with her hand and put it over her head. He heard her talking, but it was not to him. "Lord, he does not need my hand, he needs Yours. I will let go of him only because I know You love him as much as I do and Your power is sufficient."

Then she did the hardest thing she had ever done in her life. She let go of his hand.

Devlin took the other rope and broke the hold they had on one another. He had never felt so bereft in his life. He could not think about that now; there was still a long way to go. He moved slowly and deliberately, struggling without a word.

"Toby, I think we are ready." The water was accelerating, and he cursed as some piece of debris knocked into him at breakneck speed.

"Pay 'ttention, you two, it's time. I'm gonna count to three and we're going to tug. You ain't going to move very far, but at least if the bridge or bank gives way, we've got you safe 'til 'elp gets 'ere or we 'ave to make another tug. One more thing…this may 'urt. I'm not sure what shape either of you is in, but 'aving a rope pulled tight 'round your chest ain't gonna be a picnic, even in the best of conditions." Toby was silent for a moment. "Are you ready?"

"Nicole, my brave stupid girl, are you ready?" Devlin quietly called to her.

"Yes, Jared," she said.

Lord Devlin gave Toby permission to start the count. Devlin heard her speaking again, but it was low. He strained to hear, but he could not make her words out.

"I love you, Jared. I am sorry for all of the pain I have caused you."

Toby began to inch Orion backward, and as he did, Devlin held his breath as he noticed the bank next to Nicole sliding dangerously. He knew if her meager weight could cause that much damage then the bridge was sure to go. He was afraid Orion might not have the strength if it fell. He watched as Toby slowly turned Orion in the opposite direction so he could pull with all his might, in one swift yank, to get them both free. Devlin knew this could backfire, but he silently congratulated the man for giving them the best chance.

"I've got Orion ready," he began. "One…two…" And without saying three, Toby hit the horse hard on the rump to make him pull forward with all his strength. The horse, startled, dug in his front hooves and pulled ahead, trying to run, not understanding the weight holding him back. Orion managed almost ten feet before he calmed down and Toby could handle him.

Both Lord Devlin and Nicole groaned as the ropes pulled hard under their arms and around their chests. The bridge split in two pieces and was carried away by the swift water. He and Nicole slid through the mud, and he knew one second's peace. Then Devlin heard a loud clap of thunder and saw the flash of lightning hit the oak tree overhead.

He also heard the crack of a branch breaking free

and watched, as if in slow motion and helpless to do anything, as it fell on top of Nicole.

His own injuries forgotten, Lord Devlin moved to her as quickly as he could, numb with cold and terror. Toby arrived at the same time. They realized as they reached her that the widest section of the limb had hit her squarely on the head, and she was no longer moving.

Devlin's heart stopped, and in a fleeting moment he thought she might be dead. He found himself paralyzed in fear.

"No, my lord," Toby said, choking back his own re-action. "She's alive. But she's bleeding pretty bad from this cut. We've got to get 'er out of this rain."

"Get Orion, Toby. I will get her to the house."

"Can you ride, sir?"

"I am scraped and stiff, but I can ride. In any event, I do not think Orion would allow you to ride him, as nervous as he is. I am not letting all of your hard work go to waste now. We would have been dead without you, and a bump on the head is not going to take her from me. If you can hand her up to me after I get on Orion, I will get to the house and send a horse back for you immediately."

The horse *was* skittish but recognized his master's voice and settled down while they seated Nicole sideways in front of Devlin. He wrapped his arms around her as her head rested on his chest, and he gripped the reins.

Before he kicked the horse's side, he looked down at Toby and said, "This is the second time you have saved my life. I am forever in your debt, Toby, and I find I do not mind owing you such an obligation. You did the work of three men today—smart, brave and loyal all." Devlin's voice cracked on his next words. "But even more than that, you protected her. I will not let you down again where she is concerned. I do not know how to thank you."

There were tears mirrored in the servant's eyes as he said, "You keep 'er safe and we'll be even, my lord."

Devlin rode off toward the house as fast as he could, while trying to avoid shaking Nicole any more than necessary. He had never felt this way before. There were so many events totally out of his control. For a brief moment he thought he understood Nicole's faith. You had to believe that *someone* controlled the situations mere humans could not. He had to trust in her God to make things right; she had to be fine. "We are almost there, love. I am sorry if I am hurting you. I need to get you warm and in bed." He knew she could not hear him, but he had to keep talking to her to keep reassuring himself she *would* survive another ordeal. Why had his pride made him such a fool?

"I am glad you *cannot* see me now, sweetheart. I am covered in mud and soaking wet. I do not believe even you would favor such a sight."

He had ridden this way a thousand times in his life and it had never taken so long. Why was it doing so today?

When he finally came into view of the house, he breathed a sigh of desperate relief. "We are here, Nicole. Everything is going to be fine," he whispered, even as he yelled to the house in general that he had found her. He saw Lady Beaumont come running outside, then heard her gasp, but he could not take the time to explain things to her now. He slid Nicole into the arms of one of the waiting footmen, then dismounted.

He picked Nicole up and walked quickly toward the house. He gave orders with each step. "Robbie, get Orion to the stable and take care of him. Send another horse down to the stream. Toby is coming back this way on foot. Bring him here quickly. Higgins, send for the doctor. Tell him it is an emergency. Mrs. Higgins, we will need plenty of hot bath water to get Lady Nicole warm. Toby will need it, too, so he does not catch his death."

Devlin was in the house now and saw his grandmother, in her chair at the bottom of the steps. Just the sight of her made him tear up; she should be telling him everything would be all right, just as she always had. But she looked pale, and they could not comfort each other now. "Ma'am, I am sorry I have no time to explain this. I do not know the extent of her injuries, but if you could keep Lady Beaumont's courage up, that will help tremendously."

Finally, as he carried Nicole close to his heart and gently up the stairs, he said, "Grandmother, could you also send for the vicar? I think Nicole would like to have him here when she wakes. She will want to tell him of all the answered prayers we have had today."

Please, God, he thought, *give us one more.*

Chapter Fifteen

Nicole lay unconscious for three days. The doctor came very soon upon the heels of Devlin settling her lifeless body into her room. He pronounced her lungs clear despite the complete drenching. He determined her limbs were sound except for the slightly sprained ankle. But he sorrowfully acknowledged that there was nothing he could do about her head wound except to bandage the cut and put ice on the swelling. The doctor had researched several such cases with his colleagues in London last year, and their only conclusion had been that no two cases were the same.

Lady Beaumont tearfully explained her concern, this having been the second time in her life that Nicole had received such a blow.

The doctor did not appear pleased with that complication, but, being a comforting man on the whole, he remained firm that they must not let their imaginations run away with them. All they could do for the nonce was give Nicole the time and rest she needed.

An express had been sent to Dr. Morrison's office

in London, informing him of this new setback in Nicole's health. The doctor had responded immediately with an urgent missive assuring them he would leave town three days hence to assist the local doctor in any way he could. He was not an expert in head injuries, but he had not forgotten the special woman who had sat in his office that day, and he vowed to himself he would do everything that he could to help.

Dr. Morrison also added an unusual postscript to his communiqué. He bade them not to lose hope, as several of his associates had recently come to the conclusion that unconscious patients might be aware of what was going on around them, even though they were unable to communicate. He encouraged them to consider her cognizant of them until he arrived.

Lord Devlin would not leave Nicole's bedside. The doctor's words had been enough for him. He read the newspapers to her in the morning and books to her during the day. Her mother had given him a Bible and showed him some of Nicole's favorite passages. He read them to her with reverence and hope.

He did his best to get water and soup into her when he could, and he kept the drapes open each day so she could feel the healing heat of the sun on her face. He kept from completely breaking down at her continued insensibility by grasping at the small hope Dr. Morrison had given them. The vicar came often, and Devlin would stand quietly holding her hand as he listened to the soft-spoken prayers the man constantly lifted up on her behalf.

But the nights were the worst. They never failed to

weaken his resolve. With the house so quiet and Nicole so still, he knew a fear stronger than he could ever have imagined. Even the rages of his father when he was a small child dimmed in comparison to the dreaded thought of losing her.

Those hushed hours also gave him time to reflect on his past mistakes. They ate at him. He knew now that he was in love with her—a love so deep it was almost beyond his comprehension. Nothing could have prepared him for such a desperate dependence on someone else to ensure his happiness. He berated himself over and over for his behavior to her when she had needed him the most. He knew love could involve getting hurt, and he had not been sure whether he was ready to risk it. But after his recent visit to his grandmother's, Peter had quietly reproached him, letting him know he *was* taking a risk…a risk that a lifetime of complete love and devotion might get away.

That problem had seemed secondary at the time, as he'd assumed Nicole would never forgive him for his boorish actions. He had, therefore, decided he must let her go. He knew now he would not be so foolish again. He intended to show her he could be depended upon in good times and in bad.

Sitting beside her bed at night, the irony of his actions haunted him. After openly accepting the fact that he loved Nicole, he had come back to his grandmother, hoping she could tell him how to soften Nicole's heart.

Yet when he had stumbled upon Nicole at breakfast the morning he had arrived, had he asked for an opportunity to speak with her? Had he thrown his arms around her and begged her to forgive him? No, he had allowed his surprise to override any intelligent action, and had actually scared her into running from his very presence. Not only bolting from him, but unabashedly entering the dangers she faced bravely on a daily basis without sight!

So he remained by her side and prayed to a God he knew only from a distance. He asked for the chance to make all of this up to her, knowing he did not deserve it. He would convince her to marry him, and they would have a partnership that even Lord and Lady Hampton would envy. *Please, God!* he prayed.

It was the worst time of his life and yet the most enlightening. As he thought about all that had come before, he realized it was what had brought him to this moment! Had he met Nicole as a younger man, before his marriage, would he have been interested in her intelligence and humor? Of course not! He would have appreciated her beauty, made her his flirt for a while and then he would have moved on to his next conquest.

Could that be the secret? Was everything that happened in life actually controlled by this all-powerful God? Did each episode in life give you the opportunity, the choice, to make you the person you will become? He did not know. He could have chosen not to marry Vivian, but then he would never have been brought to this exact moment. Apparently the choices he made *did* play a major part. He should have been gaining wisdom from each of his experiences, but he *chose* to respond with a hardened heart and the attitude that life owed him much. Then Nicole entered his life. Only now did he see that she had responded to the hardships in her life with unselfishness and a loving heart.

He sat holding her hand in the dark, and the words poured forth from his own heart asking forgiveness and promising different responses from now on. He would do it whether Nicole accepted him or not. But was it too little, too late for God to consider his prayers for Nicole? No! He would spend his life learning from her, if God, the one he now recognized as being the true God, gave him the chance.

But Devlin was not the only one who was loath to leave Nicole alone. Lady Beaumont was constantly present, and Devlin could not hear enough about Nicole's childhood. They vowed they would include her in their conversations whether Nicole acknowledged them or not.

In addition, Toby came to the sickroom like clockwork and usually carried Lady Augusta with him. Thus they joined in a vigilant effort at willing consciousness back into Nicole.

One day when they were all gathered together, Toby spoke his mind. "My lord, me and the doctor was talking a while ago and 'e said 'e saw a case once where a lady like Miss Nicky finally come out of 'er stupor by 'earing familiar voices and 'aving familiar things about her. 'E says we're still doing all the right things now, you know, reading to 'er and all, but I was thinking maybe I could ride and get Miss Chelsea. Surely Lady Nick would recognize that bundle of mischief."

Lady Beaumont was the first to respond. "Toby, that sounds like such a good idea, but I do not know what to do." Her expression went from joy to nagging fear in the blink of an eye. "What do you think, Lord Devlin? Might it be too much activity for her? And there are already so many of us imposing on you and Lady Augusta. Oh, I wish I knew what to do," she cried, as bottled-up emotions flowed freely. "I cannot bear the thought of losing her again."

"Now, none of this talk of losing anybody, Beatrice," Lady Augusta chided. "I think Toby's idea to get Nicole's sister is a sound one, and would at least allow us to do something for Nicole besides boring her to tears." Devlin appreciated her practicality and gruffness; it became a balm to the flammable situation. "But you are a better judge, dear. Would seeing Lady Nicole in such a state be harmful to her sister? From what Jared has mentioned, your youngest daughter sounds a resilient child, but you know best."

Lady Beaumont was not the least hesitant in her response. "No, Lady Augusta, Chelsea would not be overwhelmed. She will be sad and a little scared, I think, but she was quite the impetus behind Nicole's first recovery."

After five days, neither of the physicians remained hopeful as to Nicole's recovery. She was not getting enough nourishment, and there had been no reaction to the presence of Chelsea.

Chelsea had been horrified when she'd heard about the accident, and had cried quietly for hours after her first visit with Nicole. She then began a brave assault on Nicky's mind. She took over Lord Devlin's role of communicator when he had to leave her.

Lady Beaumont and Lady Augusta tried to keep their spirits up, especially when Chelsea was about. The pall that settled over the house, however, made it seem as if death had already claimed Nicole.

Late one night, Devlin awoke with a start. His head had fallen forward in sleep, and his stiff muscles screamed to move about. The candle in Nicole's room had long gone out, leaving only the light of a very dim moon. But it was still high in the sky, and looking out the window he suspected it was only a little after midnight.

He went over to the fluttering curtain billowing into the room, deciding to close the window against any chill Nicole might feel. He stayed there awhile, fear overwhelming him. Lowering himself to the window seat he put his head in his hands, the welling tears a contrast to his physical strength.

He spoke softly, but aloud. "God, I do not know how to pray yet. I do not know how to put it into words that arouse Your compassion and induce You to respond. I do not even know if that is how it works." He stilled and remembered the vicar, only this morning, talking to God as a friend, no prosy sermons, only feelings from his heart. *That* he could do.

"God, I know I cannot offer my life in exchange for hers, at least not physically. But I offer my life to You for whatever purposes You have for me. I think Nicole would laugh at me, trying to make a deal with You."

He felt useless and inadequate. Could God possibly be listening to this? He determined to trust that He was.

"I no longer ask that You return Nicole for myself. I do not deserve her. But, God, I ask now on her behalf. She has been through so much, and yet she enriches everyone she comes into contact with, even amidst the trials. She is much more valuable to You here, God. Please allow her to flourish again. And if that means—" tears rolled freely down his face "—life without her, so be it. Please just bring her back to us." He mumbled a quick "Amen," then sat listening to the silence.

The opalescence of the moon shining through the window naturally turned his thoughts to another night when he had gone to get fresh air on a secluded balcony and had been enchanted by the woman who lay so still behind him now.

How sorely he wanted to be on the terrace with her again. He imagined them teasing and flirting in the way he had come to need from her. He wanted to be married to her and to sit in the moonlight with their eyes closed, identifying smells around them. He wanted to be kissing her; he could not let go of the dream.

The decision came as quickly as a flash of lightning during a summer thunderstorm. It was a sudden revelation disrupting his longings. He would take her out to his grandmother's terrace this night and enjoy his musings, holding her, talking to her. No one would know, and he thought God would forgive him this selfish act.

He went to the bed and lifted her, the coverlet still around her. Her head seemed to naturally rest on his shoulder, and he tucked the blankets about her sides and legs for warmth. He carried her down the main staircase back to his grandmother's sewing room. He went directly through it to the terrace that overlooked his grandmother's favorite view.

He slowly lowered himself into one of the many chairs his grandmother had randomly placed to enjoy her beautifully manicured lawns. But he had no interest in the landscape; he turned the chair so they would be facing the moon. He settled her in his lap and made sure she was covered completely, then sighed as he rested his cheek on the top of her head.

He talked to her as he had on that night weeks ago when they'd first met. He teased her about letting him "blow a cloud," and knew if they were married she would tell him what a nasty habit it was. He reminded her of their misunderstanding that night, that he had assumed she had followed him out onto the terrace to trap him into marriage! His eyes welled with tears as he recalled the anger that had flashed in her eyes for just a moment. They were eyes that he wanted to look into and read the feelings there. He wanted to "show" her what she could not see.

He could pretend no longer. He shut his eyes in quiet agony. Theirs was a once-in-a-lifetime relationship. *When* she awoke, he would not doubt God's love for her, he would try to woo her back and prove he could be worthy of her love. He buried his face in her hair and continued to hold her in the moonlight.

"Mmm, that feels good," was the whisper he conjured in his head.

Now he was not only remembering their time together, he was imagining the responses he anticipated from her. He must get her back inside before he lost his mind altogether.

As he tightened his grip, preparing to rise with her, she spoke, sending an overpowering shock through his very soul.

"Can we please stay out here a little longer? The air feels so fresh, and it is so warm inside. Please let me stay."

Devlin was afraid for the second time in his life. He was afraid to move. He was afraid to breathe. Nicole was definitely speaking to him, but he did not know if her words were lucid or demented. Had the blow caused damage they had not even considered?

"Nicole," he said softly, trying to hold her still as she struggled to submerge further into his embrace. Fighting to keep excitement and relief out of his voice, he said, "Are you sure you are warm enough?"

Nicole stiffened a little as he waited for her response. "Jared?"

"Yes, sweetheart, I am here. You have had an accident, and we have been very worried about you."

"I know. It was a fire." She shook her head, trying to remove a week of cobwebs brought on by her concussion. "But I did not know you then, did I?"

He felt the sound of panic in her voice. He sensed her trying to understand the confusion, and he wanted to keep her calm.

"No, my sweet, shh," he said, keeping his head firmly resting on hers. "Not the fire. I think I better get you inside and we can talk about it." What was going on? Was he delusional? Would she come out of a coma in one quick second? He must get her inside and wake Dr. Morrison.

"Can we talk here? I have been dreaming, I think. We shared another evening like this, did we not? Yes, it was at a ball…oh dear, I cannot recall where…and you did not know I was blind and we talked ever so comfortably. I should not tell you, but it was the most special night of my life."

Devlin's mind was racing. Obviously hers was, too, and the fear of her senses being damaged quickly faded. Was this the familiar thing the doctors had said might affect her? Of course not! It was an answer to his prayer, pure and simple! God had given him a miracle!

"Nicole, we can stay out here a little longer, but you must remember that you have been sick. You cannot catch cold." Repositioning her slightly, he continued, "And you must not talk overmuch. In fact, you will listen to me very carefully. I command it."

She giggled, and he was encouraged. But it did not last long. He grew indecisive. He was not a doctor. He did not know if he should clear up her confusion, but could think of nothing else to do. He spoke against her hair again. "Do you remember the day at the bridge, Nicole? The day Toby had to rescue us?"

Again he felt her stiffen as she tried to focus her thoughts. He could imagine her frustration at the fog that must surely be in evidence after a week of dreaming.

"Jared, I *think* I remember." She was agitated. "You

were under the bridge and we had ropes tied about us, and there was lightning. Your hand was hurt. And Toby, is he safe?"

She must be back to normal if she was worrying about everyone else! But her concern made him uneasy.

"Shh, love, everything is fine. Do not try to speak yet. Just relax, lean against me and listen." He began speaking in a very soft, calm voice and explained the past week to her. She was shocked to hear she had been unconscious so long, and upset that she had caused so much trouble. He explained how Dr. Morrison had urged them to let her hear their voices, and how Dr. Bishop had wanted them to get many familiar items around her to jog her memory. Devlin told her Chelsea had been with her for the past few days.

Nicole interrupted his explanation in a slow, deep voice. "But Jared, it was this, was it not? You brought me to the terrace, that was the most familiar to both of us. How did you know?"

"I did *not* know, love. I, too, was longing for that very special night we met, and I desperately wished for you to be well. I wanted to share that experience with you again. I could not face coming out here alone, so I brought you with me." He swallowed hard, fighting back all of the emotions he was feeling. "And I prayed, Nicole." He tried to hold back the tears by teasing her. "I doubt God has ever heard a more pitiable prayer. Indeed, it would likely not even qualify as such," he choked up again, "but He heard them, all of our prayers. *He* gave us this miracle, sweetheart."

Devlin could feel the silent crying against his chest.

It broke the dam he had been holding back, and tears streamed down his own face. "I am sorry, Nicole. I must get you inside. You probably feel terrible, and here I ramble on." He felt her shake her head vehemently.

"No, Jared. You cannot know how much all you have said means to me." She sighed and took a deep breath. "Sometimes, in my dreams, I pictured us together like this. We were sharing our prayers as well as our time." She tensed a little. "I do not know if you have forgiven me, but I have missed you dreadfully, my friend." She was a little confused, but she knew what was in her heart.

It made his heart break into a million pieces. She had missed his friendship, but only his friendship. But that was all he had ever offered her: friendship. She did not know the depth of love he had come to feel for her. But he had not stipulated terms when he had prayed for her, so he would be thankful, though it would kill him to pretend happiness. How could he be with her and not hold her?

"Nicole, I need to get you out of this night air, but there are so many things I need to say. I owe you so many apologies…" She tried to interrupt him, tried again to lift her head, but her head hit his chin. They both mumbled "ouch" at the same time.

"No, you had your say at my house that night. It was the night *I* should have been apologizing to you. But now it is my turn. I treated you abominably, and I cannot think of it without abhorrence. I accused you of the most awful things, but I was so hurt that you felt you could not tell me about your…eyes.

"So many times after you left Town, I thought about how happily I would have been your 'Toby' when we were out. Then I knew the truth. I wanted more than your friendship. And because I thought you did not trust me enough to tell me about your sight, I made it easy on myself and walked away."

Devlin could hear her quiet sobs, and he pulled her closer. But that did not stop them.

"But sweetheart, it was *not* easy. I could no longer contemplate a life without you. My grandmother had once offered to help me smooth our differences. When I thought you never wished to see me again and when I realized I could never fix things on my own, I decided to take her up on her offer." He paused and became a little less frenzied. "I knew that you and she would love each other," he added with a quiet pleasure.

He became agitated again the next instant. "When I walked into the breakfast parlor, I was unprepared to see you. I foolishly scared you out into the storm, and it almost killed you. Please forgive me for everything, Nicole, and give me a chance to prove my love to you."

Devlin finally moved his head so she could raise her eyes to his. He had to see what effect his words had on her. He wanted to somehow find a way to communicate the emotions he was feeling for her, without sight. He decided if he could win her heart, it might prove to be the most pleasurable experience in the world. To learn to kiss her with just the right sentiment, he wanted her to understand, would bring him endless joy. Indeed, he hoped it would take the rest of their lifetimes to get it just right!

He carefully lifted her face to his with his finger under her chin. Her eyes were wide and vivid, so different from her usual downcast pose.

He was amazed at the love he saw there. Tears welled in them. No wonder she had preferred downcast eyes; they clearly revealed her innermost soul. He leaned down ever so slightly to whisper against her lips, "Nicole, please marry me. Pray teach me the love and courage you show so naturally. I promise I will love you with all my being." He sat up straighter, nervous now at her prolonged silence. He did not wish to break the mood, but his insecurity made him tease her. "I promise we shall find something else for Toby to do."

Still he waited for her response. By now, any response would do. Slowly he watched a lone tear trickle from the corner of her eye.

He pulled away slightly, and she lowered her face. "Nicole?" he asked.

"Jared, I… You…" Her tears flowed freely now.

"What it is, love? No more secrets, you may tell me anything."

She was trying to master her emotions. "Jared, I cannot marry you."

He went rigid with fear at what she would next say.

"You will never know how much it means to me that you asked, especially after the way I treated you. But you know I will never marry. You have known that from the beginning. I will always be thankful that we were reunited through this. I will always be thankful you have found faith in something other than yourself. And I will always accept whatever form of friendship you are willing to offer me. Jared, you must know how much I...care about you, but we cannot marry."

He felt like the wind had been knocked out of him.

"I fear I *am* a little tired now, Jared. Can you take me back inside?" For the first time since her accident her senses failed her. She could detect none of his emotions.

"No."

"No? Jared, it has become a little chilly, I..."

"No," he said again while pulling her tightly against him. "Nicole, please do not consign us both to mere friendship. Please, Nicole. Having never known love, real love, I made a stupid vow that cost me nothing. I had already experienced a marriage, you see, and I vowed I would not do so again. I..."

She laid her head back on his chest and relaxed against him before she spoke. "I know, Jared." She put her arm up around his neck. "You must not upset yourself. She treated you abominably, I know."

"Nicole, do you not see—that is my point. I gave up any notion of happiness because of that. You have changed everything. The word *marriage* no longer even means what it once did to me." His frustration was palpable. He had to make her understand. "Nicole, I know I ruined our relationship on that day we were to go to Richmond, but I love you enough for both of us. I believe you might truly come to love me as I love you. It will grow in our time together. Please give me that chance."

She sighed. "It is not because I do not love you enough that I must refuse you. I never realized the power that loving someone else had over your life. I think I have loved you from that first night...on the terrace."

"Nicole." He let out the breath he did not realize he had been holding. He put his fingers under her chin to raise her lips to his, but she put her fingers on his mouth.

"Jared, wait." She kept her eyes level with his, as if she could see him as clearly as he saw her. "I love you too much to marry you."

"What?"

"My vow never said anything about not falling in love. I knew that to be beyond my control." She spoke softly and lovingly. "I knew I could never be a burden to anyone. That is why *I* vowed never to marry." She paused, then continued, "You see, you teased, but I will always need Toby. That is his one purpose. You have too many other important obligations."

She felt his shock physically even before he spoke it. "Do you believe I see you as a burden?"

"Of course not, Jared. I could refuse you easier if I did."

"Then why?"

"Jared, with my family and friends at home, I am not a burden. I love them too much. I taught myself not to be a hardship on them, and with Toby's help I live a relatively normal life. Not the one I would have chosen, but if it is God's plan, it is the only one I will accept.

"You, my darling friend, are an entirely different matter." Her voice choked back tears. "You do not see me as a burden because you have not felt the burden.

You have only been with me as a person who could see."

"Nicole, please say you know me better than that. Quickly, before I believe you."

"Jared, it was not a criticism. My own family and friends took years to come to grips with it, and even now on occasion treat me differently. It is a simple fact that you have no idea what you would be taking on. I, on the other hand, know very well and would not ask it of you." She paused and cleared her throat. "I could only hinder a man with so much power at his fingertips, right in the heart of the government. You will need to travel, entertain Society's most elite, and…you must have heirs. You already know my fear of crowds. How would I handle even the basics of what would be required in the woman you marry?"

He said one word. "Together."

"I beg your pardon?"

"We will handle them together." A new strength came over him. "Nicole, all I *require* is you. The happiness I have known as your friend alone is more than I have ever shared with anyone else."

"It is that way for me, too, Jared, but…"

"No 'buts.' Now you will listen to me." Devlin was terrified she meant to stand firm out of some misdirected sense of honor. He realized the most important speech of his life would not be one given in Parliament!

"Nicole, if you are so bent on *my* feelings and what is best for *me,* then listen and I will tell you. I contend that you have only been with me while I was ignorant of your blindness. You have no notion how I would respond to your needs. But I tell you now: I will do everything in my power to prove to you that your physical incapacities mean nothing to me. We will share each and every hurdle, every joy, every disappointment, every success and anything else God brings into our lives. All married couples face trials, sweetheart." He whispered the last. "The love we feel for each other is beyond the physical."

He did not know if he was getting through to her, and he tried one last-ditch effort to keep her from making them both miserable. "Where is your faith, Nicole?"

She sat up straight, tense and agitated. "I do not know what you mean."

"I think you do. I thought your faith, and now mine, would be what we depended on. You could certainly not depend on me for everything, and I could not depend on you for everything. Circumstances will arise beyond our control. I have learned that the hard way! But my understanding, quite new I grant you, is that we must put our faith in God on a daily basis, blind or not."

He found it very hard to convey his full meaning when he was not totally sure of it himself. Yet he knew beyond a shadow of a doubt he must convince her she was wrong. "I have heard you say many times that you believe God's plan for you is in helping your neighbors and tenants, either alone or married to that no-good doctor. Is it possible that is *not* God's plan at all?" He growled, "I do not know how to word this." He set her a little away from him, squeezing her upper arms, trying to make her understand. "Could it be that this has all come about because of God's plan for *my* life…for *our* lives?"

"Jared?" she asked, perplexed.

"I know, you will say I am arrogant to the last, but during the long, lonely nights sitting beside your bed, I felt that mayhap everything we have both been through has brought us to where we are now. Could it not have been to prepare us for this moment? Perhaps we could not know a love so strong if not for so many obstacles, if not for the friendship we shared first." He paused pointedly. "Perhaps we would not have the strength to handle what lies ahead separately. Conversely, we would have each other to share in the joys that lie ahead."

Devlin could have sworn she could see him at that moment. Her eyes clearly showed the thoughts running through her head, from doubt to surprise to joy! He had known those eyes, seeing or not, would be windows into her soul.

She surprised him by throwing her arms around his neck in a hold much stronger than someone who had been abed a week should have been capable of. It did not, however, stop him from returning the embrace.

"Jared, could it be so?" She whispered the question directly into his ear. "I should be so afraid you will be sorry someday when it becomes too much to bear. That would hurt me more than refusing you."

"Then do not think of it, sweetheart. Has your family ever complained about you being a burden? Of course they have not, their love is unconditional. Can you let yourself believe that I am capable of that kind of love?

Even more than that…I believe our love is a miracle. It is a miraculous love that will survive any hardship. It has been given to us by the miracle maker Himself."

She sighed so poignantly into his ear that it spoke volumes.

He slowly loosened her arms from around his neck, and with his hand guiding her chin, he lowered his lips to hers in the most intimate, loving kiss either of them had ever felt. He knew he would always need to express his emotions to her in ways that she could not see. He saw a lifetime ahead of a love only God could have given them.

Nicole drew away first, her forehead resting against his in her shyness. "I believe I shall pray for many more terrace miracles in our lives, Lord Devlin. It seems all of our firsts have occurred on one. And having found my soul mate tonight on *this* one, I do believe that with such miracles we can weather any storm. Perhaps it *was* God's expected end all along."

Nicole wrapped her arms around Devlin's neck and put her head on his shoulder as he carried her inside. She smiled as she realized that though her vision was impaired, she could *clearly* see a future ahead filled with laughter, love and God's promises.

* * * * *

Dear Reader,

I hope you enjoyed the story of Devlin and Nicole. They have become personal friends of mine, and characters who I hope have spoken to you and inspired you.

As you may have surmised, one of my favorite passages in Scripture is Jeremiah 29:11-12. I have relied on its strength through some of my own struggles, and I wanted it to permeate the story, especially in regards to Nicole. She began to claim verse 11 after the accident that left her virtually blind, but without the context of the verses that followed, she saw only a glimpse of God's goodness. Verse 11 told her that He had a plan for her life and she held on to it like a lifeline. But she was convinced that God had only *one* plan. Oddly enough, it wasn't until Devlin's own revelation that she received the full blessing of verse 12—not only a plan, but a future filled with hope. I know I want God planning my future!

There were so many precious insights God gave me as I wrote this story, and I pray that you found something to touch your heart, as well. If so, I pray that God receives all of the glory. I hope, too, that you began a love for the Regency era that will last a lifetime.

Thank you for taking the time to read *The Aristocrat's Lady*. I would love to hear from you. Visit my website at marymooreauthor.vpweb.com and drop me a note.

God bless you,
Mary Moore

Questions for Discussion

1. Did you become emotionally involved in any one character's story? Why?

2. Regency London, while elegant and romantic, had strict codes of conduct. Devlin and Nicole flouted Society by becoming friends of different genders. But in the end, their love was stronger for being the best of friends first. Do you believe people today take seriously the importance of marrying their best friend?

3. Nicole believed God had only one plan for her life, because the one time she deviated from that, she was hurt again. Have you ever restricted God by doing whatever was easiest?

4. Nicole's inner fears of rejection also played a large part in her decision not to tell Devlin the truth. Has the fear of rejection ever played a part in your decisions? How?

5. Devlin's grandmother devoted her life to protecting and caring for him, especially in terms of praying for his salvation. Is there someone you have been praying for many years to trust in Jesus? Talk about the process and where it stands now.

6. Devlin also had a special bond with his grandmother that influenced him his entire life. Can you think of someone who played that role in your life? How?

7. Nicole didn't want London Society to know she is blind, because of her own insecurities. How does hiding our insecurities often make them worse? How does this affect God's ability to work in our lives?

8. Forgiveness was required of both Nicole and Devlin—hers for hiding the truth and his for his treatment of her when he discovered it. Have you had an experience with a lack of forgiveness either on your part or someone else's?

9. Nicole believed wholeheartedly in her heavenly Father, but she often felt she was of limited use or little worth. Don't we all feel that way at times? Relate an example from your own life.

10. Toby had to defend Nicole at great risk to his own safety. Have you faced a time in your life where you risked public unpopularity to defend a friend or your beliefs?

11. Nicole had very strong convictions in an almost Godless society. Have your convictions ever made you stand out?

12. List some key themes in the story and discuss.

13. Nicole and Devlin had a happy ending, despite the fact that she did not get her sight back. Have you experienced a time when you thought if God would just fix "this one thing," life would be perfect? How did the situation actually turn out?

INSPIRATIONAL

Inspirational romances to warm your heart & soul.

Love Inspired.
HISTORICAL

TITLES AVAILABLE NEXT MONTH

Available October 11, 2011

REQUEST YOUR FREE BOOKS!

2 FREE INSPIRATIONAL NOVELS
PLUS 2
FREE
MYSTERY GIFTS

Love Inspired
HISTORICAL
INSPIRATIONAL HISTORICAL ROMANCE

YES! Please send me 2 FREE Love Inspired® Historical novels and my 2 FREE mystery gifts (gifts are worth about $10). After receiving them, if I don't wish to receive any more books, I can return the shipping statement marked "cancel." If I don't cancel, I will receive 4 brand-new novels every month and be billed just $4.49 per book in the U.S. or $4.99 per book in Canada. That's a saving of at least 22% off the cover price. It's quite a bargain! Shipping and handling is just 50¢ per book in the U.S. and 75¢ per book in Canada.* I understand that accepting the 2 free books and gifts places me under no obligation to buy anything. I can always return a shipment and cancel at any time. Even if I never buy another book, the two free books and gifts are mine to keep forever.

102/302 IDN FEHF

Name	(PLEASE PRINT)	
Address		Apt. #
City	State/Prov.	Zip/Postal Code

Signature (if under 18, a parent or guardian must sign)

Mail to the **Reader Service:**
IN U.S.A.: P.O. Box 1867, Buffalo, NY 14240-1867
IN CANADA: P.O. Box 609, Fort Erie, Ontario L2A 5X3

Not valid for current subscribers to Love Inspired Historical books.

Want to try two free books from another series?
Call 1-800-873-8635 or visit www.ReaderService.com.

---

* Terms and prices subject to change without notice. Prices do not include applicable taxes. Sales tax applicable in N.Y. Canadian residents will be charged applicable taxes. Offer not valid in Quebec. This offer is limited to one order per household. All orders subject to credit approval. Credit or debit balances in a customer's account(s) may be offset by any other outstanding balance owed by or to the customer. Please allow 4 to 6 weeks for delivery. Offer available while quantities last.

Your Privacy—The Reader Service is committed to protecting your privacy. Our Privacy Policy is available online at www.ReaderService.com or upon request from the Reader Service.

We make a portion of our mailing list available to reputable third parties that offer products we believe may interest you. If you prefer that we not exchange your name with third parties, or if you wish to clarify or modify your communication preferences, please visit us at www.ReaderService.com/consumerchoice or write to us at Reader Service Preference Service, P.O. Box 9062, Buffalo, NY 14269. Include your complete name and address.

LIH11B

*Sophie Bartholomew loves all things Christmas.
Caring for an orphaned little boy
makes this season even more special.
And so does helping a scarred cop move past his pain
and see the bright future that lies ahead...*

Since the moment Kade had appeared at Ida June's wreath-laden door behind a spotless, eager Davey, Sophie had had butterflies in her stomach. A few hours ago, they'd been having pizza and getting better acquainted, but she felt as though she'd known him much longer than a few jam-packed days. In reality, she didn't know him at all, but there was something, some indefinable pull between them.

Maybe their mutual love for a little lost boy had connected their hearts.

"Christmas is about a child," she said. "Maybe God sent him."

One corner of Kade's mouth twisted. "Now you sound like my great-aunt."

"She's a very smart lady."

"More than I realized," he said softly, a hint of humor and mystery in the words. "A good woman is worth more than rubies."

"What?" Sophie tilted her head, puzzled. Though she recognized the proverb, she wasn't quite sure where it fit into the conversation.

"Something Ida June said."

"Ida June and her proverbs." Sophie smiled up at him. "What brought that one on?"

Kade was quiet for a moment, his gaze steady on hers. He gently brushed a strand of hair from the shoulder of her sweater, an innocent gesture that, like a cupid's arrow, went straight to her heart.

"You," he said at last.

Sophie's heart stuttered. Though she didn't quite get what he meant or why he was looking at her so strangely, a mood, strong and fascinating, shimmered in the air.

Their eyes held, both of them seeking for answers neither of them had. All Sophie had were questions she couldn't ask. So far, every time she'd approached the topic of his life in Chicago, Kade had closed himself in and locked her out.

A woman above rubies, he'd said. Had he meant her?

Sophie senses Kade's eagerness to connect. But can she convince him to open his heart to love—and to God? Don't miss THE CHRISTMAS CHILD by Rita® Award-winning author, Linda Goodnight, on sale October 2011 wherever Love Inspired books are sold!

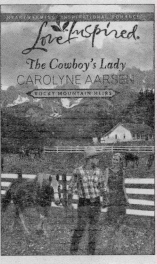

Love Inspired

Cody Jameson knows that hiring gourmet chef Vivienne Clayton to cook for the Circle C Ranch *has* to be a mistake. Back in town for just a year, Vivienne wonders how she'll survive this place she couldn't wait to leave. To everyone's surprise, this big-city chef might actually stand a chance of becoming a cowboy's lady forever.

The Cowboy's Lady
by Carolyne Aarsen

◆ ROCKY MOUNTAIN HEIRS ◆

Available October 2011 wherever books are sold.

www.LoveInspiredBooks.com

LI87698